<u>Ghetto</u>
F

Copy...
Revised 2014 Edition
Cover art by Laura Shinn

This is a work of fiction. Names, places, brands, media, and incidents are either the product of the author's imagination or are used fictitiously. The author acknowledges the trademarked status and trademark owners of various products referenced in this work of fiction, which have been used without permission. The publication/use of these trademarks is not authorized, associated with, or sponsored by the trademark owners.

Dedication
This book is dedicated to the men and women of the National City Police Department, both sworn and civilian. I hope you enjoy the book as much as I enjoyed working with you.

Acknowledgements
Thanks most of all to my wife, Doreen, for her help and encouragement. To my brother Stan, for the same, and to all the first readers.

"Ghetto"
"(noun) An impoverished, neglected, or otherwise disadvantaged residential area of a city, usually troubled by a disproportionately large amount of crime."
-- *The Urban Dictionary*

So he starts to roam the streets at night
And he learns how to steal
And he learns how to fight
In the ghetto
-- *Elvis Presley (In the ghetto)*

Preface

"124 John in foot pursuit westbound Division Street from Harbison."

The sudden radio call startled Ben after hours of quiet. They had been parked in the Walmart parking lot since 2:00 AM, he in the driver's seat of the black and white police patrol car, studying a detailed street map of the city and Corporal George Zobriskie, his Field Training Officer, apparently asleep in the passenger seat.

"Well don't just sit there, dickweed, let's go," Zobriskie calmly stated.

The rookie officer started the car and drove out of the parking lot westbound.

"Turn around numbnuts, Hopkins is up at Division and Harbison." Obviously Zobriskie had not been sleeping.

Ben whipped a U-turn and headed eastbound, recalling now that Harbison Avenue was in the eastern part of the city. He had started out westbound because Hopkins, call sign 124 John, patrolled the western part of the city. What was the veteran cop doing way off his beat? As he sped eastward Ben reached for the radio microphone to inform dispatch they were enroute. Zobriskie grabbed the mike out of his hand and said, "Stay off the radio. Screw dispatch. Hopkins needs the channel clear and he can't talk if you're blabbing away with the dispatcher. He'll know we're coming when he hears our siren. Of course, he won't hear the siren unless you turn it on."

Holy cow, Ben thought. Not only did he start off in the wrong direction but he forgot to hit the lights and siren as well. As he hit the switch to go code three he heard other sirens starting up in the distance.

"124 John south on Drexel. HMA, black hoodie, 11350." Wayne Hopkins was a ten year veteran who was badly overweight. He was already winded and talking in short bursts to save his breath. The suspect he was chasing was a Hispanic male adult wearing a black hooded sweatshirt who was in possession of narcotics, a felony violation of section 11350 of the California Health & Safety Code. With only a few days on the job, Ben was secretly pleased he was able to interpret the police lingo.

The radio crackled again. "124 John westbound south alley East 1st Street."

By some minor miracle Ben pulled into the south alley of East 1st Street without any wrong turns or having to ask his FTO for directions. As the patrol car's headlights lit up the alley he saw the suspect turn south and run into an open field. Hopkins was nowhere in sight. Ben turned to drive into the field but had to brake suddenly when he saw piles of construction debris blocking the way. Zobriskie was out of the car and running after the suspect even before the car was fully stopped.

"Tell dispatch we're here," he yelled over his shoulder.

Ben radioed "125 Edward 10-97 south alley East 1st Street, in foot pursuit southbound through a field."

He put the car in park, turned off the lights and siren, and took off after his FTO. The field was pitch black. How could it be so dark in the middle of a city? He used his big Streamlight flashlight to illuminate the ground in front of him. Unable to run fast due to the construction rubble, he tried to strike a balance between speed and caution, nearly falling several times. Up ahead of him he could see his training officer's flashlight bobbing as he ran.

Moments later, Zobriskie was yelling, "National City Police, get on the ground! Get on the ground!"

The old hand was getting to his feet when Ben caught up to him. The suspect was laying on the ground facedown, with his hands cuffed behind his back, sweating hard, breathing heavily and making no attempt to get up. Zobriskie was as cool and calm as he had been seven minutes earlier in the Walmart parking lot. He turned to his trainee and said, "Tell dispatch we're code four and have one in custody."

Ben radioed, "125 Edward code four, 10-16." He heard several sirens abruptly cut off when the rest of the patrol squad heard he and his FTO had the suspect in custody and no longer needed any assistance.

Zobriskie said, "I'll watch the prisoner, you keep your eyes peeled for other people. This is a bad area and we don't need any of this guy's buddies sneaking up on us."

Hopkins finally came chugging into view. He was badly winded and sweating profusely, moving at a pace barely faster than a walk. Ben turned away from the prisoner and kept a lookout for any other dangers, as his FTO had ordered. He wondered why Hopkins was so far off his beat, and why he had never radioed he was contacting a suspicious subject, per standard procedures, before the guy ran away. Behind him, Ben heard a thud and a loud "Oomph." He turned and saw Hopkins standing over the prisoner, who was curled up in a fetal position on the ground, moaning.

"I told you not to run from me you piece of shit." Hopkins grabbed the prisoner by the arms and roughly jerked him to his feet. They all walked back to Ben's patrol car. The suspect was mumbling in Spanish the whole way. Sergeant Wilfred Ruffin was waiting for them at their car.

Upon seeing the sergeant the prisoner nodded his head towards Hopkins and said in heavily accented English, "This asshole kicked me when I was laying on the ground handcuffed, doing nothing. I want to make a complaint about him."

"He's full of shit, Sarge," Hopkins said. "Zobriskie and his rookie took him into custody. I wasn't even there. I just walked him back to the car."

"He's a lying motherfucker, man." Jerking his head towards Ben, the prisoner said, "This cop here saw the whole thing."

All eyes turned to Ben, and he morosely thought, my first week as a police officer and I'm already screwed.

Chapter One

"Trainees are lab rats."
- Corporal George Zobriskie, Field Training Officer

    Booooring! Ben Olsen's first two days as a police officer reminded him a lot of his first days as a new Marine Corps officer. Paperwork, gear issue, gun qualifications, and more paperwork. He never even left the police station. Finally, on his third day as a cop he started field training.
    Corporal George Zobriskie was a sixteen year veteran police officer, married with two children. He worked the weekend graveyard shift, Friday through Monday, and was assigned as Ben's Field Training Officer for the first four weeks of his training . He would also be Ben's training officer for the last four weeks of training. In between Ben would have two other FTOs for four weeks each.
    Ben started his first patrol shift as a police officer by attending the pre-shift briefing, held by the squad sergeant in the police station. He was introduced to the squad members and asked to tell them about himself. As was his nature, he said little and deflected any questions from his squad mates. At the end of the briefing, Sergeant Wilfred Ruffin welcomed him and said, "There's only two kinds of people on graveyard shift - cops and assholes. All the businesses are closed. All the citizens are in their homes. Anybody you see on the street is up to no good."
    As Ben and his FTO loaded up their patrol car, Zobriskie took the opportunity to explain his version of the police department chain of command. "While you're in field training, think of the PD as a laboratory. Trainees are lab rats. Experimental subjects in a maze. Your FTOs will guide you through the maze. Think of us as cats. Cats play with rats. Sometimes we tease them, sometimes we torture

them, but cats never leave rats alone. If the rats learn from the cats they can find their way through the maze and finish field training. If not, the rats are discarded as laboratory waste. Sergeants are dogs. Dogs chase cats, but dogs will also chase rats. Rats who come to a dog's attention are in trouble. Any questions?"

Ben was amused, and happy to see Zobriskie was not going to be strictly serious all the time. "That's it? What about the lieutenants and captains?"

"Okay, think of the maze as the city streets. The rats and cats and dogs all run around on the streets. Lieutenants and captains are cars and trucks driving around, never looking out for and randomly crushing any rats, cats or dogs who happen to get in their way. Avoid lieutenants and captains at all costs.

Laughing now, Ben asked, "And the chief?"

"The chief is God. Or the Devil. If you see him during field training it means you're dead." The trainee was no longer amused.

His first two nights on graveyard shift were uneventful. The shift started at 9:00 PM and lasted ten hours, as did all patrol shifts. He filled the time by studying the department rules and regulations, trying hard to memorize every street in the city, and absorbing Zobriskie's wisdom. He quickly decided his FTO was a good cop and a good man who could teach him a lot. Of the hundreds of pieces of advice he received his first two nights, a few stood out.

"Don't be afraid to grab some nuts," the old timer had said. "Criminals always hide stuff in their crotch, especially weapons and dope. If you feel squeamish about getting a handful of balls it might cost you your life. The same goes for a woman. Gang bangers love to have their girlfriends carry the guns, thinking the cops won't search them. Search a woman's crotch with the back of your hand, and tell her what you're going to do before you do it. That way you won't get complaints and you will find the contraband. And if you do get a complaint, so what? There's an old cop saying, "It's better to be judged by twelve than carried by six."

Another little Zobriskie gem of wisdom that impressed Ben was "Two is one, and one is none. When you're out patrolling on your own, always assume some essential piece of equipment is going to fail right when you really need it. Your backup gun or backup flashlight will save your life." He was fast coming to realize nearly everything Zobriskie told him related to simply surviving on the streets.

His third night as a cop they responded code three (lights and siren) to assist Officer Wayne Hopkins, who was in foot pursuit of a suspect. Ben was not happy with his reaction. He started off in the wrong direction and completely forgot to turn on his lights and siren. But that was nothing compared to what happened when they all returned to the patrol car with Hopkins' prisoner, where Sergeant Ruffin was unexpectedly waiting for them. Upon seeing the sergeant the prisoner nodded his head towards Hopkins and said, "This asshole kicked me when I was laying on the ground handcuffed, doing nothing. I want to make a complaint about him."

"He's full of shit, Sarge," Hopkins said. "Zobriskie and his rookie took him into custody. I wasn't even there. I just walked him back to the car."

"He's a lying motherfucker, man." Jerking his head towards Ben, the prisoner said, "This cop here saw the whole thing."

All eyes turned to Ben, and he thought, "My first week as a police officer and I'm already screwed."

Ben felt Hopkins' eyes burning into him. The sergeant and his FTO were looking at him expectantly. The prisoner was now staring meekly at the ground; his shoulders slumped, as if he expected to receive another kick for daring to open his mouth. Ben realized immediately

Hopkins expected him to cover for him and lie to the sergeant. He had a bad feeling about the whole situation. Was this incident even real or could it be a training scenario, designed to test his integrity, like they did back at the police academy? Perhaps the supposed "prisoner" was actually a police officer himself, just playing a role for training purposes. Why had Hopkins been so far off his beat? Why had he not radioed he was making contact with a suspicious person? How had Zobriskie taken the suspect into custody so fast and easily? How come no other patrol units showed up at the scene? Why was the sergeant here? All these thoughts flashed rapid fire through Ben's mind. He knew if this was a training scenario and he lied to the sergeant he would be fired. If it was real and he told the sergeant Hopkins had kicked a compliant, handcuffed prisoner the veteran cop would be suspended and Ben would be a pariah with all the other officers. His mind was reeling.

"Officer Olsen, did you see Officer Hopkins kick this prisoner?" asked Ruffin.

Was the sergeant speaking formally for the prisoner's benefit or because this was training? Real or not, it doesn't matter, Ben thought. I am not going to lie to cover for Hopkins. It's just not the right thing to do. But maybe...
"No, sir, I did not."

The dejected prisoner scuffed his feet on the ground. "Aw, shit. You cops always cover for each other. This sucks."

Ruffin persisted, "Officer Olsen, this is a serious accusation. Are you sure you did not see Officer Hopkins kick the prisoner?"

"Sergeant, Corporal Zobriskie had taken the suspect into custody. He told me we were in a bad area and ordered me to keep a look out for any people who might approach us. I turned away from the prisoner to follow his order. I didn't see Hopkins kick anyone."

"Hopkins, when you get your prisoner to the station let me know so I can have him fill out the complaint paperwork," the sergeant said.

The prisoner said, "Just forget about it. I know it would be a waste of time anyway."

The sergeant told Zobriskie and Ben to return to duty, and they got into their patrol car and drove away. His FTO told him to drive to the nearby 7-11 so they could get some coffee and discuss the incident.

Once they had their coffees and were back in the patrol car, Ben thought, here it comes. This is where Zobriskie tells me how badly I messed up and how much trouble I'm in.

"Ben, did you tell Sergeant Ruffin the truth?"

"Yes, sir, I did."

"Good. You need to understand something. There are no cops out here worth risking your career by lying for them. And believe me; nobody is going to lie for you. But I want you to think about something. Did you notice the sergeant didn't ask you what happened? He specifically asked if you saw Hopkins kick the prisoner. And he didn't ask me anything at all. The district attorney will tell you in your first court case, when you testify you never volunteer any information, you simply answer each question you are asked. No more, no less. All experienced cops know that, including our sergeant. I saw the prisoner rolling on the ground and moaning, just like you did. Did Hopkins kick him when he was laying there on the ground? Probably. He has a reputation for that kind of thing. But it's also possible the prisoner faked the whole thing to try to get some leverage against Hopkins and maybe get his charges dropped. We don't know, and the sergeant was looking for facts, not opinions. Very few things in our world are black and white. We work in a world of gray, and all you can do is be true to yourself."

Gray is right, thought Ben. He still didn't know if this incident was real or if it had been staged for training purposes. All his life he had thought of himself as a straight arrow, a right and wrong type of guy. Even in Iraq things had been pretty clear - you killed the guys who were trying to kill you. Police work was going to be a much bigger challenge than he thought.

He got off duty Monday morning at 7:00 AM. He was still keyed up, thinking over everything that had happened last night, and not used to being awake all night and trying to sleep in the daytime. At the pre-shift squad briefing Sergeant Ruffin had announced there would be an award ceremony for Sergeant Selby at 9:00 AM in the police station conference room, and he encouraged everyone to attend. Ben had always enjoyed award ceremonies in the Marines and he believed they were important for morale, so he decided to go.

Still in his uniform, he entered the conference room. It was early and no one was there, but there were pastries and beverages on a side table. He had just sat down with a bagel and orange juice when a nicely dressed, good looking young black woman walked in. He stood and introduced himself. "Hi, I'm Ben Olsen, the new guy in field training."

"Jackie Greene. Nice to meet you."

"Are you a detective, ma'am?"

Laughing, she replied, "No, I'm not a cop. I'm just here for the ceremony."

"Oh, you must be Sergeant Selby's wife, then."

"Nope, I'm his sister. The different last names should have clued you in to the fact I'm not his wife. I thought cops picked up on stuff like that?"

"I've only been a cop for a few days. And sometimes wives keep their own last names for personal or professional reasons. So Greene is your married name?"

"Nope, wrong again. I'm his half-sister. We had different fathers. I'm not married."

Now it was Ben's turn to laugh. "OK, I guess I need to work on my detective skills. You look like you're dressed for work. What do you do for a living, Jackie?"

"Actually, I'm a full time student at San Diego State. I only work part time to pay for school."

"I went to San Diego State myself. I loved the campus but I didn't get along with most of my professors."

"Oh, really? Why was that?"

"I was there on a Navy ROTC scholarship and I majored in poli-sci. Most of my professors were very liberal and anti-military so we didn't get along real well. I just tried to keep a low profile and get through the semesters."

Jackie smiled to herself, knowing exactly what he was talking about. "So, did you finish school and join the Navy? See the world, and all that good stuff?"

"No, after graduation I became a Marine Corps officer. The only part of the world I saw was Iraq."

"Oh, I'm sorry."

Ben smiled. "Don't be sorry. I'm not. It's what I wanted to do."

"You wanted to go to Iraq?"

"I wanted to do something. I had to do something. I just felt so helpless and outraged after 9/11."

A few people started arriving for the ceremony. Jackie waited for him to go on but he didn't, so she changed the subject. "Do you work for Rod?"

"Rod?"

"My brother, Roderick Selby? The guy we're here for today. Don't you know him?"

"No, I've seen him around but I've never met him. I work on graveyard shift and have a different sergeant."

"Then why are you here? Shouldn't you be sleeping right now?"

"Well, I figure if somebody does something to earn an award the least I can do is be there to see them honored."

"Wow, you are new! Nobody goes to these things unless they're ordered to or they work day shift and use it as an excuse to get a break from work."

The ceremony was brief. Sergeant Selby was given an award for saving the life of a heart attack victim by giving him CPR until the paramedics arrived. After the ceremony people milled around, talking and snacking, and congratulating the sergeant. After talking with her brother Jackie looked around for Ben but was disappointed to find he was gone.

As she walked to her car in the police station parking lot she saw him in civilian clothes walking towards his car. "It was nice to meet you, Ben. You're different than most of the cops around here. Good luck with your training."

He walked over to her and said, "Jackie, I wanted to ask you something, but I'm not sure how to say it."

Here it comes, she thought resignedly. Every time I go to the police station some cop hits on me for a date. And I thought this guy was different. "I'm very busy, Ben. I go to school full time and work part time, remember? And you've got to be super busy with training."

"Oh, sure. But I wanted to ask you... When I interviewed with the police department, the hiring board was concerned as a former Marine officer with a college degree I wouldn't fit in with the patrol cops. They thought maybe I wouldn't take orders well and would resent having to start at the bottom of the ladder again. They almost didn't hire me because of it. Except for the internal affairs cop who did my background investigation none of the guys here know what I've told you. So, I wanted to ask you not to tell anyone. I can't believe I even told you. I guess I must be tired from being on duty all night, and you seemed genuinely interested."

Embarrassed she had misread Ben's intentions, she said, "OK, Ben. Your secret's safe with me."

Ben spent his second week of field training responding to infrequent, routine calls for service. He had plenty of time to study the policies and procedures manual, or P & P, as it was universally known. The P & P was the bible of National City police procedures, and it was several hundred pages long. As long as a cop followed P & P he was pretty much guaranteed not to get himself in trouble, either with his superiors or a citizen. If he strayed from P & P he opened himself up to disciplinary action. In addition to trying to memorize the policies & procedures manual, he also had to memorize all the police unit call signs, the police radio codes, and of course all the city streets. It seemed like an impossibly overwhelming task but Zobriskie assured him everyone learns it all eventually.

"Or they don't learn it," he said gruffly. "And they get fired."

At the end of week two Ben was in the locker room changing into civilian clothes, prior to going home to get some sleep. He overhead some of his squad mates discussing choir practice and asked them what they were talking about.

Scott McFadden, the beat 3 patrol officer, said, "At the end of each work week the squad meets somewhere, everyone drinks a few beers, and we kind of decompress from the week. It's a good way to start your three days off and it builds squad unity. Sometimes we discuss the hot calls, or unusual calls, so we all learn a few things, too."

Ben was astonished. "You guys go out and drink beer at seven in the morning?"

Irritated at his tone of voice, McFadden said, "Yeah, rookie, we do. After you have more than five minutes on the force you'll understand. When you spend an entire year on graveyard shift your nights are days and your days are nights. You get used to it."

"Why do they call it choir practice?"

"It started way back in the day in the LAPD, I think. Some of those guys didn't want their wives to know they were out drinking instead of being home with them, so they told them they had formed a squad choir and had practice once a week after shift. Some ex-cop wrote a book called The Choir Boys and after that police departments all over the country started using the term."

Ben wasn't interested in going to choir practice. The thought of drinking beer at 7:00 AM turned his stomach, and he was exhausted after another week of being up all night and not sleeping well in the daytime. But, he figured, in order to fit in and to get to know his squad mates better he probably ought to go. "Where's choir practice at?"

A half-naked Wayne Hopkins walked over, his fat, hairy belly preceding him like an ugly dog walking ahead of his equally ugly master. "It ain't none of your fucking business where we do choir practice, boot. Rookies aren't allowed to attend. Sometimes things get a little wild and we wouldn't want a probationary employee to be fired for some goofy stuff. A year from now, if by some freaking miracle you're still around, you can go to choir practice."

McFadden was nodding his agreement. "That's the way it is, man. Always has been."

Ben tried to look disappointed but he was smiling inside. Now he could go home and get some sleep.

After a few hours of poor quality sleep he got up and decided to go to the beach. He had three days off and already loved working a four day week. The other graveyard patrol squad could keep the city safe while he goofed off. Having grown up in Wisconsin he relished the San Diego weather, and the magnificent white sand beaches most of all. It was beach weather in San Diego almost all year round and today was no exception. He packed a large, colorful beach umbrella, a cooler, and a portable radio and headed off to Coronado. Once he got set up in the shade of the umbrella he broke out his copy of the policies and procedures manual and started studying. It wasn't long before he was sound asleep.

The next afternoon he was at home trying to decide if he wanted to go to the beach or go fishing at a lake when his cell phone rang. "Hi Ben, it's Jackie Greene. Do you remember me?"

"Of course I do, Jackie. How are you? Is everything OK?"

"Sure, everything's fine. I hope I didn't wake you up?"

"Nope, I was just trying to decide what I want to do today."

"Good. If you don't have any plans, I wanted to talk to you about something. I'm in my senior year at SDSU, but my advisor just informed me I'm lacking a social science class I need to meet the graduation requirements. The only classes available are poli-sci classes, and since you were a poli-sci major I wanted to get your opinion on what class to take."

"I'd be happy to help you out, Jackie. I was thinking of going to the beach. Would you like to meet there?"

"Perfect! I love the beach. How about we meet in an hour or so at the Children's Pool in La Jolla? I like watching the seals and it won't be crowded on a Wednesday."

"Okay, I'll see you there," he said. "Bye."

They met in the parking lot and carried their few items down to the beach. Jackie was struck again by Ben's good looks. He was 6'3" tall and 235 pounds of solid, rippling muscle, with classic Scandinavian features and blond hair. It was a beautiful July day, but neither one of them was in a swim suit, since swimming is not allowed at the Children's Pool. Jackie wore short blue pants and a yellow tank top edged with lace. A floppy sun hat and sandals completed her beach attire. Despite her casual dress, he couldn't help but notice her trim, athletic figure and pleasant face.

Ben wore cutoff jeans and one of his old Marine Corps olive drab T-shirts, with flip flops on his feet. He grew up on a farm, wearing snow boots in the winter and work boots in the summer, so he appreciated the opportunity to wear flip flops every chance he got. They were his standard footwear in San Diego.

"This is one of my favorite spots in the whole world," said Jackie.

"I like it, too," Ben said, "although I've only been here once before. I usually go to Coronado. The beaches there are always less crowded and parking is easier. Do you know any of the history of this place? Why is it called the Children's Pool?"

Jackie smiled. "Actually, the story is fascinating. It was built in the 1930s by a wealthy, civic minded woman who wanted there to be a safe place for children to swim in the ocean, without fear of being swept away by the surf. Using her own money, she had this large concrete and rock breakwater constructed to form a small cove. Once it was completed she donated it to the city. It served its intended purpose wonderfully for many years until the local seals and sea lions started using it as their playground, and eventually as their place to have pups. For many, the presence of the seals and sea lions made it even better, but then it was determined the prodigious amount of fecal matter constantly produced by the seals had badly fouled the water in the cove. Federal laws passed in the 1970s made it illegal for people to co-mingle with the marine mammals, so the city placed it off limits to people. As long as the seals were there it could no longer be used as a place for children to swim in the ocean, or even use the beach. Years of legal battles between those who wanted the pool restored to its original use and those who wanted it left to the seals resulted in an uneasy truce of sorts. The pool is still off limits to swimming, as you know, but people are allowed to use the beach provided they remain a certain distance from the seals. Neither side is very happy with the result, but to me and thousands of others it's still one of the most beautiful spots in southern California."

Ben was impressed. "Wow, Jackie, that was quite a history lesson. Did you learn all that at SDSU?"

Laughing, she said, "No. I don't recall where I heard it. Maybe from my mom. Anyway, that's enough about the seals. I want to hear about you, Ben. Tell me about yourself. We didn't have much time to get acquainted at the police station."

"There's not much to tell, really. I grew up in Barron, a tiny town in northwestern Wisconsin, on my parents' farm. The life options there are either family farming or working for Jennie-O, which is a huge turkey farming company. My two older brothers both work for Jennie-O. I guess everyone was expecting me to take over the family farm from my Dad when the time came. I wasn't interested in that or in dealing with turkeys for the rest of my life. I was really starting to hate the long winters, so I accepted a Navy ROTC scholarship to San Diego State. After my stint in the Marine Corps I wanted to stay in the San Diego area, so here I am."

"How was your time in the Marines?"

"At the start of my junior year of college 9/11 happened. Call me old fashioned, but it absolutely enraged me, and I wanted some payback. Three thousand innocent Americans killed, just because they were Americans. Did you know some of the terrorist hijackers lived and plotted the attacks right here in San Diego before going to New York? We might have bumped into one of them somewhere! I felt I had to do something to avenge the deaths of all those innocents, so I changed my NROTC program from Navy to Marine Corps. I knew it wouldn't be long before we were fighting them somewhere, and I wanted to get my licks in.

"After graduation from college I was commissioned as a Marine Corps officer and eventually assigned to a unit at Camp Pendleton, just an hour up the road from here. My unit deployed to Iraq three times in the four years I was in. On my first deployment we fought in the Battle of Fallujah. I don't like to talk about it, so I'll just say it was very bad. War is not like in the movies."

Ben went quiet. Jackie could see he was disturbed by his memories, so she changed the subject. "Why did you decide to become a police officer?"

"I enjoy helping people, and I've always had a strong sense of right and wrong, which I must have inherited from my Dad. Let me tell you a story about him. When I was very young, one of our neighbors had a family emergency and had to leave Wisconsin to deal with it. He asked my Dad to take care of his farm animals for the two days he would be gone. That night we had the worst blizzard in years. Power was out everywhere and all the roads and airports were shut down. It was six days before our neighbor was able to come home. We were okay with Mom and my older brothers taking care of things, so Dad spent six days trudging back and forth to the neighbor's place through the snow, feeding his animals, milking his cows, keeping his house warm with a wood stove so his pipes wouldn't freeze - all kinds of things. When the neighbor returned Dad refused to accept anything in payment for all his work. He said he didn't do it for money; he did it because it was the right thing to do. It made a very strong impression on me. After that, when I was in town I started carrying groceries for elderly people, and I shoveled old Mrs. Knutsen's sidewalk every winter until I left for college. Never took a dime from her, though she always offered. So, being a police officer seemed like a natural choice for me. At a career fair on the base a lot of law enforcement agencies showed up. The FBI and CIA were especially interested in me because I was an officer with combat experience, but I was tired of huge bureaucratic organizations like the Marine Corps. Even the Los Angeles and San Diego police departments sounded too big for my taste. National City was perfect, a small police force in a mostly inner city area with a high crime rate. I felt I could do a lot of good there. People call it 'Nasty City.' Geez, you already know all this from your brother. Sorry."

Jackie laughed. "That's OK, Ben. You're right about National City, though. Rod calls himself a ghetto cop."

"How about you, Jackie?"

"Well, my mom and her husband lived in San Diego and my brother Rod was born here. A few years later his father was killed in a street robbery when he was walking home from work after an overtime shift. I don't think he would admit it, but I believe that's why Rod became a police officer. I never knew my father. My mom wasn't married to him and he disappeared when I was still a baby. I don't know where he is now. Rod kind of took over as the man of the house. He's as much a father to me as a brother, even though he's only ten years older than I am. Just like your Dad, Rod made quite an impression on me when I was young. One time some of my friends made this crazy plan to go into Walgreen's and steal some cosmetics. We were like eight years old. I refused to go along with them, even though they razzed me a lot. Later I told Rod about it, expecting him to praise me. He scolded me instead, saying I should have talked them out of it, or turned them in.

"My mom started living with a guy a few years ago. It just felt awkward to me. I guess I wanted them to get married, and I kind of felt like I was in the way all the time. Shortly after I started college mom's boyfriend's company transferred him to Atlanta, and mom went with him. I couldn't afford a place of my own so I moved in with Rod."

"You wanted to talk about poli sci classes," said Ben. "What are you majoring in?"

"Early childhood education. As part of that program I'll get certified to teach elementary school. I'd like to go on for a master's degree but that would be very difficult financially, so I think I'll start teaching after graduation, at least for a few years, then hopefully go back for a master's. Somehow I messed up and never took a social science class I needed. Now the only classes available are political science classes. That's why I asked for your help."

"Well, in that case I'm glad you messed up then. I thought with my being in field training and you so busy with school and work I'd never see you again. You made it pretty clear in the parking lot last week you weren't interested in seeing me."

Laughing, she said, "I felt a little silly about that later, Ben. Every time I go to the police department some cop hits on me for a date. I thought you were going to do the same. I swear, cops are all horn dogs, even the married ones. It gets old pretty fast and I guess I just go into an automatic mode to stop it. You struck me as different, though. Maybe it was the fact you called me ma'am." She laughed again. "I think that might be the first time in my life anyone ever called me that! I realized later I wished you had asked me out, so I got your phone number through Rod and called you up. I really do want your opinion on which poli-sci class to take, though. I don't have any interest in politics, and I don't want a hard class or a bad professor."

They spent a pleasant afternoon with the seals, enjoying the day and getting to know each other. Although they had been raised in completely different circumstances, they discovered each was kind of old fashioned and shared a similar outlook on life.

When they were back at their cars getting ready to leave Jackie said, "Ben, I had a great time. I hope we're going to see each other again."

"Count on it, Jackie. This was one of the best days I've had in a long time."

"Good. I wanted to ask you a favor, though. I told you I dated a few cops before. One in particular became pretty demanding and controlling after a while, so I broke it off. I made the mistake of telling Rod about it and he got very upset. If we're going to be dating I'd like to keep it just between us."

Ben said, "Of course. Now we each have a secret."

The last two weeks of phase one field training went by fast. Ben was getting to know the cops on his graveyard squad and some of the cops on other squads as well. Swing shift and graveyard shift overlapped by several hours so the officers on those squads frequently ended up on the same calls. National City cops work a ten hour shift four days a week. As Zobriskie had explained to Ben, each shift has a weekday squad and a weekend squad, with one day where the two squads work together. "We call it the 'barrel day.' Barrel day for graveyard shift is Friday, so double the number of cops are on the street every Friday night, and we usually need them all. Friday nights rock and roll."

For those not used to it, the four day work week can be confusing. Cops call whatever day they start their work week "their Monday" and whatever day their work week ends is "their Friday," regardless of the actual calendar day. So, Ben's Monday was really a Friday and his Friday was really a Monday. His "weekend" was Tuesday-Wednesday-Thursday.

No one was allowed to start their three days off without having all their paperwork reviewed and approved by the squad sergeant. If you didn't get your paperwork done on time you had to stay on overtime to finish it. That irritated the sergeant and especially irked the civilian bean counters who always screamed about the overtime pay. Worst of all, it meant you got a late start on your weekend.

"You don't want to get a reputation as a booger eating spazz," Zobriskie told Ben. "Spazzes are constantly making traffic stops and pedestrian stops and getting into all kinds of crap that screws up the whole squad. Remember, every time you make a stop another patrol unit has to cover you. If everyone's trying to get their paperwork finished or even just on a coffee break they're not going to be very happy with you. New cops are always gung ho and can't wait to get into some action. We all understand that, just don't go crazy about it and be a spazz."

There was no need to worry about being a spazz in phase one of field training. With the mountain of material Ben had to memorize, every minute he and Zobriskie were not responding to calls from dispatch they were parked somewhere safe and Ben was studying.

One Sunday night about midnight he pulled their patrol car into a 7-11 parking lot. There was already another NCPD police car parked there, and Ben could see the patrol officer inside the store. He went in to get some coffee while Zobriskie remained in the car, filling out the never ending reams of paperwork all cops must do, but especially field training officers.

All the convenience store employees in the city loved it when cops dropped in for coffee. The presence of a marked NCPD patrol car in the parking lot guaranteed the store would not be robbed. All the clerks tried to give free coffee to the cops to encourage them to stop by, but NCPD regulations did not allow the officers to accept gratuities, even free coffee. Ben recognized the officer inside as Allen Gerhardt, a swing shift guy who would be getting off duty soon. They had met a few times on calls but never had a chance to talk very much.

He got his coffee and went to the register to pay for it. As usual, the clerk, a cute young Hispanic woman, told him there was no charge. Ben pulled out his wallet anyway, telling her he would pay for both his and Gerhardt's coffee.

Gerhardt said, "That's all right, I already paid for mine," and he winked at the young lady. She smiled back and rang up Ben's coffee.

He wondered what that had been about but Gerhardt interrupted his thought with, "Let's go outside and talk for a few minutes, Ben. We haven't had a chance to get to know each other."

Once outside, the two cops stood in front of the store entrance drinking their coffees. For the 7-11 clerk, it was like having two armed guards posted outside the store, and she loved it. She had been working here for less than a year and the store had been robbed twice already. She really needed the money and wanted to keep her job, but she was terrified of being robbed. Thankfully, she had not been working either time.

Ben said to Gerhardt, "I'm surprised you're drinking coffee so late in your shift. Aren't you going home in an hour?"

"I am, but it's my Friday and the squad's doing choir practice. The coffee won't keep me awake because I'm planning on balancing it out with a few beers."

After a few minutes of idle talk, Gerhardt said, "So, I heard you backed up Hopkins on a foot pursuit a couple of weeks ago."

"Not really. Corporal Zobriskie chased the suspect down and took him into custody so fast, by the time I got there it was all over. I didn't do anything."

"No, that's not what I mean. Hopkins told me you covered for him with the sergeant. I think that's cool. People need to know who's got their back."

Ben felt his face flush with shame and hoped Gerhardt didn't notice it. The swing shift officer thought he had lied to the sergeant to cover for Hopkins, and he was praising him because of it!

"Allen, I told the sergeant the truth. If Hopkins kicked that guy, I didn't see it, and that's what I told him."

"I gotcha, Ben. There are lots of things I don't see, either."

Now he was getting angry. "Look, Allen, I don't want you to get the wrong idea. I didn't lie to the sergeant, and I never would. He asked me what I saw and I told him. Period. If Hopkins thinks something different happened, he's wrong."

Gerhardt looked at Ben like he was something he had scraped off the bottom of his shoe. "Okay, rookie. I hear you. Since you're up on your high horse maybe you ought to start calling me Officer Gerhardt while you're in training, as the P & P manual requires, and I'll call you shithead, since that's how you strike me." He walked away shaking his head.

Puzzled, Ben took a minute to think about what just happened. He knew this conversation would get back to Hopkins. Should he discuss it with Zobriskie? Maybe he had misread Gerhardt, but he didn't think so. Still, he decided not to mention it to his training officer.

He completed phase one of field training without having experienced anything out of the ordinary. He and Zobriskie had responded to burglar alarms, prowlers, street robberies, drunk and disorderly calls, gang fights, traffic collisions, prostitution complaints, suspicious persons calls, and of course, numerous narcotics complaints and domestic violence situations. Domestic violence and narcotics calls were the bread and butter of policing in National City, and it was a rare shift when an officer went home without responding to one or both of them.

Chapter Two

"Crooks drive cars."
-- Corporal Alberto Salazar, Field Training Officer

For phase two of field training Ben was assigned to weekday day shift. He was pleased to find out Sergeant Selby would be his squad sergeant for the next month. Ben and Jackie had gotten together twice more since their first date at the Children's Pool, and he was curious to meet her brother.

Corporal Alberto Salazar would be Ben's field training officer for the next four weeks. Salazar was a six year veteran of the National City PD and one of several highly motivated young FTOs. He was born and raised in National City and still lived there, a rarity in the police department. He was married with one young child.

Their first day together Salazar told Ben the difference between day shift and graveyard shift was like night and day, figuratively as well as literally. "Graveyard shift is pretty much cops and robbers, as you know. Day shift is completely different. All the bad guys are still out there, but there are lots of good people on the streets as well. And of course, all the PD bosses and their bosses, the city politicians, work during the day. That means as cops we always have to be on our best behavior. You never know when a lieutenant or captain might be watching you. This is a small city. The city council members and the mayor are out and about all day long, and they always eyeball the cops. Some of the city council members are very anti-police. Most of our citizens support the police and are friendly towards us, but there is a segment out there that doesn't like us and they are always alert to any police misconduct. Citizen complaints are common on day shift. A frequent complaint is a citizen saw too many cops at

Starbucks or Denny's, so we're not going to spend any time on coffee breaks. If you need some coffee we'll stop in a 7-11 and drink it in the car.

"Another big difference between graveyards and day shift is the amount of traffic in the city. Even with lights and siren it's difficult to get anywhere fast during the day. There's just too much traffic to deal with.

"We don't get a lot of violent crimes on day shift. The bad guys usually stay in their hidey holes until it gets dark, although we do get some robberies once in a while. Mostly we deal with homeless people and traffic collisions, and whatever we can dig up on our own. Fortunately we have several officers right now on light duty status. They can't work in the field so they get a temporary transfer to day shift and work as a telephone reporting unit. They handle a great number of routine case reports over the telephone, which allows us to stay in the field and do real police work."

Salazar asked Ben, "Do you speak Spanish?"

"No. I took a year of Spanish in high school but I never used it and forgot everything I learned."

The FTO shook his head in disappointment. "Well, if you're going to make a career as a National City cop you need to learn to speak Spanish, the sooner the better. Pick up one of the law enforcement Spanish booklets and start studying."

Great, Ben thought. Just what I need - more stuff to memorize. I don't think I did this much studying in college.

Salazar went on, "Most of our population is Hispanic, Ben. Many of them speak English but many of them don't, or don't want to. It's never a problem when you're interviewing a victim, there will usually be a family member or friend to help with translation if needed. The victims want justice, so they'll work hard to communicate with you.

"Hispanic crooks will almost never speak English to you. Why should they? They have no interest in telling you anything, other than to get stuffed, and they'll say that in Spanish as well. You need to know some Spanish right away. I'll teach you some key Spanish phrases for your safety. 'Stop. Put your hands up. Get on the ground. Don't move. Police officer.' That type of stuff, not what you learned in high school. When giving orders to a Hispanic suspect always repeat your English commands in Spanish. If you don't, and he truly doesn't understand English, you might have a tragic misunderstanding. Let me give you an example. When I'm concerned about a suspect possibly fighting with me I usually tell him three or four times to get on the ground. If he refuses, then I use force to take him to the ground. Say you tell a Hispanic suspect to get on the ground in English several times, and he refuses, so you use force to take him to the ground and handcuff him. Was he really refusing your order or did he simply not understand what you said? If he truly didn't understand and you used force, he might have a valid complaint against you. Experienced Hispanic criminals will pretend they don't understand even if they speak English well, to confuse you as things are happening, or to file a false complaint against you later."

After Salazar explained the need for law enforcement Spanish Ben understood it and felt better about having to learn some phrases.

"I got a pretty good report on you from Corporal Zobriskie, Ben. He says you wanted to do more proactive policing. Well, that's never gonna happen in phase one of training, but in phase two, with the telephone reporting unit sucking up most of our routine reports we should be able to scratch that itch for you.

"Here's my philosophy in a nutshell - crooks drive cars. The more traffic stops we make the more crooks we're going to find, and crooks are stupid. If they don't happen to have any active warrants for their arrest they always have something illegal in their possession. It's just their nature. They can't be on the street without a weapon of some kind - they wouldn't last very long here in National City without one. And they usually walk around with dope, too. Either they're addicted and carry it for their own use, or they carry it to bargain with. Dope is the same as money here, maybe even better, since money is just a means to buy dope."

Ben was excited about proactive policing, but he was also somewhat confused. "So, we sit around and wait for someone to run a stop sign and then what? I guess I don't see how we get from the traffic stop to finding guns and dope."

Chuckling, Salazar replied, "You have a lot to learn, Ben, and it's not all in the policies & procedures manual. And it's surely not like the politically correct nonsense they taught you at the police academy. A cop's best friend and greatest tool is the California Vehicle Code. It's about a million pages long and lists violations most people have never even heard of. The vehicle code is your ticket, sorry about the pun, to pull over anyone you want to stop. You don't need to wait for a driver to commit a moving violation to stop him. If you really know the vehicle code you can find an equipment violation of some sort on any car or truck within seconds, and that's all you need to pull them over. Once you pull them over, then you have the legal right to demand identification, and all the fun starts from there."

"Corporal, I don't want to sound like an ACLU lawyer, but this is all new to me. Is what you described even legal?"

"It's perfectly legal, Ben, and good policing. And call me 'Berto,' unless we're with a sergeant. What I described is called a pretext stop, and even the United States Supreme Court has ruled it's legal and is a valid policing technique.

You can't pull over a motorist for no reason, but any reason, no matter how nitpick a violation, is all you need. As I said, once they're pulled over, since they're driving a car they are required by law to have a driver's license and to carry it with them. Naturally, you have the legal right to see that license. If they don't have a license they must produce some other form of ID. They also must carry the car registration and proof of insurance. If they claim not to have it you have the legal right to search any area of the car where those items are commonly kept, such as the glove box or the center console, to look for it yourself. Nearly everyone will give you permission to search their entire car and their person if you ask them. They either don't know they have the legal right to refuse or they feel if they do refuse it will make them look like they're hiding something, which they usually are. And as I said before, crooks are stupid. They actually think they've hidden their gun or their dope so well the cop won't find it. I'll show you all the most common places criminals hide things in their cars and on the persons."

This was sounding better and better, but Ben knew he was missing something here, because he still didn't quite get it. "Don't you get a lot of citizen complaints doing this? You stop John Q. Public for some minor equipment violation he didn't even know about and then you ask him if you can search his car?"

Shaking his head sadly, Salazar told him, "I think maybe you listened too closely in the police academy, Ben. You're in the real world now. We don't stop John Q. Public at random. We use our training and experience to recognize the signs of criminal behavior or gang activity on the part of a driver, and that's the driver we stop for whatever reason we can find."

"So what you're saying is you profile people. They taught us in the academy profiling is illegal."

"Ben, I told you that you listened too closely at the academy. Profiling is illegal, but that wasn't what I described. I'm your FTO and no FTO is going to teach you anything illegal. Now, maybe some lawyer might try to make an issue of it, but if you stick with what I said, your training and experience, to observe a pattern of criminal or gang behavior, you'll be fine. Here's an example: you see a young Hispanic male dressed in gang attire driving slowly through a known gang neighborhood at midnight. You watch as he drives aimlessly, circling the block several times. Okay, if the driver is granny with her grand kids, maybe she's lost or looking for an address. But he's not lost. He's a gangster looking for a dope dealer, or a rival gang member, or a prostitute, or casing a business he wants to rob or burglarize. Do you see the difference?"

"Honestly, Corporal Salazar, it seems to me that the only difference is the way the drivers look. And that's profiling."

"I can see how you might feel that way, Ben, but you're wrong. Remember, it's not just the way they look, it's what they do. Behavior, appearance, time of day, location, and your police experience and training all combine to tell you what is most likely occurring. The legal jargon for it is 'the totality of the circumstances.' Profiling is based solely upon appearance. That's the difference. What I'm describing is called good police work."

"And what if you're wrong and the young Hispanic male really is just lost?"

Berto smiled. "No problem. Remember, you found a legitimate violation of the vehicle code before you stopped him, otherwise you couldn't have stopped him. You tell the driver you stopped him because his car has no front license plate, let's say, and you ask for his driver's license, registration, and proof of insurance. He gives you all three. You do a record check and learn his license and registration are valid and he has no wants or warrants. You realize you've stopped Jose Q. Publico instead of a notorious gangster about to commit a felony. So, you give him his paperwork back and send him on his way with a verbal warning. He's happy because a cop cut him a break instead of writing him a ticket."

The first day of phase two started out with a long code three (lights and siren) run for Ben right out of the station. Just as the day shift units went in service the beat 1 unit was dispatched to an 11-8 male lying in the street in the 600 block of E.8th Street. That block of E.8th Street was at the far eastern end of the city, and the police station was on the west side. Corporal Salazar got on the radio and told dispatch he and Ben would respond to the call for training purposes. As the squad corporal with a trainee, it was always the FTO's prerogative to preempt another unit so his trainee could get more experience. Salazar wanted Ben to have the experience of a long code three run in day time traffic, and he knew from his turn over briefing with Zobriskie that Ben had not yet responded to an 11-8 call. 11-8 was the police radio code for a person down and unresponsive, circumstances unknown. The fire department and paramedics always responded to 11-8 calls, and the police went in case the person was down on the ground due to criminal activity.

Most commonly in National City, a person was lying on the ground due to intoxication or drug overdose. Sometimes they were down because of a medical reason such as a seizure or heart attack, and occasionally it was because they were an assault victim or even the victim of a hit and run traffic collision. The cop never knew until he got on scene.

The lights and siren run was quite a frustrating and educational experience for Ben. He had done a few code three runs on graveyard shift with Zobriskie, flying through the city at high speeds and slowing only to make sure intersections were clear of traffic before blowing through the traffic lights or stop signs. They were a lot of fun. This code three run was the complete opposite - a nightmare. With the morning traffic commute in full swing all the streets were jammed with cars. Upon hearing the siren and seeing the emergency lights most drivers did their best to stop and pull over to the right as required by law, but with all lanes of the roadway full many drivers were not able to move over very far. Ben was forced to crawl between cars, usually driving in the oncoming traffic lanes or straddling the center lines. Some drivers either didn't hear the siren or didn't know what to do. Some just kept driving. Some stopped in place and blocked the roadway. Worst of all, some drivers pulled over to their left and stopped. The drivers that moved to their left while Ben was also moving to his left set up potential rear end or head on collision situations. It was nerve wracking and extremely irritating. He realized the ambulance and fire trucks were also out there crawling through the same traffic he was, and the person down might very well be dying as they all tried their best to reach him as quickly as possible.

In fact, the person down was dead when they finally arrived. The fire trucks and ambulance had arrived on scene moments before he and his FTO pulled up. The first fireman to reach the victim saw a hypodermic needle on the sidewalk next to the man, who was lying on his back. The fireman checked for a pulse and breathing and found neither. The paramedics saw the syringe and noted the dozens of black needle tracks on the man's arm and immediately injected him with Narcan.

Salazar explained to Ben was what happening. "Narcan is a drug that counteracts opium based narcotics, and nothing else. If this guy OD'd on heroin, as it looks like he did, the Narcan will bring him back to life if he hasn't been gone too long. But when overdoses come around they are sober, pissed off, and disoriented. Remember, the last thing this guy knows is he slammed some smack into his arm and went off into la la land. Instead of his usual blissful high he suddenly wakes up with some cops and firemen in his face. It can get ugly. Glove up, get close to him and be prepared to hold him down on the ground."

Sure enough, a few moments later the man came around. He didn't wake up gradually like a sleeping person, but rather he startled awake and immediately tried to get up off the ground. Ben put his hands on the man's shoulders to pin him to the sidewalk. The bewildered man swung his head side to side like a trapped animal looking for an escape route, and tried again to get up. Ben told him to calm down. He paid no attention at all and started yelling in Spanish. When he had calmed down a bit one of the paramedics started asking him questions. The man finally focused on the paramedic, who asked, "When did you last use heroin?"

"I don't use heroin."

Like all paramedics who work in rough neighborhoods, this one was cynical and laughed in his face. "Dude, you're a heroin addict. I can see the tracks on your arms. Your needle's right over there."

"I didn't use any heroin."

"Hey asshole, I'm a paramedic and I just saved your worthless life. I gave you a shot of Narcan. It only works on heroin. You were dead and I brought you back, but the Narcan is just temporary. We have to get you to a hospital for more treatment and monitoring. I need to know when you shot up and how much you did so you can be treated properly."

The man glanced over at Ben and Salazar, turned away and stayed silent. The frustrated paramedic said, "Listen dude, the cops don't care. They got better things to do than bust your balls. You're not going to jail with them, you're going to the hospital with me. Now help me out here."

That convinced him. "I just shot up. I shoot up about every eight hours. A spoonful, like always," the man said. He looked at the cops like he still expected to get arrested. Ben turned to his FTO for guidance. Salazar motioned him back towards their patrol car as the paramedics strapped the man onto a gurney and rolled him towards the ambulance.

"What's your plan, Ben?" Salazar asked.

"Well, he obviously is under the influence of narcotics, which is a misdemeanor. And he was in possession of a syringe, which is also a misdemeanor unless he has a prescription for it, so I guess we should arrest him."

Salazar said, "You're right that he broke some laws. Misdemeanors. In National City, with very few exceptions, we don't take people to jail for misdemeanors. The jails are already overcrowded and if we booked every misdemeanor there would be nobody left on the street."

Berto continued, "We could still arrest him, issue him a citation and release him, which is what we do with misdemeanor arrests. But what's the point of that? The guy has to go to the hospital for treatment. We would have to follow him there and try to get through the arrest and citation process while the hospital staff is working on him. Not gonna happen. Besides, the guy literally just died and came back to life. I think he's been punished enough for one day, don't you? We'll get his horsepower and do a warrant check on him. If he's not America's most wanted we'll go back in service."

"Horsepower?"

Salazar chuckled. "You never heard that before? Everyone we contact, we get their name, date of birth, address, ID or driver's license number, and any other pertinent info so we can positively identify them and run a warrant check. We call all that info a person's horsepower."

Ben asked, "Aren't we going to search him for more drugs or needles?"

Salazar replied, "If we were arresting him we could do a search incident to the arrest, but we're not arresting him. We can still pat him down for weapons for our safety if we feel the circumstances lead us to believe he might be armed. I don't believe they do and besides, I watched the paramedics go over his whole body pretty thoroughly. They always do. They would have told us if he had any weapons or more needles."

"So that's it? Get his info, run a warrant check, and if he's clean we go back to patrolling?"

"You got it," Salazar said.

"It seems like we should be doing more," said Ben. "The guy's a heroin addict."

"Ben, in many ways this guy is more of a victim than a criminal. Sure, he put that heroin into his arm. He made that choice a long time ago, but it's not a choice for him anymore, it's a way of life. The medical folks will advise him of all his treatment options and opportunities to get straight, but heroin addiction is usually for life. If he starts burglarizing houses and robbing people to support his habit then the police will get involved. Until that happens there's not much we can do."

Shortly after his squad went in service Sergeant Roderick Selby walked up the stairs and entered the dispatch center. Dispatch was the nerve center of the National City police station. It was off limits to non-supervisory police personnel, and to virtually all civilian employees except those who actually worked there. Inside the steel reinforced door was a state of the art communications center and integrated computer system. That system allowed the dispatchers to access large numbers of state and federal law enforcement databases and simultaneously communicate via radio with National

City police officers in the field and citizens on regular or 911 phone lines. The dispatchers also had the capability to communicate via radio with all the other police agencies in southern California. That major communications upgrade had been paid for by the federal government, shortly after the terror attacks on the World Trade Center in New York.

National City dispatchers were all civilian employees, and mostly women. Unlike most cities, National City dispatchers routinely functioned as both 911 operators and police dispatchers - one person doing the work of two. It was an unbelievably difficult job few could do, and even fewer could do well. They were the best in the business.

Selby said hello to Nora, the lead dispatcher on duty, and after a minute of pleasantries he said to her, "I have a new trainee on my squad for the next four weeks - Officer Ben Olsen. I haven't had a chance to speak to him yet and as you know my squad is already on the streets. Would you get me Olsen's home and cell phone numbers so I can update my personnel notebook?"

The dispatcher asked, "Did you lose them?"

Confused, Selby said, "What?"

"I gave those numbers to your sister Jackie about two weeks ago. She called and said you needed them to update your notebook."

Selby was surprised and disturbed to hear that, and he wondered why Jackie would have done such a thing. Not wanting to get her in trouble with Nora, he said, "Oh yeah. Jackie wrote them on a piece of paper and I never transferred them into my notebook. The paper's buried in the mess on my desk at home somewhere."

"Ok, you got your notebook ready this time?" Nora asked.

Showing her his notebook, he said, "Go for it."

After getting the phone numbers he left the dispatch center, already becoming angry with his half-sister. At home that evening after dinner, out of the blue, he asked her, "What's going on with you and Ben Olsen?"

Jackie couldn't have been more stunned. She and Ben had agreed not to tell anyone about their blossoming relationship until they both felt it might continue for a while. Had he told Rod? She carefully said, "Ben and I have seen each other a couple of times. Did he speak to you about it?"

"No, we've been so busy I haven't had a chance to talk to him yet. Nora in dispatch told me you asked her for Olsen's phone numbers a couple of weeks ago. That's privileged information, Jackie, and you used my name to get it. Not only is that unethical, it's a violation of policy and could get me in trouble. What in the world were you thinking?"

"I apologize, Rod. I don't know what I was thinking. I guess I wasn't thinking at all. I met Ben at your award ceremony and we kind of hit it off. Then later I found out I needed a political science course to graduate. He was a poli sci major at SDSU so I wanted to get his advice on which class to take."

"Olsen went to San Diego State?"

"Yes, he was there on a Navy ROTC scholarship. He graduated and joined the Marines, and fought in Iraq. He's keeping it quiet because the hiring board made a big deal about him maybe not wanting to follow orders, given his recent experience as a Marine officer, where he was the guy giving the orders."

"Well I'll be damned. Yeah, I guess I could see that."

"I really do apologize, Rod. I know how much you love your job and the last thing I want is to get you in trouble." She quickly got up to leave the room.

"Whoa! Hold on just a minute, Jackie. We're not done talking yet. You know how I feel about you dating cops. I'd trust any of them to watch my back on the street and mostly they're all good guys, but when it comes to women they're worse than animals. They treat women like meat and then brag about it in the locker room."

She knew this was coming. It was one of the reasons she had wanted to keep her relationship with Ben quiet. "I pretty much agree with you, Rod. None of the cops I dated in the past worked out. And all the cops still hit on me every time I go to the PD, even some of the married ones. But Ben is different. He didn't hit on me at all. In fact, I called him."

"He's no different than the rest of them, Jackie, he's just got a new angle he fooled you with."

"Rod, we've had three dates so far and he hasn't even tried to kiss me. The other cops I dated tried to get me in bed on the first date! I'm telling you, Ben is a gentleman."

"All cops are the same when it comes to women, Jackie. They're all after the score and the bragging rights. You'll see."

"You're wrong, Rod. You're wrong about Ben, and there's another cop I know who treats women like royalty. You! I love you for worrying about me, but I'm twenty two years old and a senior in college. I'll be fine."

The next day at his squad's pre-shift briefing Selby called Ben up to the podium at the front of the room. "We didn't have time to do this yesterday. Introduce yourself to the squad, Olsen."

He looked around the room at the five police officers and said, "I'm Ben Olsen. I grew up in a small town in Wisconsin. They didn't have many job prospects there. I hated the long winters, so I moved down here to San Diego County to get warm, and here I am."

He left the podium and was walking back to his seat when Teodore Liwag, an eight year veteran of Filipino descent stopped Ben in his tracks by saying, "Holy shit! That's the fastest squad intro in the history of the world. Maybe we have some questions for you, boot."

Remembering what Jackie had told him about Ben wanting to keep his personal history private, Sergeant Selby said, "Teo, just because you never shut up doesn't mean everyone has to chatter away like a squirrel on meth. Go sit down, Olsen."

Brenda Stockwell, the only woman officer on the squad said, "Yeah, and women really go for the strong silent types. Damn, they grow 'em big back there in cheesehead land, and good looking, too. You and I will talk later, Ben, or I'll talk and you just listen."

Unaccustomed to women being so brazen toward him, he was blushing furiously as he sat down, his beet red face quite a contrast to his blond hair.

Stockwell said, "I don't fucking believe it! Farmboy's blushing like a virgin at a gang rape. I didn't think that shit happened anymore."

As she continued to needle Ben, Sergeant Selby interrupted with, "All right, people. Let's hit the streets and serve the citizens. Be safe."

Ben and Corporal Salazar went in service and were on their way to pick up some coffee when a radio call came out. "224 John with 225 Edward to cover on a disturbance at W.20th Street and Coolidge Avenue. Several people fighting in the street. No weapons seen."

"224 John 10-4, responding from two blocks away."

"225 Edward 10-4."

Ben and Salazar were not far from the location of the reported fight and traffic was not too bad on the west side of the city, which was largely an industrial area with some scattered homes. Ben was about to hit his lights and siren when Salazar told him not to bother. The beat 4 officer had radioed he was responding from only two blocks away and should already be coming on scene.

"224 John on scene, contacting one person. Everyone else is already gone."

Ben and his FTO rolled up a minute later. "225 Edward on scene."

Salazar told Ben, "Let's let Eddie handle this. You just watch and learn."

Edgar Keaton was the beat 4 officer. Beat 4 was statistically the quietest beat in the city. Most squad sergeants allowed their officers to choose their beat assignments by seniority, and usually the most senior officer on the squad chose beat 4. Keaton was no exception. As Ben and Salazar walked up to him Keaton radioed to dispatch he was code four, not in need of any assistance.

Keaton was talking to an Hispanic male who looked to be about fourteen years old. He was wearing a white tank top, black baggy shorts and white socks pulled up almost to his knees. Salazar explained to Ben the teen was dressed in the classic hot weather Hispanic gang attire. The kid was bleeding from a split lip and had numerous abrasions on his arms and face from rolling around fighting on the pavement. He refused Keaton's offer to call an ambulance. The cop asked him what happened.

The surly teen replied, "Nothing happened. Can I go now?"

Keaton said, "No, you can't. I want you to tell me what happened."

"I told you, homes. Nothing happened. I didn't do nothin'. I'm gonna be late for school."

The veteran cop said, "Yeah, I can tell you're a real Rhodes scholar. Listen to me. I'm conducting an investigation and until I figure out what happened you're not going anywhere."

"OK man, five or six black guys jumped me. No big deal."

"Stop lying to me. When I rolled up I saw a bunch of your home boys running away. There weren't any black guys. They were jumping you in, weren't they?" Using the parlance of the street, Keaton was asking if this had been a gang initiation.

The kid's face lit up with pride. "Yeah, man, that's what it was. I'm West Side now, homes. OTNC." Keaton filled out a field interview form and took a photo of the kid, who happily posed displaying his gang's hand sign. He asked him again if he wanted an ambulance and was again refused.

"OK, we're all done here. I'll give you a ride to school."

The kid was laughing as he walked away. "Yeah, right. That'll happen, in your dreams. Later, homes."

Salazar asked Keaton to tell Ben about the call. Keaton said, "I knew before I even got here it was probably some kid being jumped in, just because of the area. Look around at all the graffiti." Ben looked around and saw "OTNC" and "WS" painted on all the buildings, sidewalks and streets, along with dozens of names and the number 13.

"As I rolled up I saw five or six gangster types running away and the kid laying in the street. Even he tried to run off but I stopped him. Anytime some Hispanic kid dressed like him tells you he was jumped by a bunch of black guys you know he's lying. Blacks and Hispanics almost never mix it up, they're too busy killing their own kind. Anyway, Berto can tell you a lot more than I can. He's a gang expert. I'm going to get some coffee."

Keaton radioed dispatch he had done a field interview and was back in service. "224 John 10-8, FI."

Salazar explained the graffiti to Ben. "OTNC stands for Old Town National City. It's the oldest gang in the city, probably as old as the city itself. The number 13 stands for the thirteenth letter of the alphabet, the letter M, which itself stands for the Mexican Mafia, a very large, international gang with ties to the Mexican drug cartels. "WS" stands for West Side, which is just one set of OTNC, representing the west side of the city. It's where OTNC got started way back in the day. So, West Side is part of the Old Town National City criminal street gang, which is part of the Mexican Mafia. Graffiti is the shorthand language of the streets. It looks like nonsense to most people, but if you can read it there's a lot you can learn from it. Let's go visit someone. It will open your eyes."

Salazar told dispatch he and Ben were going to conduct a probation check on Coolidge Avenue and gave the address. He explained to Ben that Hector Ramirez, a 19 year old Old Town National City gangster, lived there. He was on probation for various convictions, and as a condition of his probation law enforcement personnel could visit his home and search his room and his person any time, for any reason.

Salazar knocked on the door and Hector's mother, a Hispanic woman in her early forties, opened it. Berto spoke to her in fluent Spanish and she gestured for them to come inside. He told Ben the woman had said she was home alone but they did a security check of the small house just to be sure. Never trust anyone except another cop, he explained. When that was done he complimented the woman on her beautiful home and asked if he could show Ben some of the family photos.

The house was meticulously clean and tidy. There were numerous religious icons on the walls and shelves. The living room wall held an arrangement of framed family photographs depicting several generations of the Ramirez family.

"Look around, Ben. I bet you didn't expect a gangster's house to look like this, did you? Neat and clean, and all about God and family. Not only is this not unusual, it's actually typical. Gang life is not as simple as it might seem. See these photos? That's Hector's father, obviously some years ago, wearing the same outfit as that new gang kid we just saw. And look at this one. It's Hector's grandfather, wearing the gang clothes of his day. And here he is again, in Vietnam. These folks are not just proud Mexicans, they're proud Americans, too. Hector is third generation OTNC, maybe more. The whole thing is just sad."

Ben asked, "Why would Hector's father allow his son to join the gang?"

"If he were alive I'm sure he'd tell Hector to get out of the life. His dad was killed in a gang shooting a few years back, and his grandfather's in prison. Social scientists have been trying to understand the gang life for a hundred years. If anyone could ever figure out how to break this cycle they'd win the Nobel Peace Prize."

Salazar thanked the mother and they left.

The first two weeks of phase two field training went by fast for Ben. It seemed like he and Salazar were making traffic stops and pedestrian stops every minute they were not assigned to something else, and as Salazar had promised, it frequently paid off in arrests. Ben became familiar with the procedures for processing arrestees at the police station, then driving them to the county jail in downtown San Diego. Women prisoners had to be driven all the way to the Las Colinas Women's Jail in the town of Santee, a 30 minute trip each way. Any arrest that resulted in the suspect going to jail took several hours to process and during that time the arresting officer was out of service and not available for calls. If more than one officer had a prisoner at the same time it left the city dangerously short of cops on the street.

Ben was enjoying working normal daytime hours and he was especially happy to have weekends off so he and Jackie could spend time together. He was starting to think perhaps his relationship with Jackie was going to be a long term one, and the prospect pleased him very much. He only hoped she felt the same way.

In fact, Jackie was thinking exactly the same thing. She looked forward to each weekend now. She and Ben were acting like tourists new to the city instead of long term residents. She had lived here all her life, while Ben had come to San Diego to attend San Diego State eight years previously. Despite that, Ben was largely unfamiliar with most of the county. While at SDSU he spent most of his time on campus, at the beach, or fishing in the many area lakes. In the Marine Corps, when not deployed overseas his unit was constantly training and Ben again spent his precious off duty time at the beach or fishing. He had never been much for nightclubbing or fancy dining.

Jackie shared Ben's disinterest in nightclubbing and their dates so far had all been daytime excursions. When she discovered Ben had never been to many of the beautiful spots in the San Diego area she insisted they explore the county together. A typical date might involve a picnic at Mission Bay, watching people fly kites and control model boats, or a sightseeing trip to the Point Loma lighthouse with its magnificent views of San Diego Bay and the Pacific Ocean. To get to the Point Loma lighthouse they had to drive through the grounds of the Fort Rosecrans National Veterans Cemetery. When they got to the lighthouse Ben was very somber. It was clear to Jackie the drive through the cemetery had deeply affected Ben.

One day they spent an afternoon slowly driving around the ritzy neighborhoods of La Jolla, gawking at all the mansions with their amazing landscaping. At the end of the day Jackie drove them to the top of Mount Soledad to watch the sunset over the ocean from the mountain top. The top of the mountain has a small park with a large cross as its centerpiece. They parked the car and walked to the western edge to admire the view, holding hands. Jackie was still waiting for Ben to kiss her for the first time, and she was running out of patience. If he didn't do something soon Jackie would have to take matters into her own hands.

It was still a half hour or so before sunset so they turned away from the west and walked towards the cross, to explore the rest of the small park. As they approached the cross Ben stiffened and squeezed her hand unconsciously. Jackie had not been here in many years and had forgotten a veteran's memorial had been built at the base of the cross. The memorial consisted of about 3,000 small plaques, many with photos, each one commemorating a deceased San Diego area veteran. Ben was entranced. He moved very slowly past the plaques, pausing to read some, but merely glancing at most of them, not speaking. Jackie asked him if he was okay, but he did not reply, nor did he even turn his head, he was so lost in his thoughts. After they made their way about three quarters around the memorial Ben finally stopped and looked at her. There were tears in his eyes, and although he was looking directly at her she knew he was not seeing her. She realized there was a side to him she did not know, and for the first time wondered if their relationship really had a future.

The following Monday morning at 6:00 AM Sergeant Selby's squad was at their pre-shift briefing. Selby noticed Ben was not present and said, "Berto, where's your trainee?"

"I don't know, Sarge. He was in the locker room with the rest of us. I'll go check on him." As he got up to leave the briefing room the door opened and Ben walked through, in uniform but carrying his boots in his hands.

Sergeant Selby said sarcastically, "Glad you could join us, Olsen. I hope we didn't interrupt your beauty sleep. Maybe I could talk to the chief and get briefing time moved back to 7:00 AM, if that would work better for you."

Embarrassed, Ben replied sheepishly, "Sorry, Sergeant. I'm having some difficulty with my boots."

"What's the problem?" Selby asked. They're shiny enough. The freaking things are damn near blinding me."

"I'm having trouble with a knot in the laces, Sergeant. I'll get it squared away."

"OK, but pay attention in briefing. I don't do this just to hear myself talk."

Ben worked at trying to unknot his boots throughout the briefing and finally got them undone and on his feet as the squad was heading for their patrol cars. As he and Salazar were leaving Selby said, "Berto, if it's not real busy today have Olsen come by my office. I still haven't had a chance to talk with him."

As they loaded up their patrol car Salazar asked Ben what the story was with his boots. He said, "Somebody tied the laces together with about fifty knots. I wasn't able to get them all undone in time to make briefing. I guess it's just another rookie hazing thing."

Salazar replied, "Maybe so, but it's a pretty stupid one, and dangerous, too. What if we had gotten a hot call and had to go in service before briefing was over? I'll talk to the squad about it at the end of shift today."

"Berto, please don't bother. It was just a joke. Besides, I don't know if it was somebody on the squad. It could have been anybody."

"What do you mean? There was nobody in the locker room except our squad."

"Yeah, but whoever did it had the whole weekend."

"The whole weekend? Didn't you lock your locker?"

"I never lock my locker. Why should I? We're all cops in a police station, for gosh sakes."

"Man, you are a country boy, aren't you? Even here stuff turns up missing occasionally. Cops are people, too, and people do stupid things. Lock your locker from now on."

Once they were in the field Salazar said to him, "As much as I'd like to have you keep making traffic stops we need to put a few more checks in the field training boxes. We'll take the next 5150 call, and in the meantime I'll introduce you to some of our homeless people. Hell, half of them are 5150 anyway, and we might end up taking one to

CMH. Make sure you have plenty of those plastic surgical gloves with you. We're going to be meeting some really filthy folks and you don't want to be skin to skin with them."

"What's a 5150? And did you say CMH?"

"A 5150 is a mentally ill person who is a danger to himself or to other people. As police officers, we have the authority, no, I'll go further than that - we have a duty under section 5150 of the California Welfare & Institutions Code to transport any mentally ill person who is a danger to himself or others to a mental health treatment facility. For us, that means the County Mental Health Hospital out near the San Diego airport. We call it CMH for short. The law allows a police officer to involuntarily commit a dangerous mentally ill person for up to 72 hours so they can be checked out by professionals. I say it's our duty because imagine the flak we would get if we knew some dangerously mentally ill person was on the street and we did nothing, and then they killed themselves. Not only would that be tragic, but we'd be sued big time. The doctors at County Mental Health can either release them after three days or keep them up to a total of fourteen days. After that, to be involuntarily held the hospital would need to get a court order."

Surprised, Ben said, "So even someone who is dangerously mentally ill must still be released after two weeks?"

"Yep, and that's what usually happens. Getting a court order to hold someone for a longer period is almost impossible. Nearly always the hospital will just dope them up so much they can't do any harm, and then they release them. Of course, when the medicine wears off and they forget to take any more of it they become unstable again, and we end up scooping them up once more. It's a vicious cycle and the best we can do is hope no one gets hurt.

"Always try to keep in mind when you're dealing with mentally ill people that they're not criminals, they're ill. You may need to use force against them and you always need to protect yourself and the public, but you also need to protect them from themselves. Now drive over to the nearest liquor store and we'll check out some of the homeless. Liquor stores attract homeless people like shit attracts flies."

They drove to a liquor store and sure enough, in the rear parking lot of the store were half a dozen homeless men, and two homeless women. Every one of them seemed to have a brown paper bag either in hand or nearby.

Berto was carefully scrutinizing everyone. "Glove up, Ben, and be safe. I recognize all of these folks and they're usually harmless, but they're all street people with very little to lose. They are either alcoholics, drug addicts, mentally ill or all three put together. Never threaten them with jail. They've all been there dozens of times and some of them like it. It's a warm place to sleep with free food and hot showers. If you decide to arrest one of them just hook them up and stuff them in the car, don't make a big deal of it."

Ben said, "When you told me last week we were going to be checking out some homeless people I studied up on the municipal code. It's illegal to be drunk in public. It's illegal to drink alcohol in public. It's illegal just to have an open container of alcohol in public. Heck, it's even illegal in National City to possess a shopping cart outside of the store parking lot. All of these people are in violation right now."

"Good for you, Ben. It's important to know the muni code. It's another tool you can use if you need to jack somebody up. But all those violations you mentioned are infractions. The best you could do is write them a ticket, which they would later use as toilet paper. They never go to court, they all have warrants for failure to appear, and nobody cares. The jail won't take them and they're never going to pay the fines, so what's the point of wasting your time writing tickets?"

"So how do we deal with homeless people?"

"Ahhh," said Salazar wistfully. "That's the million dollar question. Like the gang problem, when you solve it they'll give you sainthood. The best we can do is leave them in peace when they're not causing trouble and take them to jail when they are. I don't know any cops who bother the homeless unless they're dispatched because of a citizen complaint. Usually we just move them out of the area, but it's like squeezing a balloon - they just show up somewhere else where we wait until someone complains, then we move them along again."

Berto found a person he wanted Ben to meet. "Hey Ben, come over and meet Zoomie."

Zoomie was an unusually tall, very skinny black man who looked to be about sixty five years old. He had an impressive salt and pepper beard and an even more impressive odor. Except for the beard, he was a dead ringer for a child's stick figure drawing. His clothes and skin were caked with dirt. He tightly clutched a brown paper bag in his right hand and was eyeing the two cops warily. "Zoomie, put the bottle down and step over here so we can talk. I want you to meet my new partner," said Salazar.

Seeing no response from the skeletal man, Ben was beginning to wonder if he was too drunk to understand, when he finally moved. The wraith slowly followed Salazar's instructions, placing his bottle down so carefully and gently it might have contained an evil genie he was fearful of disturbing. He walked over to them sluggishly and with great effort, like he was walking underwater, but he kept glancing back at the paper bag with his bottle in it, as if the bag would disappear if not watched. "Zoomie, this is my new partner, Officer Olsen. Officer Olsen, this is Zoomie."

Ben knew better than to shake hands, and Zoomie made no move to do so, either. Instead, he very deliberately reached into the breast pocket of his raggedy shirt and removed a crumpled, greasy piece of paper. Fiercely concentrating, bit by bit he straightened out the paper and handed it to Ben. The homeless man apparently functioned at only two speeds - slow and slower, so of course he was known as Zoomie.

Ben took the paper from him and read the words written there in bold, neat pencil: "My name is Xvztrylntl. I am from the planet ZpklQnrdClnpw. Please help me. The Chula Vista police arrested me and stole $85,102,446,302 from me. Then they drove me here. I need my $85,102,446,302 back. Thank you."

Ben gave the note back to him, and he returned it to his pocket at his usual breakneck speed. Then he cupped his hands in front of Ben and waited. Ben asked, "What do you want?"

Zoomie did not respond, but slowly moved his hands back and forth, looking at Ben expectantly. Realizing he was not going to speak, Ben asked Salazar, "Do you know what he's asking for?"

Smiling, Berto said, "Yeah, he thinks we're the Chula Vista police and we've got his 85 billion dollars. He wants it back."

Ben couldn't help but laugh. He motioned for Berto to step back with him, and when they were out of earshot of the pathetic fellow he said, "Are we going to take him to County Mental Health on a mental illness hold? He's obviously mentally ill."

Salazar said, "Ben, you're right that he's mentally ill. You don't need to be a doctor to see that. But remember the 5150 criteria. Is he a danger to himself? You could ask him if feels suicidal and he'll shake his head no. Is he a danger to anyone else? I haven't seen anything that would indicate that, have you? He's got money enough for booze which means he can buy food when he wants it. So we can't take him to the county psych hospital, and we shouldn't. He's a nut, but he's a harmless nut."

Ben asked, "Shouldn't we at least run him for warrants?"

Berto laughed. "Yeah, sure, you go ahead. Make sure you spell his name right for the dispatcher. As far as I know nobody knows his real name. He's been arrested and fingerprinted under John Doe. The fingerprints come back clean. Maybe he really is from a different planet."

As they were driving away Salazar asked Ben, "So, what do you think of Zoomie?"

"Well, you'll probably laugh and call me a softie, but I feel sorry for him. An older man, mentally ill, living on the streets, and if that isn't hard enough, mute."

The field training officer chuckled. "Ben, you are a softie. He's not really old, he told me he's forty two. He just looks ancient. Life on the street will do that to you. And he speaks just fine when he feels like it. He'll speak to you sooner or later. You've got to stop taking things at face value. On the street everybody lies to the cops. It's the natural order of things. Although I do believe him when he says the Chula Vista cops drove him here. Those guys dump their homeless in our city all the time."

They drove all over the city so he could become familiar with the various homeless encampments. There were homeless people throughout the city, but they tended to congregate in groups near Plaza Bonita mall, liquor stores, and freeway off ramps. Just when he thought the tour was complete Berto said, "I've saved the best for last. Head over behind the bowling alley."

They parked behind the bowling alley but Ben could not see any homeless people at all. Berto was busy sketching something. When he finished, he showed his work to Ben. "OK, this is not to scale. Think of the paper as the whole city. All the lines I have drawn represent storm drain tunnels beneath the city. These are not sewers, Ben, they're huge storm drains designed to dump water into the Sweetwater River in major rain events."

Ben looked at the paper and was surprised to see a depiction of a complicated network of tunnels crisscrossing all through the city. "Wow, I had no idea there were this many. It must add up to miles."

"Yes, and I'm sure there's a lot more I don't know about and aren't pictured here. Wait until you see them from the inside. Let's go."

They got out of the car and walked over to a tunnel entrance. It was landscaped so well Ben had not even noticed it until they got close. Then he realized how large it was. The tunnel was at least six feet high and ten feet wide. Berto was able to walk upright and Ben had to bend over some, but not too much. Before they went in the training officer radioed dispatch they would be in the tunnels and out of radio range. The radio signals were unable to penetrate the thick concrete underground structures.

After walking in about fifty feet they needed flashlights to see. "It's pitch black in most of the tunnels. There are some areas beneath storm grates where sunlight comes in. Those areas are where the homeless live."

They approached a sunlit area and saw an elaborately constructed room. It had makeshift shelves, boxes for tables, buckets for chairs. Some small areas were curtained off for privacy. It looked like a family lived here. There was food in cans and boxes, and jugs of water. A blackened area indicated a small fire had been made not too long ago. No people were around, and Ben asked where the occupants were. Berto replied, "They always hear you coming and disappear. The tunnels carry sound. Somehow they seem to know it's the cops coming and not some other homeless person. If it's another homeless person they'll stay to protect their turf."

They continued on until they reached a junction of two tunnels. The tunnels met at angle and formed an X. Berto shined his powerful flashlight down one of the shafts and Ben could see another intersection at the far end of the light beam. "This is what I wanted you to see, Ben. These things are like a maze. If a suspect goes into a tunnel he could pop up anywhere in the city. If you try to follow someone down here you probably won't find him and you stand a good chance of getting lost. With no radio comms you'd be in serious trouble. Never go into a tunnel alone, and always let dispatch know before you go in. There are urban legends about people going into these tunnels and never being seen again."

As they were walking out Ben asked, "There's something I don't get. If these are designed as storm drains won't all this stuff clog them up? Why doesn't the city come in here and clear everything out?"

Berto replied, "Well, first of all, it hardly ever rains here, and when it does it's not very heavy or for very long. These tunnels are designed for a thousand year flood event. They're dry almost all the time, or just have trickles of water. The city used to come in once in a blue moon and clean all the stuff out, but it's like playing whack-a-mole. As soon as they clear it out the homeless just build it all up again. They say back in the late 1980s when they had some serious rain the water washed all this crap into the Sweetwater River and out to sea. Supposedly a few bodies washed out along with all the junk. Don't worry about the water, Ben. I just wanted you to get an appreciation for the size and scope of the tunnel network, so you don't just blindly rush in here one day."

Near the end of shift Salazar phoned dispatch to see what calls for service they were holding. Nothing important was waiting to be assigned, just several minor calls dispatch would hold until the swing shift went on duty. He then called Sergeant Selby and confirmed he was clear and still wanted to meet with Ben. "Ben, return to the station. Sergeant Selby wants to meet with you and I've got to catch up on your daily progress reports. We're done for today."

Back at the station, Ben unloaded the car, cleaned himself up as best he could, and knocked on Sergeant Selby's office door.

"Come in."

"Officer Olsen reporting as ordered, Sergeant."

Selby slouched in a swivel chair behind a standard issue city desk. "Shut the door and sit down, Olsen." He pointed to an armless chair against one wall. "And knock off that military shit. I told Berto I wanted to see you to give you the standard welcome to the squad pep talk and all that hoohah. Seeing as you're already in your third week with my squad it's a little late for that. Berto is an outstanding training officer and I know he's got you on the right track. I really called you in here because I wanted to talk to you about Jackie."

Trying to hide his astonishment, he thought, Oh boy, here we go. I wonder why Jackie didn't warn me this was coming?

Hard eyed, Selby said, "Are you in there, Olsen? Did you hear me?"

"Yes, sir, I heard you. I was just kind of surprised. Jackie and I had agreed to keep our dating to ourselves until we decided it was going to last."

"Is it going to last? Never mind. I told Jackie I wouldn't say anything to you but that was a few weeks ago. I was hoping she would come to her senses but since she's still seeing you I guess she hasn't, so you and I need to talk. I know she told you I don't approve of her dating cops. Now I'm telling you. I don't like Jackie dating cops, and that includes wannabe trainee cops like you."

Ben tried to put Jackie's brother at ease. "Sergeant, I think I understand your concerns. I want to assure you my intentions towards your sister are completely honorable. We enjoy each other's company and share very similar views on virtually everything. She's a wonderful woman."

Irritated to start with, Selby was infuriated by what he perceived as Olsen's condescension. He sat up so fast the back of the chair slammed against the wall. "Are you patronizing me, rookie? You sure as hell don't need to tell me how nice my sister is. And give that hayseed bullshit a rest, would you? 'My intentions are honorable.' Jesus Christ, nobody talks like that anymore. I'm not one of the guys in the locker room that wants to hear you brag about your conquests. I'm her brother."

"Sergeant, I've told no one that I'm seeing Jackie. And that's all I am doing - seeing her. We are not having sex, and with respect, if we were it would be none of your concern. She's a grown woman."

"You've got some balls to talk to me that way, Olsen. I'll give you that. My concern, as you put it, is the welfare and good name of my sister. I won't stand for you or any cop to use her and then toss her aside like an old toy you've become bored with."

Trying to contain his growing anger, Ben said, "I would never do that to any woman, and especially not to someone as special as Jackie."

"Yeah, I bet she's special to you, isn't she? You ever date a black woman before? I bet they don't even have any blacks back home in Cornpone, Wisconsin, do they? That's what this is really all about, isn't it? Country boy coming to the big city to take a walk on the wild side."

Ben was shocked and outraged, and no longer bothered to hide his resentment. Jackie had warned him her brother didn't want her dating cops, but she never mentioned that he was prejudiced against whites and country folk. "Sergeant Selby, Jackie thinks the world of you. She told me she thinks of you more as her father than as a brother. I am not going to dignify your coarse comment with an answer, and out of respect for Jackie I'm not going to mention it to her, either. Are we through here?"

Without waiting for the sergeant to answer he got up and walked out of his office, closing the door behind him in a not quite slam.

The shift was over and Ben went into the locker room to shower and change into civilian clothes. He was seething. Salazar had already changed and was just leaving. "Ben, what the hell? I've never seen you look so angry. Sarge give you some bad news? I told him you're doing well."

"I don't want to talk about it, Berto. It's between me and him."

"Okay, Ben. You know I'll listen if you want to talk."

"I just need to calm down. Don't worry, I'll be ready to go tomorrow morning."

"All right, Ben. See you in the morning."

But Salazar did not go home. He was curious to know what had set Ben off. If Sergeant Selby had a problem with Ben it was a direct reflection on him as his field training officer. Ben was doing well, far better than most trainees, so it puzzled Berto even more. He knocked on Selby's closed office door.

"Who is it?"

"Corporal Salazar, Sarge. You got a minute?"

"How about we talk tomorrow, Berto? I'm getting ready to go home."

"I think it needs to be now, Sarge."

"All right, come in then."

Salazar entered and shut the door behind him. One look at Selby was all he needed to know something was badly wrong. "What's going on, Sarge? You and Olsen have a knock down drag out in here? I'm his FTO and if you have a problem with my trainee then I should be the first to know about it. Olsen wouldn't tell me anything."

Selby wearily fell back into his chair. "Ah, Berto. It's not about you. And it's not about Olsen's performance. He's doing fine. It's me. You know how I am about cops dating my sister. Those other assholes she dated treated her like trash. It drives me crazy."

"Olsen's dating Jackie? When did that start?"

"About two months ago now. You saying you didn't know?"

"Sarge, nobody knows, or I would've heard. Olsen hardly opens his mouth except in the line of duty. He's one of the quietest guys I've ever met."

"Yeah, I know. I've heard that about him. I also heard he doesn't swear. Is that true?"

"Well, I never thought about it, but yeah, now that you say it. I've never heard him cuss. Pretty rare for a cop."

"Rare? It's a first. Anyway, he pissed me off big time and I said some things I shouldn't have said. He's probably gonna grieve to the union about it."

"I'll talk to him, Sarge. I don't see him going to the union for anything. He's not that way. He's kind of an old school throwback, if you know what I mean."

"Yeah, okay, Berto. I'm going home. Guess I'll talk to Jackie and take my lumps."

Ben drove to his house in Pacific Beach, a small beach area community in San Diego. Pacific Beach is kind of seedy and it's known as one of the least desirable beach towns to live in. It was the best Ben could afford, however, and he thought it was just fine. His landlord had been happy to rent to a new police officer and Ben enjoyed the beach town atmosphere. If he had the time he still preferred to go to Coronado for a day at the beach, but if he only had a couple of hours he would drive the five minutes to the beach near his house.

On the thirty minute drive from the NCPD station to his house Ben mentally reviewed his conversation with

Sergeant Selby. It had certainly not gone well, and he realized in hindsight he could have handled things better. Walking out on the sergeant without permission was probably not the best way to end the conversation. Still, Selby had infuriated him with his blunt insinuation he was only dating Jackie for the thrill of dating a black woman. Yes, she was the first black woman he had ever dated, he'd been right about that, but her skin color had nothing whatsoever to do with his attraction to her. Ben was about as racially color blind as a person could ever be. He had not even seen a black person until he was sixteen years old. There had been none in his hometown of Barron when he was a kid. He came across a black kid occasionally, playing basketball and football against the nearby high schools. Sometimes the parents of the boy would be sitting in the stands. Ben's family, friends and neighbors never talked about race for the same reason they never discussed kangaroo husbandry - it just wasn't part of their world.

At San Diego State there were plenty of African Americans, of course, as well as students representing virtually every race and ethnicity on the planet. He had not befriended any of them, and except for the occasional mandatory ROTC social event he did not socialize with blacks, either. Of course, it was just Ben's nature. In truth, he did not socialize much with anyone.

His first close and prolonged interaction with African Americans was in the Marine Corps. Blacks were well represented there all up and down the chain of command. The military had led America in racial integration and by the time Ben joined the Marine Corps men and women of all races working together was taken for granted. Everyone in the Marine Corps was the same color - Marine green.

He became close to his men in Iraq as only comrades in battle can. He routinely put his life on the line for them, and they for him. He anguished as much over the occasional loss of one of the men in his platoon as he would over the loss of one of his own brothers. Those men were his brothers, in all the ways that counted, regardless of their race, ethnicity, religious beliefs or anything else. They were Marines, and they were his Marines.

Lost in his thoughts, he was surprised to find himself turning into his driveway. His anger at Selby had faded, and instead he felt only sadness. He hoped the sergeant's attitude would not come between him and Jackie. He decided not to even mention the ugly conversation to her.

Rod Selby was also reflecting on his confrontation with Ben as he drove home. He felt like a fool and was ashamed of himself. He was a fair man, not a bigoted man. Wasn't he? His remarks to Ben caused him to question his own beliefs. He had lost his temper and said some stupid things, but how could he even have thought those things? Unlike Ben, Selby had spent his entire life dealing with racial prejudice, both subtle and overt. He thought he was beyond that, but his comments to Ben made him think again. Certainly he had been treated fairly in all his years with the National City police, and he owed it to Ben to treat him the same way.

The next morning, at the end of the pre-shift briefing, Sergeant Selby said he wanted Ben and Berto to stay behind a minute. After the rest of the squad filed out, Selby spoke to them. "Ben, I wanted to apologize for the way I acted and for what I said to you yesterday. Berto knows what happened, and I feel like I let him down, too. I don't know what came over me. Jackie is the only family I have here and I still think of her as my little sister. I was out of line and just lost my mind. I'm sorry."

He extended his hand to shake and Ben grasped it firmly. "That means a lot to me, Sergeant. Thank you. Everyone deserves a mulligan now and then. As far as I'm concerned it never happened."

I heard today Jackie is dating Ben Olsen, the new guy in field training. At first I didn't believe it, but then I heard it from two other cops. I had to know for sure, so I asked Berto. He's Olsen's FTO and he's tight with Selby, so he would have the straight poop. He confirmed it!

What could Jackie possibly see in Olsen? He and I are nothing alike. It's got to be just a stage she's going through, on the rebound from me. It won't last, and she'll come back where she belongs, to me. She has to.

Berto said Selby was pissed about Olsen dating his sister. Hah! He gets upset anytime a cop dates Jackie, so fuck him. But Olsen better not be fucking Jackie. That would not be acceptable. Jackie is mine.

On the last day of phase two Ben and Berto were tying up loose ends. They were discussing the few items on the field training check off list they still had not taken care of when the radio came to life. "222 John with 225 Edward to cover on a suicidal person outside room 742 of the Holiday Inn, 802 Roosevelt Avenue. Adult female sitting on the balcony railing threatening to jump."

"222 John 10-4."

Berto grabbed the radio microphone. "225 Edward 10-4. We're already on scene. We'll take primary." By coincidence they had been parked in the underground parking area of the hotel doing their paperwork and thus were already on scene.

They left the patrol car and went to the elevator. As they rode up to the seventh floor Berto told Ben, "This is not the time for training, Ben. I'll talk to the woman, you just cover me. Usually these folks are not serious but you never know."

They left the elevator on the seventh floor and turned the corner to the west side of the building. Berto told dispatch to keep the radio clear for them. The view of the bay and the ocean beyond the balcony was spectacular. A well-dressed white woman in her 30s was sitting on the railing, facing outward, with her legs dangling over the side of the building. She was in an extremely precarious position, as likely to accidentally slip over the side as to go on purpose. This woman was not just making a suicidal gesture, she was seriously considering it.

She saw them approaching and said softly, "If you come any closer I'll jump." They both stopped.

Several people were watching through their partially open hotel room doors. One of them must have called 911. Berto quietly said, "My name is Alberto. What's yours?"

"I'm Barbara Stills. I know what you're trying to do and it's not going to work. I'll jump when I'm ready."

"I just want to talk with you, Barbara, that's all. Is that OK?"

"Yeah, that's OK. But I don't like all these people gawking at me." She looked over her shoulder at the people with their room doors open.

Berto did not want to raise his voice to order the people inside, so he said "Ben, walk over and tell all those people to shut their doors and stay in their rooms." He started forward but Barbara said, "No! Stay away from me!"

Ben stopped. Berto said, "Go around the other way and get those people inside." Ben sprinted on the wrap around balcony until he was back on the west side. As he came to each open door he told the person to close it and stay inside. When he was done he and Berto were on opposite sides of the woman.

Berto said, "Barbara, they're all inside now. Why don't you come onto the balcony and we'll talk some more?"

"No, I don't think so. I'm going to look at the ocean another minute and then I'm going away." Her calmness was chilling.

The beat 2 officer, Paul Woodruff, came around the corner from the elevators, walking rapidly, then stopping short when he saw everyone. Barbara became agitated and her voice was cracking. "There's too many cops here. I know you guys are going to try something."

Berto said, "Paul, go back to the elevators and keep everyone else away from here."

He was quickly out of sight. While the distraught woman was focused on the other officers Ben silently shuffled several feet closer to her. He had received exactly one hour of training in the police academy on dealing with suicidal people, and at the moment he could recall none of it.

Berto started to say something else when the hotel room door between him and Barbara suddenly jerked opened. A man in a business suit started to step outside, saw the woman sitting on the railing and the cops right outside his door, and was so shocked he stopped in mid stride, one foot off the ground.

Barbara let out a startled "Oh!" and pushed herself off the railing into space. Acting purely by instinct, with reflexes honed by years of high school sports and sharpened in combat, Ben lunged towards her. The woman's entire body was already below the railing when he caught her right wrist in his right hand. Her body weight caused Ben to slam into the side of the concrete balcony and bent him over the railing at the waist. He needed every bit of strength in his well-muscled body to hang onto her and not follow her over the railing himself. She was screaming, flailing both her legs and her free arm as she dangled seventy feet above the concrete parking lot.

"Let me go! Let me go! Let me go!"

Gripping her even more tightly and adjusting his lower body, Ben said, "No way, Barbara. It's not meant to be. You know that now. Help us help you. Stop kicking and give me your other hand."

To his great surprise, she stopped kicking and reached her free hand up to him. He grabbed her other wrist, and with Berto bracing his legs, he lifted her up to the railing. "I'm OK now, Berto. Get a hold of her and let's get her over the railing."

They lifted her over the railing, with Barbara now helping by bracing her feet on the outside of the balcony. They got her onto the balcony but both cops were afraid to release their grip on her for fear she would try to leap over the side. The businessman was still standing there astounded, like a deer in the headlights. He finally lowered his foot to the ground.

Berto said, "Sir, step outside and leave your door open. We need your room."

The man said, "I was just leaving anyway," and he walked out. They led Barbara inside the room and closed the door, Ben leaning back against it to prevent her from leaving. She was sobbing uncontrollably.

Berto informed dispatch they were all secure in room 744 and asked for paramedics to respond with a gurney. Ben started to speak to the woman but Berto shook his head no. They sat silently while she sobbed, until the paramedics arrived, strapped her down, and wheeled her away.

Saturday morning Jackie went over to Ben's house and they sat at a picnic table in his tiny backyard. They both wanted to go to the beach but knew it was pointless. It was Labor Day weekend and the weather was perfect. They probably couldn't get within a mile of any beach in the county today for all the people, so they settled for Ben's backyard.

Jackie told Ben she had a long conversation with her brother in which Rod told her all about his unfortunate talk with Ben. "He's really ashamed of himself, Ben. He was so sincere I couldn't even be mad at him."

"I've already put it behind me, Jackie. I wasn't going to bring it up unless you mentioned it. There're no hard feelings on my part."

"Good," Jackie said. "Did you want to take a walk to the beach? I know it's kind of far but we'd never find a parking space."

"Nah. I rode my bicycle down there earlier this morning and it was already packed. I could hardly see the sand for all the people. As much as I love the weather here sometimes I miss the peace and quiet of Barron."

"Yeah, you're just a regular party animal, Ben. Lucky for you I'm a low maintenance girl."

"Jackie, I am lucky. You're the best thing that's ever happened to me."

Laughing, she said, "Oooh, you'll turn a girl's head with that kind of talk, Benjamin."

They kissed each other deeply. They hadn't been kissing long, and each time it seemed to get better and longer. "You know, Ben, this picnic table isn't exactly made for romance."

He blushed slightly as he said, "I know, but I'm afraid if we go somewhere more comfortable I might not be able to control myself."

Jackie giggled and said, "What makes you think I want you to?"

He replied, "Jackie, I'm starting to hope you and I will be together for a long time. I don't want to ruin that by getting into something we're not ready for yet."

"Ben, you are so sweet, but we're both adults, and we've been dating for almost two months now. I'm ready to move on to the next level in our relationship."

"Would you be mad at me if I told you I wasn't ready?" It's not that I don't want to, it's just that it doesn't seem right to me yet."

"God, Ben, you really are an old fashioned guy. It's one of the things that attracted me to you, so I guess I can't complain about it now. All right. I like you too much to try to make you do something that would make you uncomfortable. Just don't make me wait too long, okay?"

Not comfortable with the turn the conversation had taken, he quickly changed the subject. "The word's out at the PD you and I are dating. Your brother was kind of forced to tell Berto Salazar, and he told someone else, and you know how that goes."

She nodded her head. "It was just a matter of time. I was mainly concerned about Rod, and he's known for a while. I'm okay with it."

Pleased, Ben said, "Well, now that people know you can come by the PD more often and you won't have to worry about the guys hitting on you."

"Ben, you're dreaming. Those horny toads even hit on each other's wives. I don't think they're serious about it, at least I hope they're not, but there it is."

They spent a long, comfortable day together.

Chapter Three

"We're not traffic cops."
-- Corporal Remy Aquino, Field Training Officer

For phase three of field training Ben was assigned to swing shift weekends, so he would work from 3:00 PM to 1:00 AM Thursday to Sunday. His field training officer was Corporal Remy Aquino, the longest serving officer below the rank of sergeant in the whole department.

On his first day with his new squad Ben was late for the pre-shift briefing. His locker, which he routinely locked ever since the boot laces incident, had been super glued shut. It took him quite a while to get it open, and he was late as a result.

Sergeant Luisa Clemente stopped her briefing and smiled at Ben when he came through the squad room door. "Hi there, Ben. I heard you had some locker trouble, but obviously you overcame it. I was wondering if you'd have to work in civilian clothes tonight. Just step right up to the podium and introduce yourself to the squad."

He gave his usual short speech, and no one seemed to mind. After briefing, while Ben and his new field training officer were loading up the patrol car, he noticed an odd clock in Aquino's equipment locker. "Corporal, what's that clock for?"

Beaming, the small Filipino man replied, "It's my retirement clock. Check it out. Three years, two months, twenty seven days, fourteen hours and fifty two minutes until I retire. It runs backwards. Pretty cool, huh?"

Actually, Ben didn't think it was cool at all. He had known a few Marines who were just putting in their time until retirement. In the Corps, they were known as "ROAD warriors." ROAD stood for Retired while still On Active Duty.

As they drove out of the underground parking garage, Aquino told him, "Let's hit Starbucks right now. They've got the only decent coffee in this whole shitty town. It's always the first thing we do when we go in service. Then we'll go back for refills right before they close at 8:00 PM. If we miss closing time we'll sneak down to Chula Vista where they've got a Starbucks that stays open until midnight."

They rolled out of the station and reported to dispatch they were in service. As they were pulling into the Starbucks parking lot the radio came to life. "423 John with 422 John to cover on a report of domestic violence at 1707 McClary Street. Female victim reports she was punched and kicked by her boyfriend. The suspect is still in the residence."

"423 John 10-4."

"422 John 10-4."

Ben was turning the car around in the parking lot when Aquino asked, "What are you doing? There's a parking space right there."

"I was going to head over towards McClary until the assigned units report they don't need any assistance. The dispatcher said the suspect is still on scene."

Shaking his head no, Ben's latest field training officer looked both amused and disappointed at his gung ho attitude. "They'll call us if they need us. Besides, we don't want to have every patrol car in the city over there. It looks bad. Just park the car and let's get our coffee."

He found a parking space and they got in line for coffee. He was surprised to see after Aquino got his coffee he sat down at a table inside the business instead of going out to the car to drink it. Ben had no choice but to join him.

"You're just itching to go to that domestic violence call, aren't you?" Aquino asked.

Ben said, "Well, I've been to a bunch of DV calls already, but they bother me. I really hate to see a woman get beat up."

"Don't worry about this one, Ben. That address is a Chud house. It's NHI."

"Corporal, I've never heard those terms before. What do they mean?"

"Call me Remy. Chud stands for Cannibalistic Humanoid Urban Dweller. It's from an old science fiction movie. Chuds are scumbags who are always getting arrested. This time they'll arrest the boyfriend, next time the girlfriend. A pimp beats his ho today, then the whore stabs the pimp tomorrow. This week's victims are next week's suspects. It's life in the ghetto.

"NHI means No Humans Involved. We're out at that house every weekend. Believe me; those morons ain't worth letting our coffee get cold."

The shift was not overly busy that night but all the patrol units were getting dispatched to calls steadily. Ben and his FTO had not been assigned once. They had been parked down at the 24th Street marina, at the far western end of the city, most of the night. Except for a trip to Starbucks just before closing, they hadn't even driven around the city. Aquino seemed content to sit in the car and listen to some talk radio show about UFOs and conspiracy nuts.

"Remy, are we going to sit here all night?"

"Well, Salazar told me you were a self-starter, Ben. Why don't you study your policies and procedures manual or the penal code while we've got some down time? Were you waiting for me to tell you?"

Irritated, Ben replied, "No, I was hoping to get into some calls. I study the P & P and other stuff at home."

Aquino's normally soft voice took on a harsh tone. "They're not paying you to study at home, Ben. These bastards don't pay us enough in the first place and they screw us every chance they get. You do your studying here while you're on duty, getting paid for it. We'll get our share of the calls, and check off all of the boxes in the training manual, don't worry about that. I've been doing this since you were in diapers, so just go with the program."

Sunday was the "barrel day" for swing shift - Ben's "Friday" and the "Monday" for the other swing shift squad, so briefing had twice as many cops as usual. As was their routine, after the briefing Ben and Remy drove to Starbucks. When they sat down with their coffees Remy said, "Sundays are good training days, Ben. The other squad will take all the calls and let us catch up on our paperwork. We'll put a lot of checks in those boxes."

Ben was frustrated. They had done virtually nothing all week long. They seldom got assigned to calls, even as a cover unit, and Aquino never volunteered to take calls for the sake of Ben's training, as Salazar and Zobriskie both had done.

Officer Allen Gerhardt walked into Starbucks. Aquino said, "Hey Allen, what are you doing here? I thought you always go to the 7-11 to be with your sweet thing?"

Gerhardt replied, "Yeah, but she's off tonight. Their coffee sucks, so when she's off I come over here."

Ben knew Gerhardt was married, and not to the clerk at the 7-11. After he had his coffee Aquino asked him to join them at the table. Staring at Ben he replied, "Nah, it smells too much like shit in here. Maybe your rookie crapped his pants worrying about getting a hot call."

After he left, Aquino asked Ben, "What did you do to piss him off?"

"Nothing, really. Hopkins and I had a little misunderstanding a few months ago and Gerhardt won't let it go."

The FTO nodded knowingly. "Ah, I see. Those guys are real tight, Ben. You need to watch yourself. Hopkins and his boys can play rough."

"Thanks, Remy. I can take care of myself."

Ben was happy to go on his three days off, but Jackie's classes and part time work schedule didn't allow them to have any real time together. They had to be content with meeting for an hour or so for lunch on campus and talking on the phone. It was so frustrating Ben was actually relieved to start his work week again and focus on his training.

"422 John with 423 John to cover on a trespassing complaint, 127 Hartford Street. Reporting party says there are people underneath the house. The reporting party may be a mentally ill person."

Both units acknowledged. Remy scoffed. "That's not trespassing and it's not a nutcase. It's the meth monster rearing its ugly head."

"What do you mean, 'meth monster?'" Ben asked.

Remy was surprised Ben had not yet experienced a call of this sort. "You're not familiar with the meth monster? We'll take this call for training, then." He grabbed the radio and said, "425 Edward, we'll take the Hartford Street call for training and advise you if we need a cover unit."

The assigned units and dispatch all acknowledged as Ben started towards Hartford Street. "First of all," Remy explained, "the dispatcher said the call involves a possibly mentally ill person, so the reporting party said something that made the dispatcher think it's a bogus call and the guy is a nut. You can glean a lot of information just from listening closely to what the dispatcher says. This is not about people trespassing under the house; it's a person who only thinks there are people under there.

"Heavy methamphetamine users become paranoid after prolonged use. These delusions are all in their screwed up minds, but it seems absolutely real to them." The call for service popped up on the patrol car's computer screen, and Remy read the details as Ben drove. "The reporting party is a 20 year old man. His father is also at the house. The dispatcher could hear the father in the background telling his son not to bother the police. The son said something about digging under the house to find the people hiding there. Oh yeah, this is a classic case of meth paranoia. These guys are almost never violent but stay on your toes just in case."

They arrived at the house and the father met them outside. "I'm sorry my son bothered you, officers, but thank you for coming. I'm at my wits end and could use some advice.

"It's just my son, Sebastian, and me. There's no one else. I was gone three days on a business trip and when I came home I found him digging through the floor in his bedroom. He's been using meth for years. I've tried to get him help but he refuses. He's never been this bad before. You'll see."

They accompanied the father inside. Ben noticed the house was clean and well furnished. They were in one of the best areas of National City, a solidly middle class neighborhood. Meth makes no social or racial distinctions, it's everywhere.

As they entered Sebastian's room Ben was taken aback by a huge pile of dirt that covered the bed and spilled over onto the floor. It had to be four feet high. Sebastian was nowhere to be seen.

Ben shot a questioning look at the father. "He's underneath the house digging. The hole's in the closet."

Ben looked in the closet and saw a two foot wide hole through the floor and sub-floor. He could hear someone moving around down there, and the sound of digging and scraping. Remy told Ben he would talk to Sebastian.

"Sebastian, it's the National City police. We're here to find the people for you. Come on out of there."

Sebastian crawled out of the hole. He was filthy and had a small shovel in his hand. Remy gently took the shovel from him and handed it to his father. "Sebastian, there's no one down there, is there?"

"No, they keep moving. I'll find them if I dig fast enough, though. Listen, you can hear them now." He turned to go back into the hole but Remy stopped him by putting a hand on his arm.

"We'll find them, Sebastian. We're the police, it's what we do. You need to go with your father to a hospital while we find the people, OK?"

The young man became upset. "You can't force me to go to the hospital. The cops tried that before and the hospital wouldn't take me. I'm not crazy. My dad can't make me, either, I'm an adult."

Remy took out his handcuffs. "You're right. I can't force you to go to the hospital, but I can damn sure take you to jail. You're under the influence of methamphetamine. They'll keep you until you come off your high. Now, it's your choice - go to the hospital with your father or go to jail with me."

Not surprisingly, the pitiful young adult opted for the hospital. Remy gave the father a card with the names, addresses and phone numbers of all the drug treatment facilities in the area, and they drove away a few minutes later, leaving Ben and Remy to lock up the house. Ben was still trying to absorb it all. "I've never seen anything like this in my life. It's unbelievable."

"You'll see plenty more of it when you work the streets a while. A few months back we had a call of six men with machine guns surrounding a house. When we arrived and talked to the guy he insisted they were still there, standing right behind us. We had another, a 911 call from a girl who said her boyfriend was chasing her down the street with an ax. That sounded so real every cop in the city responded. We found her running full tilt down Hoover Avenue with no one else around. It's really scary and sad. The problem for us is they're stoned, not mentally ill. All we can do is take them to jail, which does no good at all. They need drug treatment, but until they decide to get it, they're on their own."

Near the end of his second week with Aquino they were once again driving from Starbucks to the marina where they would park and Ben would study. As they approached a four way intersection a car coming from the cross street blew through the red light at about 20 MPH. Ben hit his police lights and turned to get behind the driver and pull him over. "What are you doing, Ben?"
"Didn't you see that guy blow the light right in front of us? I'm going to pull him over."
"Look, we're not traffic cops. Turn your lights off and head over to the marina."
Ben was astounded. "Remy, that guy blew the light big time, right in front of our marked police car. He was only doing 20 in a 35 zone. He's probably drunk out of his mind. He still hasn't seen our lights and pulled over."
More sternly this time, Remy said, "Ben, turn the lights off." He reluctantly complied.
"Now, head on over to the marina. As I said, we're not traffic cops, we're patrol guys. If we pulled over every traffic violator we saw we'd never get anything else done. That's what we have a traffic division for. We need to stay clear and available for calls. Patrol guys should never be doing proactive stuff. It takes you out of service, and it takes your cover unit out of service, too. There're only five units on duty in the whole city right now, and you want to make two of them unavailable just because some citizen pissed you off. If the city really wanted proactive policing they would hire a bunch more cops."

"Remy, that guy was probably DUI. Don't we have an obligation to take him off the road?"

"You don't know he was drunk. Are you basing that on your years of police experience, or your own personal experience?"

The snarky insinuation angered him, and Ben responded heatedly. "I hardly ever drink, and I never drink and drive."

"Relax, Ben, it was a joke. You need to lighten up a bit. Let's say that guy was drunk, and we arrested him for DUI. Have you done a DUI arrest yet?"

"No, I haven't, and that's another good reason to go after him."

"DUI training is in phase four, Ben. Zobriskie will get you all the drunk drivers you want. Until you get trained there's no point in making a DUI arrest. The lawyers would just beat it in court.

"DUI arrests involve a lot of paperwork. They are very time consuming, maybe three hours from start to finish. You're out of service the whole time and some other cop is taking your calls. It might be worth it for some major felony but drunk driving is only a misdemeanor offense. Depending on how your squad sergeant wants to play it the guy won't even go to jail, you'll write him a notice to appear in court and release him at the station to a sober driver."

Ben had to admit much of what Remy was saying made sense, but he still didn't like it.

The next day they were parked out at the Plaza Bonita mall for a change, in the far southeastern corner of the city. At least it was a change of scenery. Ben had figured out Remy intentionally had him park at the far reaches of the city. That way, when the occasional call for a cover unit came to them Remy could truthfully respond they would be enroute from a long distance. Upon hearing that, the dispatcher would usually cancel them and assign another, closer unit. Everyone on the squad was on to the trick and the dispatchers only assigned Remy as a last resort. What a change from Alberto Salazar. The few times his phase two FTO grudgingly had Ben park to do paperwork they always parked in the heart of the city, ready to respond to any call.

"Remy, why are you on swing shift? You hate the hours and you complain about working nights all the time. With your seniority can't you tell them you want day shift?"

"Ah, these dickheads have a policy to spread out all the different types of cops. They try to have a Spanish speaker on every squad, a female cop, a Tagalog speaker, whatever. It's like they're loading freaking Noah's Ark or something. 99% of the Filipinos in the city speak English, so I'm never needed anyway. I earn the extra money for language pay they give me just for the aggravation, though."

Ben still didn't get it. "I just came from dayshift with Corporal Salazar. He's only got six years with the PD and his squad also has a really young Filipino guy."

Remy said, "Salazar is senior to me as a corporal. I just made it last year. No offense to you, Ben, but I had no interest in training new guys so I never tried for promotion. I had it made as the senior slick-sleever in the department. I always got the squad assignment I wanted. Then I took a hard look at my finances and realized I wasn't going to do very well in retirement. I could have stayed a slick-sleever and worked a lot of overtime for the last few years or promote to corporal. I chose the easier way."

Now there's a shocker, thought Ben.

Phase three was a frustrating time for Ben. He was doing all of his studying in the car which left him tons of free time on his days off. Unfortunately, he and Jackie had very little opportunity to spend that time together, and Ben missed her so much he didn't have any interest in doing anything on his own. He ended up at the beach most days, or fishing out at Santee lakes. He might have done the same things with Jackie, but it wasn't the same without her.

One night it was really hopping and all the units were busy, including Ben and Remy. Even when the graveyard shift came on duty it stayed busy for both squads. Ben loved it. When it finally settled down and the graveyard guys were handling the calls Remy told Ben to drive down to Chula Vista to the Starbucks. They had not had time to get their second cup of coffee before the National City Starbucks closed for the night.

Ben was worried about leaving the city limits without permission. He knew from his relentless studies of the policies and procedures manual patrol units could not leave the city without at least informing dispatch. Remy assured Ben it wasn't an issue and everyone did it. Sure enough, there were two other NCPD patrol cars in the Starbucks lot when they got there. The business was just over the city boundary and the units could be back in National City within moments if needed.

As they sipped their coffee his FTO said, "Ben, the P & P manual is not the bible. For the most part it gives us broad policy guidelines and allows officers the flexibility to use their best judgment in the field. If you try to follow the manual to the letter you won't get much done and you won't be a very good cop." It was the first good advice Remy had given him.

In his last week with Aquino another unit was assigned to take a report of a residential burglary. To Ben's surprise, Remy got on the radio and said they would take the call for training. It was only the second time Remy had volunteered to take a call. Ben had already taken several burglary reports and he wasn't too happy about it. Burglary reports involved gathering evidence, taking photos, dusting for fingerprints, and interviewing the victims. It was routine, cold crime police work and pretty boring.

When they arrived on scene Remy told Ben he would take the lead and Ben should just watch. The victim was an older Filipino man. He explained to the officers he had come home from work after cashing his paycheck and left six hundred dollars cash on his bedroom dresser near the window when he went to bed. The window had been partially open during the night. When he got up in the morning the money was gone. The story sounded fishy to Ben, and even though Remy questioned him quite closely, the guy stuck to it. Ben was thinking it wouldn't take long to dust the window and the dresser for fingerprints and the report would be simple. Remy suddenly barked out, "Bulaan!" and then went off into rapid fire Tagalog. He and the victim went back and forth in the Filipino language for a minute or so, then the guy gave up and stopped talking. Ben had no idea what they were saying, but it was clear from the body language and the tone of his voice the victim had lost the argument. He looked like a whipped dog who knew he was about to get another beating. Remy told Ben they were through and they left.

"What the heck was that all about?" Ben asked when they were back in the car.

Remy smiled. "I knew from the call details the victim's story about a burglary was bullshit. I've taken a dozen of these false calls over the years. The real story is the guy went to a casino last night and lost his paycheck. He knows his wife will fry him over it so he makes up this crock about a burglary to save his ass. I had to make him more afraid of me than of his wife to get the truth out of him. I told him I was going to pull the surveillance tapes at the Barona casino and when I saw him on the tape I was going to arrest him for making a false police report. That's when he finally admitted he made it all up."

Ben was impressed. "There're half a dozen different Indian casinos around here. How did you know he went to Barona last night.?"

The older cop said, "There's a Barona 'dreamcatcher' talisman hanging on their front door, and I saw a book of matches with the Barona name on the kitchen counter when we walked inside. Seemed like a reasonable guess. There's a point in all of this, Ben. Everyone lies to the police. It's just human nature. Even legitimate victims will only tell you some of the truth some of the time. Everybody's hiding something. Never forget that."

Ben's last training officer, Alberto Salazar, had told him almost exactly the same thing. This exceptionally important bit of street wisdom from a twenty seven year veteran cop was worth all the frustration Ben had suffered in phase three of his field training. Unfortunately for him, he didn't pay a lot of attention to it.

Chapter Four

"Phase four never ends."
-- Corporal George Zobriskie, Field Training Officer

    Per the training program curriculum Ben was assigned to Corporal George Zobriskie again for his fourth and final phase of field training. The idea was, having seen Ben since day one, Zobriskie would be the best person to judge his progress through the program. Zobriskie did not have the final decision on whether to let Ben work the streets on his own, but his recommendation carried a huge amount of weight with the training staff.
    On his first day of phase four with the weekend graveyard squad, Sergeant Ruffin welcomed him back. Friday was the "barrel day" for graveyard shift, with the weekday squad here on "their Friday" and Ben's weekend squad starting their work week on "their Monday." Ben was already known to everyone, so they went right into the briefing. He looked around the room at the eleven cops. Sergeant Ruffin had treated him fairly the first time, and Ben thought Zobriskie was a good cop and an excellent training officer. He wondered about the rest of the officers on his squad, and which ones might be making his life difficult with all the rookie pranks. Hopkins clearly did not like him, and McFadden was tight with Hopkins. Carlos Delacruz, the beat 2 officer, never talked to Ben except when he had to. He couldn't decide if that was because Delacruz was a friend of Hopkins or it was just the way he was. He didn't seem to talk to anybody very much and Ben never saw him at any of the coffee spots or paperwork hiding spots where the squads congregated when they weren't busy. Crystal York was the only woman officer on Ben's squad. She seemed friendly enough to him and she usually hung out at the coffee spots. Plus, as a woman it

was unlikely she would go into the men's locker room to set up some of the pranks. Ben decided she was not someone he had to worry about.

The cops from the other graveyard squad all seemed okay to Ben. Vernon Jefferson was an African American on beat 1. Arnoldo Bungabong was a Filipino on beat 2. He told Ben to call him Arnie but most of the cops called him Bungie, or Bonger, or Boingo. He was a happy go lucky guy and Ben thought the nickname Boingo suited him perfectly. Tara Morris was a young black woman assigned to beat 3. Leslie Hougardy was the beat 4 officer. He was called Horse by everyone, never Leslie. Since Hougardy was of average height and weight, back in phase one Ben had asked Zobriskie why he was called Horse. Zobriskie replied, "Well, the politically correct answer is, if you were a man named Leslie, wouldn't you want to be called anything except that? But the real answer is he's got a dick about a mile long. He's a legend around here. If you don't believe me check it out for yourself."

Ben had managed to avoid checking it out so far, and he still didn't know if Zobriskie was kidding him or not. The other squad's Corporal was Te Kawanishi, a Japanese American who seemed squared away. Ben thought back to Remy Aquino describing the squad assignment policy as "loading Noah's Ark," and it certainly seemed true of the weekday graveyard squad. Their sergeant was on extended injury leave and Ben had never met him. Corporal Kawanishi was the squad supervisor until the sergeant returned to duty.

As the squads were loading up their cars Hopkins found Ben. "I haven't had a chance to talk to you since that foot pursuit a few months back, Olsen. People tell me you had some questions about it."

Sure, Ben thought sardonically, you haven't had a chance to talk to me in three months. "Nope, no questions.

Corporal Zobriskie and I talked about it and he answered all of my concerns."

"Yeah, well if you ever have any questions about me in the future, I hope you're man enough to ask me to my face instead of whining to your training officer."

"Corporal Zobriskie and I talked about it because we debrief every call we go on, Hopkins. Yours was nothing special."

The beefy old timer scoffed. "Yeah, that's exactly right, rookie. It was nothing special."

Ben had had enough of Hopkins' macho man act, and decided to ruffle his feathers some. "I do have a question for you, though, Hopkins, now that you bring it up. What were you doing so far off your beat that night? And why didn't you radio you were contacting a suspicious person before the foot pursuit started?"

Hopkins face went red with anger and Ben could see a vein pulsing in his forehead. The veteran street cop closed the distance between them, and Ben could smell his nasty coffee breath. "That's two questions, asshole. And here's my answer to both of them - fuck you. When you get some time on the street, IF you make it through training and probation, then ask me again. Until then, mind your own fucking business."

Ben and his training officer headed out of the station into the night. He had worked every shift, graves, swings and days, and although it was hell on his social life, he really enjoyed patrolling the mostly empty streets on graveyards. Every car was much more likely to hold criminals, every pedestrian more likely to be a dope dealer, or prostitute, or one of their customers. Small groups of young Hispanic males walked the streets. He didn't need to be in the gang unit to know they were virtually certain to be gang members. Had he so quickly resorted to profiling? No, he decided, it was the totality of the circumstances, just as Berto had taught him. Basically, it was common sense.

No decent, sane person would be walking the streets of the ghetto past midnight.

Zobriskie spoke as Ben drove. "Ben, you're in phase four now. Four weeks from being on your own as a cop. I know you don't think you're ready yet, and you're not, but you will be ready four weeks from now. It won't feel like it, and your first shift in service on your own is a pretty scary thing. We all went through it. I can tell you at this point unless you suddenly get goofy and stupid over the next few weeks I'm going to tell the bosses you're good to go, so just put that out of your mind. Phase four is the time to hone your skills and fill in your knowledge gaps. We still have a bunch of boxes to check in the field training manual, but mostly you're going to tell me what you want to work on. We'll try to get into things you haven't seen or done yet, and whatever doesn't come up we'll talk it through or maybe get some of the squad to role play on a quiet night."

Hallelujah, thought Ben. What a change from Aquino! "Corporal, I was hoping to make a drunk driving arrest. Corporal Aquino told me those are programmed for phase four."

"Call me George, Ben. We'll get some deuces, don't worry."

"Deuces?"

"DUIs. We call them deuces. A drunk driver is a deuce driver, or just a deuce."

Ben said, "Gosh, is there anything in the English language cops don't change or abbreviate?"

The old veteran laughed. "Nope. Between the radio codes, the penal code, abbreviations and street slang, it's a whole other language - copspeak. After a few years you'll need to make a conscious effort to speak normal English with people or they won't understand you." Turning serious, he said, "You might make note, though, parolees understand copspeak perfectly, so when you are around one, for your safety you need to watch what you say."

They cruised the streets and responded to a few burglary alarm calls, which turned out to be false alarms. Statistically, burglary alarms turned out to be false 98% of the time. Cops and dispatchers know this and assume each call to be false, so there is no urgency to respond to them. Most people think cops respond urgently to alarm calls, with lights and siren, because that's what happens on TV and in the movies. The reality is the dispatchers will often hold a burglary alarm call ten minutes or more before assigning a unit to respond, and the responding officers will just drive there at normal speeds, obeying all traffic laws. In the rare case the alarm was valid and the house or business has been burglarized, the crooks are long gone by the time the cops show up. Ben thought paying money for a burglary alarm was a big waste of money.

"Ben, we've been all over the city tonight except for beat 4. Head on over there."

Hesitantly, Ben said, "I had a little run in with Hopkins after briefing and I was hoping to avoid bumping into him."

Zobriskie scoffed out, "Screw Hopkins. The whole city is my beat and you're with me. Head over there. He's not going to stop me from doing my job."

He made a turn and drove towards beat 4.

As they rolled through the quiet and dark streets, George said, "Are Hopkins and his asshole buddies still pulling rookie crap on you?"

"Somebody is. I'm sure it's Hopkins, but I can't prove it. Most of it is harmless stuff like shaving cream inside my boots or an official looking note on my locker to go see the Chief and turn in my badge. Berto introduced me one day to some of the regular prostitutes on the stroll, including a transvestite named Joey. The next day I found a pink ribbon tied around my baton with a note that said, 'Beat me anytime, big boy,' supposedly signed by Joey. That was pretty funny, actually. Not funny at all was somebody soaked all the clean underwear in my locker in pepper spray. And I've been late for briefing twice due to knots in my boots and my locker glued shut."

The training officer had a concerned look on his face. "Some of that stuff is pretty extreme. I don't recall any rookie ever having their locker glued shut. What if we had a hot call to respond to?"

"That's exactly what Berto said about the knots in my boots."

"I'll talk to Hopkins and tell him to knock off that horseshit."

"I'd prefer you didn't George, but thanks for the thought. What might help me is knowing who Hopkins' buddies are. That way I can keep an eye on things better."

"Okay, let's see. Hopkins' buddies… McFadden on our squad. Horse Hougardy on the other graveyard squad. Gerhardt and Wilson on swing shift. Paul Woodruff on days. There might be others. Most guys just tolerate him. Those guys I mentioned are his drinking buddies. Personally, I'm sick of his crap."

"How about Carlos Delacruz?"

"What, as one of Hopkins' buddies? No way. If you ain't white, you ain't right. That's his motto."

Ben was surprised. "Really? I can't believe the chief puts up with that stuff. When he interviewed me he made a huge deal about it. No room for it in my department, etc. etc."

"Yeah, and he means it, too. He's really brought us out of the dark ages. Hopkins flies under the radar, though. He gets more citizen complaints than most guys but he always seems to skate out of trouble."

Sunday night shortly before midnight they pulled into the 7-11 parking lot. Ben needed some coffee to stay awake. He had spent all day with Jackie instead of sleeping. He was exhausted, but it was worth it.

There was another NCPD patrol car parked in the lot, which was otherwise deserted. "That's Gerhardt's unit. You want me to go in with you?" George asked.

"No, I know you want to finish up that report. Can I bring you some coffee?"

"No, thanks. If Gerhardt gives you some crap just leave."

Ben smiled. "Thanks, Dad."

Ben entered the store to the tinkling of the door chimes. As he went to get his coffee he looked around and saw no one else. The cashier's station was deserted.

In the bathroom, the young clerk was sitting on the toilet giving oral sex to Allen Gerhardt. "Shit," she said. "Somebody's in the store."

Gerhardt groaned. "Don't stop now, baby, I'm almost there. Nothing's gonna happen with my car out front."

"Oh, Allen, I can't do this with somebody in the store."

"Tiff, it's my Friday! I ain't gonna see you for three days and I can't go home without finishing. I'll go crazy."

Ben was waiting at the cash register with his coffee. Finally, he called out, "National City police. Anybody in here?"

"Shit, Allen, that's it. We're done." The flustered young woman pushed him away and walked out into the store.

As Ben paid for his coffee he asked the young clerk, "Where's Officer Gerhardt? His car's out front."

"I don't know. He was in here before but he left. Maybe he went around back. Sometimes we have homeless people hanging out there and he clears them out for me."

Moments later Gerhardt stepped out of the restroom, frustrated beyond belief and in a very foul mood. "What the fuck, rookie? Your whole squad's down at the Chula Vista Starbucks."

Ignoring his comment, Ben said, "I thought you were supposed to be around the back checking on homeless people. What were you doing in the bathroom?"

"What does anybody do in a bathroom, you moron? I was taking a Ben and wiping my Olsen," Gerhardt replied, and laughed uproariously.

"Yeah, right. With Tiffany in there at the same time." The clerk turned quickly away and pretended to rearrange something under the counter. Ben could see her face was bright red.

Gerhardt growled out, "It ain't none of your fucking business what I was doing in there, asshole. You got your shitty coffee, now get the hell out of here."

When Ben returned to the car his training officer was just finishing his report. "George, I think I just walked in on Gerhardt and the clerk having sex in the bathroom."

"No shit? I heard he was banging the chick but I didn't think he had the balls to do it on duty. You saw them?"

"No, but it couldn't have been more obvious. They were both in the bathroom when I came in, then she came out and lied to me about it."

"Maybe he was in there helping her with something and she was just embarrassed about what you might think."

Ben shook his head no. "She was embarrassed all right. Her face was beet red. And Gerhardt's fly was open. He didn't even deny anything. Actually, he seemed kind of proud of himself."

George hated having to deal with crap like this. "OK, Ben. I'm sure you're right. What do you want to do about it?"

"He already thinks I lied about Hopkins' foot pursuit my first week of training. If I don't say anything about this he'll think I'm turning my cheek again. I can't let this slide."

Zobriskie was shaking his head. He knew the politics of the police department as well as he knew the city streets.

"Look, Ben. You said you didn't really see anything. An Internal Affairs beef won't go anywhere and all you'll do is piss everyone off."

Ben was incredulous. "Are you telling me to just let it go?"

George sighed. "You do what you have to do, Ben. I'm telling you Internal Affairs won't bother with it. Luisa Clemente's his sergeant. How about if I talk to her about it? She'll read him the riot act and be on him like white on rice after this. If you really feel you have to tell someone, it's about the best you can do."

"OK, George, but I'll go with you. It's only fair I tell her myself."

As they drove away an angry set of eyes watched until they were out of sight.

He's seeing way too much of Jackie. I followed them around town the other day, all cuddly and kissy. It was sickening to watch. Olsen's got to go. I can tell Jackie is becoming infatuated with him just as she did with me. But with me it was true love. That fucking farm boy just has her confused.

The following Friday the graveyard squads finished briefing and Ben went down to the underground parking garage to load his patrol car. Following standard procedure he carefully checked the entire car to ensure all the required equipment was present and working properly. He also searched the rear seat prisoner area to make sure a prisoner from the last shift, if any, had not dumped any contraband back there while being transported.

His training officer joined him, gave the car a cursory once over, and loaded his personal equipment. Ben radioed to dispatch "125 Edward in service," as they rolled out into the city.

A few hours later they returned to their car after responding to a domestic violence call. They had quickly determined there had not been any domestic violence, just a loud argument that caused a neighbor to call the police. Ben unlocked the patrol car and was about to get inside when he noticed a small dead bird on the driver's seat. "George, check this out. On my seat."

"Huh. That's pretty strange. I wonder how it got there."

"I locked the car and the windows are rolled up," said Ben.

Pointing at the rear windows, George replied, "The back windows are down a few inches, and this old car doesn't have window mesh. The bird must have flown in through one of the rear windows."

"How did it get past the plexiglass?" asked Ben. There was a solid plexiglass shield separating the front seats from the rear seats.

"There's a small gap on both sides. Too small to matter to a prisoner but that bird could have squeezed through. Maybe it got injured doing that and died," George said.

"Maybe so," mused Ben. "Or maybe it's a message to me."

"A message?"

"Yeah. I told Sergeant Clemente about Gerhardt last Sunday. Today is the first day since then Gerhardt and I are working at the same time. I think it's a message from Gerhardt."

"Come on, Ben. You're getting paranoid."

"Sergeant Clemente ordered him not to go anywhere near that 7-11 unless he's dispatched there on an official call. You know he's got to be sore about that," Ben said.

George laughed. "Oh yeah. I'd say sore is putting it mildly. So what's the message?"

"Maybe the message is 'the bird who sings gets dead.'"

George laughed again. "I think you've been watching too many old Mafia movies, Ben. You're giving Gerhardt way too much credit. He isn't smart enough to figure out something like this."

Ben laughed along with George. "Yeah, I guess you're right."

After the shift ended and they had changed into civilian clothes they walked to their cars together. "Hey Ben, I've been thinking about that dead bird."

"Yeah?"

"Watch your back."

The second week of phase four was the most eventful yet for Ben. True to his word, George and Ben found some drunk drivers - two on the same night. Ben spotted the first driver at about 1:30 AM, crawling down the road at 15 miles per hour, with his right side tires over into the bicycle lane. It was a 35 MPH road. Since the bars closed at 1:00 AM, the hour from 12:30 AM to 1:30 AM was prime time for deuce hunting.

When the driver finally stopped after ignoring Ben's police lights and siren for almost two minutes, it wasn't hard to predict he would be drunk. There was little training value in the arrest for Ben, however. When he asked the driver to get out of his car he opened the door and fell to the ground. He was so drunk there was no point in trying to do field sobriety tests.

At the station, it took Ben two and a half hours to complete all the DUI arrest paperwork and fingerprint and photograph the driver. He was released to his wife with a written notice to appear in court. It was past 4:00 AM when he and George finally went in service again.

"Head over to 7-11 Ben. We'll get some coffee and talk about that arrest."

On the way there Ben spotted another car moving very slowly ahead of them. "George, here's another one. You want me to stop him or blow it off and get some coffee?"

"I'm surprised at you, Ben. We're sort of obligated to stop him for public safety reasons, don't you think? What if we don't and he kills somebody down the road? Stop him quick and maybe we can still get home on time."

Ben was irked. "George, Remy Aquino said… Ah, never mind." He grabbed the radio microphone and said, "125 Edward on a traffic stop E.18th Street and A Avenue. California plate 4NQE550 on a gold Toyota Camry." He hit his police lights and siren. The driver in front of him immediately floored it and took off in a cloud of dust.

The never nervous or excited Zobriskie coolly told Ben, "I'll handle the radio for the pursuit. You just drive. And don't kill us."

While George informed dispatch of the pursuit Ben tried hard to keep up with the driver ahead of him. The car had blown through the four way stop at the intersection of E.18th Street and D Avenue and looked to be going about 70 MPH on a residential street. Ben was forced to slow way down at the intersection to make sure it was clear. George radioed the Camry had turned south onto Highland Avenue.

Dispatch announced, "125 Edward your plate comes back on a 2005 Toyota Camry reported as stolen." A stolen car! Other units throughout the city were racing to get into the chase. Ben turned south onto Highland Avenue and he could just make out the taillights of the Camry far ahead of him. George radioed, "Suspect vehicle is southbound Highland approaching 24th Street. His speed about 80." As the Camry blew through the red light at 24th and Highland it clipped the rear end of a car on 24th Street going through on the green light. A few seconds later the whole neighborhood went dark.

George radioed, "Suspect crashed at 24th and Highland. Two car collision at 24th and Highland."

Ben rolled up to the intersection and shut off his siren but kept his police lights on. The Camry was on its roof in the 7-11 parking lot, having crashed right through a bus shelter, rolled over and smashed into a car parked in the lot. The driver's side door was open and there was no one inside. The other car had spun out and ended up smashed into an electrical pole, which had sheared off, knocking out power in the area. The driver was still in the car, slumped over the wheel and bleeding from the head. George informed all units via radio of the situation and two units rolled up as he was still talking. He ordered a perimeter established to try to box in the suspect. He also requested the fire department and paramedics for the injured driver and told dispatch the electrical pole had been broken, power was out and San Diego Gas & Electric repairmen would be needed.

Next the veteran cop requested a police helicopter and a K-9 unit to assist in the search for the suspect. The graveyard squad did not have a K-9 officer, so one was requested from Chula Vista PD. San Diego PD was asked to provide the helicopter. National City was too small to have an aviation unit. Dispatch radioed a few minutes later that the SDPD helicopter was out of service for maintenance and the Chula Vista K-9 unit was busy on a call in Chula Vista. With an officer at each corner of the perimeter and George and Ben busy with the traffic collision there was no one available to search, so George ordered the perimeter broken down and asked for two units to assist them at the traffic collision scene. One officer was needed to direct traffic, and the other to process the stolen car. Ben and George would document the traffic collision and write the report. The paramedics had arrived and were medically evaluating the injured driver. One of them waved Ben and George over. "The driver's deuce, man."

Ben had been expecting a report of his injuries. "What?"

"The guy's drunk off his ass. He has alcohol on his breath, he's slurring his words, the car smells like a brewery, and there're empty beer cans all over the place," the paramedic said.

"What are his injuries?" George asked.

"He's got some facial lacerations and contusions. He's not seriously hurt but we'll have to transport him to the hospital just to be safe."

"Jesus Christ," said George. He radioed the info to dispatch and requested an officer meet the paramedics at the hospital to get a blood sample from the driver and arrest him for drunk driving. Four of the five patrol units on duty were now out of service dealing with the collision and its aftermath. Only one unit was still available for radio calls, and if a call came out requiring two units the sergeant would have to be the cover officer.

"Well Ben, I was hoping this was one box we wouldn't get to check off."

"What box is that?" Ben asked.

"The bucket box," George replied, with a grimace on his face.

"Bucket?" said Ben. "I don't get it."

"Let me run it down for you. We pursue a stolen car that crashes into a drunk driver who takes down an electrical pole which knocks out power. The stolen car also destroys a city bus shelter and plows into a parked car. Our whole squad is out of service, the suspect is in the wind, some poor guy's stolen car is totaled, some other schmuck's car is wrecked, and the city is minus a bus shelter and without power. We call that a bucket. A bucket of shit."

Chagrined, Ben asked, "All right, George. What do you want me to do first?"

"Go over to 7-11 and see if the coffee is still warm. It's gonna be a long night."

The following evening Ben walked into the patrol squad briefing room and was surprised to see a Chinese-American man in a suit and tie sitting in the back. He had no idea who he was. When the whole graveyard squad was present Sergeant Ruffin did the usual briefing then said, "As you can see, Sergeant Yang is sitting in tonight. You might assume having Internal Affairs sitting in our briefing room on a Sunday night is not a good thing, and you'd be right. Sergeant?"

"Thank you, Sergeant," said Yang, who then addressed the squad. "I'm here because one of the dayshift guys found two marijuana joints in a small baggie on the men's locker room floor this morning. The most likely explanation is one of you guys dropped it when you got off shift this morning. I will interview each of you individually and I'll have everyone piss tested if no one admits to this. But, I was hoping to do this the easy way and have the person responsible step up now."

Ben patted his breast pockets, then immediately spoke up. "They're mine Sergeant. I found them on the ground by the bus stop that was destroyed in the traffic collision last night. We were so busy I forgot all about them. They must have fallen out of my pocket when I was changing my clothes."

"OK, Olsen. Report to my office when your squad breaks from briefing. Corporal Zobriskie, I'll inform Sergeant Ruffin when we're done. Meantime, I suggest you load up and go in service on your own."

Ben was puzzled. Why should George load up and start patrolling without him? He was sure he would only be a few minutes with the IA sergeant. He'd already explained what happened.

Sergeant Ruffin said, "All right, people. We're through here. Be safe and try to stay out of trouble."

Ben waited outside of Sergeant Yang's office. He arrived and told Ben to go inside and sit down. "First off,

Olsen, you have the right to have a union representative present during this interview. If you choose one who is not on duty tonight we will reschedule the interview at a time and place that works for all of us."

"I don't need a union rep, sergeant. I didn't do anything wrong."

"Of course you did, Olsen, or you wouldn't be sitting here right now."

"I told you, I found the marijuana at the bus stop while we were documenting the collision scene. It was crazy busy with the stolen car, the other wrecked cars, the broken electrical pole hanging there, power out, early commuters starting into the city, the drunk at the hospital. I meant to ask dispatch for a case number so I could impound the dope for destruction, but the radio was so busy I couldn't get on right away. Then it just slipped my mind."

Sergeant Yang said, "Even if what you say is true, you violated policy by mishandling narcotics. Who do you want for a union rep?"

Ben said, "I made a mistake. I hadn't thought about it, but you're right, I did violate policy. I'll take my lumps for that without a union rep."

"OK, Olsen. Sign this waiver of your rights and then we'll talk." He signed the waiver and gave it to the sergeant.

"So, tell me the real story," said Yang.

Ben was irritated. "Sergeant, I've told you the real story twice already. There is no other story."

Yang scoffed, "Olsen, nobody takes the time to scoop up two joints on the street, draw a case number, impound the stuff at the station, and then write a report about it. Some guys wouldn't even bother picking it up off the ground. Most guys would just crush the joints under their boot and be done with it. Nobody does what you say you did. So why don't you just admit it's your dope and you were going to use it to unwind after shift?"

"Sergeant, the policies and procedures manual requires any contraband found be impounded for destruction. I was just following policy."

"Don't tell me what policy is, rookie. I've been doing this since you were just a gleam in your daddy's eye." He looked hard at Ben for a long moment, then he seemed to come to a decision. "You've been taking a lot of shit from Hopkins and his crew, haven't you? They call you the Boy Scout. Did you know that? Hopkins has been a pain in my ass for ten years. Anything you want to talk to me about?"

Is that what this is really all about? Ben wondered. IA is looking to nail Hopkins for something and Yang thinks he can use this marijuana incident as leverage to get me to help him. He was certain Hopkins and his friends were responsible for much of the stuff that had been happening to him, but he couldn't prove it. Maybe now was the time to talk to internal affairs about it. Still, he didn't know for sure it was Hopkins or his buddies, and it went against his nature to pass along his personal problems for someone else to take care of.

Ben had thought so long the IA sergeant became impatient. "Are you still with us, Olsen? Or are you so stoned right now you lost track of the conversation?"

He made up his mind. "No, I'm fine, sergeant. It's just rookie hazing stuff from Hopkins, if it's even him doing it. Nothing internal affairs would be interested in. I'm not being treated any differently than any other new guy."

Yang said, "OK, I think you're full of shit, but I'll let it go for now. You ready to take that piss test?"

"Yes, sir. I'll give you a gallon a day if you want. I've never used drugs in my life."

Yang shook his head. "Nah, I knew you'd say that. I did your background investigation when we hired you, Olsen, and I've read your military record. I'm not allowed to talk about it with anyone else, and I know you don't talk about it, but you did some serious shit over there, and you came home with a chest full of medals to prove it. That's gotta count for something." He tossed the marijuana to Ben. "Now, go draw a case number for that marijuana, impound it for destruction, and write your report. Then call Zobriskie and tell him you're ready to hit the streets. We're done here."

At the end of shift the next morning Ben spent a long time in the shower. He was drained. He loved police work but all the hazing incidents and the tension between him and Hopkins and his friends was wearing him down. He was all alone in the locker room putting on his civilian clothes when Hopkins walked in. He had already been in civvies and left before Ben even hit the shower, so he figured the jerk had come back to hassle him. He was right.

"So, doofus, what did you and Yang talk about? The price of tea in China? Hah!"

Ben could smell beer on Hopkins' breath. "7:30 in the morning and you're already drinking. Nice."

"I'm off duty, rookie, and I'm over 21. You spent an awful long time in with IA over that marijuana thing, but you came out smelling like a rose. No punishment at all, not even a slap on the wrist. Did you spit or swallow after you sucked off Yang's wang?" He laughed uproariously at his own joke. "Yang. A stupid name for a stupid asshole."

Ben was exhausted and in no mood to tolerate this racist nonsense. "Hopkins, why don't you go home and crawl into your coffin? It's past sunrise."

"Hey! The new guy has a sense of humor. I bet you make that nice piece of dark meat you're banging laugh like a baboon."

Ben was livid. He balled his fists and took a step towards Hopkins. "You're going to seriously anger me one of these days, Hopkins, and you don't want to do that."

"Oooooh, I'm shaking in my boots, jarhead. What, you thought no one knew about you being the big war hero?

There ain't no secrets around here, Olsen, except the ones I keep."

Enraged, he took another step towards Hopkins. The two were now almost toe to toe and the older man didn't back down an inch. "Take your shot, asshole," Hopkins growled, showering Ben with spittle. "I got ten years on the street in this fucking ghetto and I've beat down assholes a lot bigger and badder than you."

He was about to knock the fat slob through the wall when he took a deep breath and stepped back, shaking his head and unflexing his tightly curled fingers. "You almost had me, Hopkins. We get into a fight and I get fired, because I'm on probation. You get a suspension and come back a week later happy as a clam. But this isn't over. I get off probation on June 28th next year. Mark it on your calendar. Any time after that, you want it, you got it."

Hopkins laughed derisively. "When the time comes make sure you bring your 'A' game, farm boy. You'll need it. But I ain't gonna mark down the date 'cause you ain't gonna make it off probation. Next time you fuck up your big secret military record and la-di-dah college degree ain't gonna save you. And you *will* fuck up again."

Ben said, "And you'll make sure it happens, won't you? You and your pals."

"You sure you ain't been smoking meth along with that pot? You are one paranoid son of a bitch. Me and my buddies ain't done nothing to you. We wouldn't waste our time. You want to see who's causing all your problems, take a look in a mirror." He walked out of the locker room.

I can't believe it! Olsen is so stupid he fesses up to the grass and still walks away with nothing! They fired a rookie for less than that a few years ago. He's a fuck up as a cop and he's trying to steal my girl. Who the hell is this guy? He's dogshit, that's what he is, and I'm going to scrape him off the bottom of my boot.

Ben was gaining more confidence in himself as a police officer every day. Now when he encountered something new he didn't feel overwhelmed. He simply applied what he already knew and modified his actions to fit the situation. Still, this time he was flummoxed. He and George had been dispatched to investigate a report of two teenagers drinking alcohol on the National City golf course. The reporting party told the dispatcher the kids were near the 9th green, and that's where they found them.

The two boys looked to be about fourteen years old and both were obviously intoxicated. There was a half empty bottle of vodka on the ground next to a crumpled paper bag. Ben handcuffed and frisked both boys then got all their information, their "horsepower." Once he had their home phone numbers he called up their parents, explained what was happening, and arranged for them to pick up the boys at the police station. As he and George got ready to escort the boys to the patrol car Ben picked up the vodka bottle and the paper bag, which was not empty as he had thought. He hoped for the boys' sake it wasn't marijuana in the bag - they were in enough trouble already. He was stumped when he opened the bag and found half a dozen tampons. What in the world?

"Hey guys, what's up with these tampons?" Ben asked.

One boy replied, "We just found 'em here, man."

George snorted and said, "You guys were butt chugging out here, weren't you?"

A boy replied, "Yeah, man, okay. Do you have to tell our parents?"

Ben had no idea what George was talking about. Was he accusing the boys of having sex out here on the golf course? How did the tampons play into that?

George asked, "Do you still have that junk in your butts?"

Both boys immediately said no. George said, "Listen, I'm going to check back at the station. Tell me now or I'll strip you naked in front of your parents."

Both boys then admitted they had tampons in their rectums. Ben still had no idea what was going on. He didn't want to ask George and look foolish in front of the boys, so he kept quiet.

At the police station they left one boy locked in the patrol car while they escorted the other one to the men's bathroom. There, the youngster removed a tampon from his rectum. They returned him to the patrol car and had the other boy do the same thing. Ben still didn't understand what this was all about. When the parents arrived they got some info from them, then sent their sons home with them.

"All right, George, I can't wait any longer. What the heck was that all about?"

George chuckled and said, "I figured you were clueless on this one, Ben. I just heard about it a few months ago myself, and this is the first time I've ever come across it. The boys want to get drunk but they're so young they can't stomach hard liquor. Some brainiac figured out if you soak a tampon in vodka and stuff it up your butt it gets you drunk super-fast. The alcohol is absorbed directly into the bloodstream without having to go through the stomach, so you get drunk faster using less alcohol, and you don't have to worry about trying to gag it down. The kids call it butt chugging. It's all over the internet."

Ben said, "This is more new guy baloney, isn't it George? It can't be real."

"You saw them remove the tampons yourself, Ben."

He just shook his head. "There are some things I'd rather never know, George."

"Welcome to police work, pal."

A few days later Crystal York, the beat 1 officer, was dispatched to Paradise Valley Hospital. Hospital staff had called the police and reported a gunshot victim had been dropped off at the emergency room. George told Ben to drive up there and they would observe York as she handled the call.

As he rolled up to the emergency room area he saw police tape around a pool of blood on the sidewalk. There was also a small trail of blood drops on the blacktop and sidewalk leading to the pool.

York was inside one of the emergency patient rooms, where a black male in his 20s was being attended to by a doctor. Ben and George joined her there. York closed her officer's notebook and said, "I've got everything I need for now." She turned to them and said, "Let's go talk outside."

George said, "Crystal, this is Ben's first homeboy ambulance call. Would you fill him in on how they're handled, please?"

Ben said, "Homeboy ambulance?"

Crystal laughed. "Ben, this guy was shot somewhere, brought here by his friends, and dumped outside the emergency room doors. You can see the trail of blood drops where they moved him from the car towards the doors. Then they either got scared or didn't give a shit and just dumped him on the sidewalk and took off. We call that a homeboy ambulance run.

"The blood here is a secondary crime scene, so I taped it off. We'll get back to that in a minute. Any time you respond to a call the first question to be answered is always, "Was there a crime committed?" If the answer is no, then life is easy. If the answer is yes, then you have to try to answer the who, what, when, where, why and how of it all. Assuming this guy didn't shoot himself accidentally, we have a crime. What's the next most important question for you to answer first?"

Ben replied, "Is the victim going to survive?"

Crystal chuckled. "Nope. As cops, that's a minor detail to us. I meant which of the who, what, where is the most important?"

"Oh. The who. We need to find out who shot him."

"Nope, wrong again. The where is the most important. Where did this happen? If it happened in National City, then it's our case and we start investigating. If it happened in San Diego, then we notify SDPD and they come and handle things. Don't waste your time investigating a case that belongs to another department."

Ben said, "But that's easy in this case. You just ask the victim. It would be more difficult if he was dead or couldn't speak due to his wounds. Where did it happen?"

Crystal said, "Well, the victim first told me it happened in El Toyon Park, which as you know is just across the street from here and it's on my beat. I've been in this area for several hours and I didn't hear any gunshots, and no citizens reported gunshots to our dispatch, so he lied about that."

Ben didn't get it. "Why would he lie?"

Crystal smiled. "He's a bloods gangster, Ben. Dressed head to toe in red. It's probably programmed into his DNA to lie to cops. When I called bullshit on him he changed his story and said it happened on Market Street in San Diego. I asked dispatch to contact SDPD and see if they could check that area. SDPD reported they were investigating a report of gunshots on 43rd Street near Market. Just before you got here they found a crime scene there, with blood drops and shell casings. A witness there saw a black SUV leaving the scene. A black SUV dropped off our boy here, so this is San Diego's case. They're on their way now. That's why the 'where' is more important than the 'who.'"

"So now what do you do?" Ben asked.

"I give whatever info I have to SDPD and go back in service. No muss, no fuss, and best of all, no report to write. Life is good."

Ben was in his final week of field training. He and George would spend much of their free time in this last week driving around the edges of the city in the streets of San Diego and Chula Vista. National City officers frequently found themselves pursuing suspects out of the city into the surrounding communities, so George wanted Ben to at least be acquainted with the areas.

He informed him, barring any last minute craziness, Ben had been approved by the training staff to go in service on his own and would be assigned to the squad he was currently training with, the weekend graveyard squad. This was a huge occasion for Ben, and it marked a major milestone in any police officer's career. He'd been expecting some kind of final exam, or an interview with the training staff, and then a formal announcement of his change in status. He wouldn't have been surprised if there was a ceremony of some type. He was disappointed to find out none of that would happen. Instead, he would just come to work next week and load up a car on his own instead of with a training officer. George told him it was traditional when reporting to his first squad the new officer provided pizza for everyone at briefing. So, no formal announcement, no ceremony, and he had to buy the pizza! What a letdown.

He told Jackie he would be assigned to weekend graveyard shift after his training period ended. He had hoped he might be assigned to weekdays so they could spend their weekends together, but he knew a weekend assignment was more likely. Great weight was given to seniority when assigning officers, and Ben was the most junior cop on the force. Jackie took the news well. Since all the officers were reassigned to new squads in January of each year, Ben might get lucky and be assigned to weekdays next year.

Over coffee the next day George told him he was happy Ben would be assigned to his squad. "You're a good guy, Ben, and you're going to be a good cop. You'll have to learn to work with Hopkins and McFadden, but they'll get bored with messing with you and things will settle down."

"Something I want you to keep in mind - for a good cop, phase four never ends. You go on learning forever. The moment you stop learning or stop caring your career will stagnate and you'll join the burnouts or the know-it-alls. Burnt out cops just punch the clock and take up space until they retire. Know-it-all cops think they've got nothing more to learn and end up on disability retirement or dead. Don't be one of those guys, be a good cop."

He started his last day of training at the pre-shift briefing with the rest of the squad. Sergeant Ruffin congratulated him on completing training and wished him luck on his next assignment. Ben said, "Sarge, I've been assigned to this squad."

Ruffin said, "You didn't get the word? Edgar Keaton on weekday dayshift tore some ligaments in his knee playing basketball and he's out on injury leave the rest of the year. You're going to take his spot on dayshift."

Ben was flabbergasted. "Nobody told me!"

McFadden muttered something that sounded like, "lucky asshole."

Hopkins said, "Gee, that's too bad, Olsen. I was really looking forward to working with you. Like I'm looking forward to another hemorrhoid. Hah! Did I say that last part out loud?"

Everyone laughed, even Ben. He was on cloud nine.

After briefing he called Jackie and gave her the good news. "They changed my assignment. I'll be working on your brother's dayshift squad Monday to Thursday! It's a miracle. We'll have every weekend off together."

Jackie was thrilled as well. "That's wonderful, Ben. We haven't had a whole weekend together in a long time."

Chapter Five

Ben finished training on a Tuesday morning. His new squad was already on duty. He was given Tuesday off and told to report to his new dayshift squad the next day.

At the pre-shift briefing on his first day with the new squad he brought two dozen doughnuts. Any leftovers would go to the dispatchers. He figured the traditional pizza wasn't appropriate at 6:00 AM, and didn't even know if it was possible to buy a pizza so early in the day.

One by one his squad mates came into the briefing room. "What the hell, new guy? Where's the pizza?" asked Teo Liwag as he took a doughnut.

Brenda Stockwell grabbed two doughnuts and said, "Doughnuts go straight to my hips, Ben. I shouldn't be eating them. Pizza would've been much better."

Alberto Salazar, Ben's phase two field training officer, stuffed a doughnut into his mouth and mumbled around it, "Good call, Ben! Way to take the initiative. I trained you well."

Paul Woodruff ignored the doughnuts and said, "Without tradition we got nothing, and the tradition is pizza. Hopkins told me you were a fuck up. Looks like he was right."

Sergeant Selby walked in. "All right people, settle down. I know you all got the word Officer Olsen will be replacing Eddie Keaton for the rest of the year. Ben, Eddie had beat 4, but you're going to take beat 1. Brenda's moving to beat 2 and Paul will take over beat 4. Can't have a new guy kicking back on beat 4. You'll stay busy on beat 1. Brenda can fill you in on all the beat 1 info later. Welcome to the squad."

Briefing went quickly and the sergeant dismissed the squad. "Ben, stay a minute. The rest of you guys hit the street."

After everyone else left Selby took a doughnut and said, "I know you and I had some words over Jackie and I think we've both moved beyond that. She's happier now than I've ever seen her before, so I know you're treating her well, and that makes me happy. But don't expect any special treatment on my squad just because you're dating my sister. You're the new guy and you're going to get all the shit details, that's just the way it is. If swing shift is short an officer for any reason a dayshift guy has to stay and work overtime until graveyards comes on and is able to cover the shortage. The overtime always goes to the most senior officer who wants it, but if nobody wants it the most junior guy gets it by default. Follow me?"

"Yes, sir. No problem for me, sarge. I'm just happy to be here."

"Was that a wise ass comment?" Selby asked sharply.

Ben was alarmed. "No! No sir. I really am happy to be here. I was assigned to graveyard weekends and this came out of the blue."

"Okay. Don't be afraid to ask anyone on the squad for help when you need it. They're all good cops and they won't mind. Berto's not your FTO anymore so don't be bugging him every minute. Any questions for me?"

"No sir."

"All right then. Hit the street."

Ben loaded up his patrol car and as he rolled out into the street he proudly radioed "221 John in service." He was on the street on his own! He couldn't help but sit up a little straighter. His head was on a swivel. What if he crashed his car? What if he missed seeing a crime in progress? What if a citizen tried to flag him down and he didn't see them? What if he was assigned to a call and he couldn't find the address? He took a deep breath and forced himself to relax.

He was assigned three cold crime reports in a row. It was the nature of dayshift. Property crimes usually happened at night and were often not discovered until the next day, so the dayshift ended up taking the cold report. Ben was itching to make his first solo traffic stop but he had three reports to write. The sergeant would fry him if he was doing proactive policing when he should be working on his reports. It was another of the many unwritten rules.

His radio crackled. "221 John with 222 John to cover on a 647F at El Toyon Park near the bathrooms. Suspect is a Hispanic male in his 20s."

Finally, his first real radio call. 647F was the penal code section for a drunk and disorderly person. Not exactly the crime of the century but it was better than taking another cold burglary report. "221 John 10-4."

"222 John 10-4."

He arrived on scene and easily found the suspect. He drove his patrol car right over the grass and parked it near the bathrooms. The suspect was sitting on the sidewalk with his back leaning against the bathroom wall. His clothes were filthy and he smelled bad. He was singing some old song Ben seemed to know, but the guy was slurring his words so badly he couldn't understand them. There was a young mother with two children on the nearby playground watching him carefully. She was most likely the one who called the police to complain, he thought, and he didn't blame her. She would have to pass right by this guy to get her kids to the bathroom.

When Brenda arrived as his back up he put on some gloves and approached the suspect. In a loud voice he said, "Hey, pal. How you doing? How about coming over here and talking to me a minute?"

The guy ignored him and went on singing. After several attempts to communicate had failed, Ben stepped close and moved an empty brandy bottle away with his foot. Then he grabbed the guy by the arm and told him to stand up. The guy finally stopped singing and said, "Leave me alone."

Ben stood him up and turned him to face the bathroom wall. He quickly frisked him, handcuffed him, and placed him in the rear seat of his patrol car. He radioed to dispatch, "221 John code four. One in custody, drunk in public." His first arrest was about as easy as they get.

Brenda said, "Nice job, big guy. Very gentle. You could be a little rougher with me and I wouldn't mind." She flashed Ben a big smile and walked away, knowing he was blushing. "222 John back in service."

Ben got into his patrol car and took out a blank arrest report form. He asked the drunk his name, but the guy had gone back to singing and ignored him. "I know that song," said Ben, finally recognizing it. "It's an old army song. Were you in the army?"

"Fuck off."

Watching the guy in his rear view mirror, he saw his big floppy hat had toppled over to the side of his head. Ben was shocked to see about one quarter of his head was missing. The large triangular indentation was mostly scar tissue with little tufts of hair sparsely covering it. "What happened to your head? You got that in the war, didn't you?"

"Fuck off, asshole." He went back to singing.

"Garryowen! That's the song. You were in the army, weren't you?" asked Ben.

"It ain't none of your business, cop."

Well, Ben thought, at least I got him to talk to me. "What's your name?"

"Nacho. Nacho Evans."

"Is that your name or your nickname? I need your real name," said Ben.

"It's my name."

"How old are you?" He needed the guy's real name and date of birth in order to run a warrants check on him.

"23."

"What date is your birthday?"

"I don't remember. Sometimes I don't remember stuff."

He was amazed the guy was even walking and talking with a huge chunk of his head missing, so a little memory problem certainly didn't surprise him. He radioed dispatch, "221 John, request wants and warrants on last of Evans, first of Nacho, age 23." Dispatch could find possible matches with the name and age but they needed an exact date of birth to be sure.

"221 John 10-4, standby."

Salazar got on the radio. "225 Adam to 221 John, switch to channel 2."

On channel two, Berto asked, "Ben, does your guy have half a head?"

"Affirmative."

"His real name is Ygnacio Evangelista, DOB 05/13/1985. I've arrested him a couple of times. I think everyone on the squad has, but only for being drunk in public. He's a homeless alky, not a criminal. Except for the smell he's pretty harmless."

"Thanks, Berto. Back to channel 1."

Nacho had apparently been listening to the radio conversation. "I smell, but I smell like a human. You smell like a turkey."

Ben ignored him. Dispatch reported he had no wants or warrants. He radioed his sergeant and asked if he was clear to leave the city and take the suspect to the detoxification center in downtown San Diego instead of to the county jail. It saved the city the cost of a jail cell, was easier for the officers, and preferred by the drunks as well. Sergeant Selby gave him permission.

"Turkey!" the drunk yelled. "You stink like a turkey. Hooweee!"

"Come on, Evans, or whatever you call yourself. I'm trying to drive. I'm taking you to detox instead of jail, so count your blessings."

The young Hispanic man became agitated. With his hands cuffed behind his back, he started flapping his arms back and forth and yelling, "Turkey! Turkey! Turkeyturkeyturkey! Gobble gobble gobble!"

"Knock it off!" Ben yelled. "I'm trying to drive. If you keep it up I'll take you to jail instead of detox."

Nacho went quiet for a few minutes and then he said, "OK, man. I won't mess with you, because you were there. You were there with me."

Ben tried to ignore him. At least he wasn't yelling anymore.

He said again, "You were there with me. I see it now."

Confused, Ben said, "Yeah, back there at El Toyon park."

"No, man, over there. You know."

"You're drunk out of your mind, pal. I've never seen you before in my life. And with a head like yours I'd remember."

Nacho snapped back, "I wasn't born this way, asshole. I got this over in Fallujah, and you were there with me."

What the heck, Ben thought. This guy's drunk and made a lucky guess. "Fallujah, huh? The Marines did some serious butt kicking over there. Were you in the Marines?"

The drunk scoffed derisively. "Shit. Even with half a head I'm too smart to be a Marine. I was in the 7th Cavalry. Garryowen. We led the way in Fallujah and you jarheads followed us."

Ben was stunned. The U.S. Army's 7th Cavalry had been in Fallujah with his Marine unit. Garryowen was their unit nickname and Nacho had been singing the Garryowen song. Okay, so this guy really had been in Fallujah with the 7th Cav, and got wounded there, but how could he possibly know Ben had been there with the Marines?

"All right, Nacho, I believe you were with the 7th Cav. You did your time in hell, and it looks like you paid a huge price for it. I respect that. I apologize for that crack about your head."

Nacho said, "That's all right, man. You can't help being a jerk, since you a cop and a jarhead."

Ben replied, "I was a Marine, and I was in Fallujah. Did one of our officers tell you that?"

"Nobody told me nothing. I just know it. Since that rocket took off half my head sometimes I know things."

"OK, whatever," said Ben. "I do respect your service, though. I knew some good dudes in the army. Now let me find the detox center. I've only been there once before."

Nacho said, "Take the next exit, then go left and stay straight until you see it at the top of the hill."

Ben was amused. The drunk had been taken to detox so many times he knew the way.

When they got there he was sleeping. Ben opened the rear door and shook him awake. "Come on, Nacho, we're here."

As he got out of the patrol car he said, "Cop, what is it with you and turkeys? You smell so strong of turkeys I can't believe you don't have feathers."

"You sure you've just been drinking? You sound like you're whacked on meth."

"Never in my life, man. That shit is poison."

He checked him into the detox center and gave him one of his police business cards. "Here Nacho, take this. Not many people have made the sacrifices you have. Call me if you want to talk."

As he was leaving Nacho called out, "Hey jarhead. You got an Irish girlfriend? O'Donnell? O'Leary?"

Ben said, "You really need to sleep it off, Nacho. My girlfriend's not Irish."

As the doors to the center were closing behind him he heard Nacho mutter, "Not O'Something. Something-O. Who's Jennie-O?"

Ben drove from the detox center back to National City on auto pilot. His thoughts were of his tiny hometown of Barron, Wisconsin. Barron, whose only major employer was the Jennie-O turkey processing plant. How could a drunken stranger possibly know that?

The next day Ben went in service and realized, with some astonishment, it was his second day on his own as a cop. He was already a veteran of the streets! He chuckled to himself. As he drove east on E.8th Street he saw one of the National City motorcycle cops had a driver pulled over up ahead. As he approached, Ben tapped his loud air horn to get the motor cop's attention. It was a courtesy among all law enforcement agencies when passing a solo cop on a traffic stop. The passing cop would stop to cover the other officer unless he indicated he was code four, not in need of assistance, usually simply by waving four fingers.

In this case when the motor cop heard the air horn he turned and waved Ben over, indicating he wanted a cover officer. Ben obliged, and radioed dispatch. "221 John covering an NCPD motorcycle unit in the 300 block of E.8th Street."

Ben stopped behind the motorcycle and got out of his patrol car. The motor cop saw him and said, "Oh, I thought you were Paul Woodruff. This is his beat."

"Yeah, I'm new on the squad. Just driving through to beat 1. I'm Ben Olsen. And this is Brenda Stockwell's beat now. Woodruff is over on beat 4."

As they shook hands the motor cop said, "Joe Vaughn. Nice to meet you, Ben."

Ben said, "Anything unusual here, or do you just want me to keep an eye on the driver?" Ben could see a female in the driver's seat and no other passengers.

Joe laughed. "Nah. I'm code four. The driver is certainly unusual, though. I thought Paul would get a kick out of her. You will, too. Let's go back and talk to her. Just play along with me."

They walked up to the driver's window together. She was a very pretty woman in her early 30s, wearing a skimpy tube top that barely concealed her enormous breasts.

Joe said, "Miss, this is my supervisor. He happened to be passing by so I waved him over. Why don't you explain to him what you told me about why you weren't wearing your seat belt."

The woman looked up at Ben and batted her eyes. "Well, officer, as I told this other officer, I just had surgery on my boobs a few days ago and they're very sore. Wearing the shoulder belt is so painful. I know I was wrong but can't you give me a break?"

Ben was flustered but recovered quickly. "Ma'am, if you had a doctor's note it might be a different story, but without any proof I think the officer is justified in giving you a ticket." There. Ben thought he had handled that rather well.

Smiling mischievously, the woman said, "Officer, I don't have a doctor's note but I'll be happy to show you the proof."

She was pulling down her tube top as Ben yelled, "No! That's all right, I believe you!"

Joe was laughing so hard at Ben he had to step away. The woman saw she had rattled Ben and went on, "It really hurts when the belt ruuubs them, officer. Look." She squeezed her breasts together and moaned loudly, smiling playfully all the time.

Ben had had enough and did not trust himself to speak, so he tore his eyes away and walked over to Joe, who was still chuckling. "Jesus, Ben, I thought you were going to go for your gun when she started to pull them babies out. What, did you think she had a couple of grenades in there?"

"Grenades?" Ben said. "More like howitzer shells if you ask me. Holy cow! Are you going to write her a ticket?"

"Are you crazy? After that show, she gets a free pass. I'll go find a grumpy old man to write up."

Ben started to say something but the motorcycle cop interrupted him. "I can tell you're about to say some stupid rookie happy horseshit thing about treating all citizens the same. Look at me, Ben, and don't turn your head. Now, if you can correctly tell me the driver's hair color then I'll write her a ticket. No guessing."

He was chagrined. "I have no idea, Joe."

"Exactly. Because you never looked above her neck. Lighten up a bit. Thanks for the cover, new guy."

The rest of the day went smoothly for the newest cop in the city. He took more cold case reports and answered more radio calls than any other unit on duty. It was the nature of beat 1, which would be his beat no matter what squad he was assigned to until an officer junior to him was assigned to his squad. Since National City only hired two to three new cops each year it could be several years before he got off beat 1. He didn't mind at all. He became a police officer to help people and he was happy to be busy.

He ended up working ninety minutes overtime in order to complete his reports, before going off duty for his three day weekend. He had Friday, Saturday and Sunday off! It was the best deal in the whole police department, and he intended to take advantage of it while it lasted.

Chapter Six

Jackie had one class on Friday and then she had to work at her part time job. She called Ben on her way to work and said, "I've got tons of studying to do and a project to work on. I'm going to pull an all-nighter tonight to get that out of the way so we can spend the whole weekend together."

Ben was elated. "That's wonderful, Jackie. It's going to be a beautiful weekend, warm enough for the beach."

She said, "The beach sounds good but have you ever been to Julian?"

"The old west town up in the mountains? No. I've heard of it but it always seemed like kind of a long drive."

She was elated. Her secret plan was going to work. "Great! Let's go there Saturday. I haven't been in years. You'll love it, Ben. The small town will remind you of home."

"Jackie, I left Barron because it was a small town, but if that's where you want to go its fine with me. Just as long as we're together."

"You are such a sweet man, Benjamin. We'll take my convertible. It's really a nice drive. I'll pick you up at 10:00 AM."

She pulled into his driveway just before ten the next morning. Her punctuality was just one of many things Ben liked about her. He had been punctual all his life and four years in the Marines had cemented the habit.

"Take a jacket, Ben. It gets cool up there in the mountains this time of year."

He got in the car and kissed her. After the kiss, he couldn't help but stare at her. She was beautiful, intelligent, loving, great fun to be with, and seemed to share his old fashioned outlook on life. He felt he was blessed.

She caught him staring and said, "Ben, is there a bug in my hair?"

Laughing, he said, "No, I'm sorry. You're just so beautiful I can't help myself sometimes."

"Why thank you, Ben. Rod told me you had an encounter with another beautiful woman yesterday."

Ben replied, "Gosh, is there anything that happens you don't know about? How did your brother find out about it? I didn't tell anyone."

"It's a small department, dear, and it's Rod's job to know what happens on his squad. Don't let it worry you. Joe Vaughn told him you practically ran away screaming when the woman started flirting with you."

He flushed with embarrassment. "I was trying to act professional. There are some things the police academy and field training just don't prepare you for."

Jackie laughed, then grew serious. "There's another thing I guess I'm not supposed to know about, Ben. Berto was over the other night visiting with Rod and he said you saved a woman's life a couple of months ago. How come you never told me about that?"

Even though he had thought about the incident quite a lot, he still didn't know exactly how to explain it to Jackie. "I guess there are several reasons. All the guys told me it isn't fair to get off work each day and tell your wife or girlfriend all the good things you did but none of the bad things that happened. They say after a while it gets so skewed it causes problems in the relationship. It's like you're bragging all the time about what a super great guy you are. On the other hand, if you tell about all the bad things that happen each day, or nearly happened, that also causes problems. So, most guys just say as little as possible. I thought it was good advice.

"Another reason I didn't tell you is I still don't know how I feel about it myself. I violated policy, first of all. Berto and I discussed it afterward and we agreed it was best not to tell anyone the details. He wrote in the report the woman was startled by a hotel room door opening and I took the opportunity to grab her and help her off the rail. I suppose that's true as far as it goes. The reality is she had pushed off the rail before I grabbed her. I didn't think about it at all, just moved on instinct. If I wasn't in such good physical condition I probably would have gone over the rail with her. That's certainly not what the policies and procedures manual calls for.

"I became a cop to help people, and I certainly helped that woman. You couldn't find a better example. Yet instead of feeling elated I felt empty inside. I didn't know that woman and she didn't know me. I'll probably never see her again. It felt different in Iraq when I was fighting alongside fellow Marines. We were like brothers and I loved those guys. That's not to say I didn't care about that woman - I did, and still do. I hope she's okay and getting her life back together, but it's not the same. I'm glad I saved her, of course. I love helping people. It just felt different somehow because now I'm a cop. I wasn't a stranger helping a stranger out of the goodness of my heart, or a Marine fighting alongside my brother Marines. I was a cop, ordered to help that woman, and I did my job. I know I'm not making any sense but it still doesn't make sense to me."

Jackie said, "You're being way too hard on yourself. Ben Olsen saved that woman, not just a cop. You said you barely held on to her without going over yourself. How many other cops would have failed to do what you did? How many cops would never even have tried? I'm proud of you. It scares me to think you might have died that day, but if you didn't try to save her you wouldn't be who you are. And I like you the way you are."

They rode in companionable silence for a while, enjoying the pleasant scenery and the closeness of each other. As they headed east on Interstate 8 the green belt of the coast faded into the rear view mirrors and the mountains grew larger in front of them. The land around them very quickly turned to desert, populated by large rocks scattered everywhere, with little scruffy bushes in between, and not much else. When they turned onto highway 79 everything changed again. The road wound through the rolling hills of Cuyamaca State Park. There were cattle guards on all the crossroads. The hills were filled with trees and shrubs. Small animals such as squirrels, rabbits and chipmunks were plentiful. Deer crossing signs were posted. They had not even driven an hour and they were in a different world. It was hard to believe they were still in San Diego County. They continued to climb in elevation until they reached the town of Julian.

Julian is a historic old west gold mining town. It had been founded after the civil war by war vets who came west to get away from it all. There was a short period of about ten years when gold mining ruled the day there, but the gold ran out and so did most of the miners. Those who stayed settled into a life of small town farming and commerce. The climate and the soil were especially well suited to growing apples. Julian farmers raised them back then and still raise them now. The town never got big, no more than 500 or so people at its peak, and it remained that way ever since.

Jackie parked the car and they got out and looked around. It was like stepping through a time warp. All the buildings were old but in good repair. There were wooden sidewalks. Tourists like Jackie and Ben were everywhere, but no one seemed to be in a hurry. It was as if time itself had slowed down. They had no idea where to start. All the people seemed to be milling about happily but aimlessly.

They decide to join them and let their feet take them wherever they ended up. Suddenly, gunshots rang out. Ben grabbed Jackie and ran for cover, hyper alert, his off-duty gun in hand. Men were yelling and women screaming, then people were laughing and pointing. It was a staged reenactment of an old west gunfight. Ben seemed to take an inordinate amount of time to realize what was happening. Finally, he breathed a sigh of relief, holstered his gun, and laughed at himself. Jackie was staring at him, not laughing at all. She sensed Ben's reaction went well beyond that of an off-duty cop. She wanted to talk to him about it, but decided it might spoil the day, so she let it pass.

    The town had dozens and dozens of small shops and restaurants. They couldn't possibly see them all in one day and it was already past noon. They decided to first get something to eat and settled on The Miner's Diner because it happened to be close by. After a family style meal they sat at the old fashioned soda fountain and had root beer floats for dessert.

    They went to an art gallery neither one particularly enjoyed. The Farmer's Market was much better for Ben - it did indeed remind him of home, and in a good way.

    They both loved the numerous stores selling old fashioned candies. The time warp feeling was dizzying in them. It was like being transported back to childhood or even back to your parents' childhood. They left each store with a bag full of old time goodies you couldn't buy anywhere else.

    There was a bird watching store, and Ben learned Jackie was an ardent birdwatcher. He bought her a small birdhouse.

    They spent a long time in a store called Crossroads Treasures. It really was full of treasures and neither one could decide what to buy. Jackie was oohing and aahing over some Indian jewelry and Ben insisted on buying a

Native American crystal pendant for her. She immediately put it on her neck.

When they finally left the store it was nearly 7:00 PM and they went to dinner at another family style restaurant. They had fresh baked apple pie for dessert. As they walked out into the cool evening air Ben was wishing they could stay here forever. "Jackie, Julian is amazing, but it's a long drive home so we'd better head out."

Now was the time for her to spring her carefully conceived trap. "Oh, Ben. It's been a really long day. I stayed up all night last night studying after work. I'm not up for the drive home."

Ben said, "Okay, I'll drive. You can catch some sleep on the way back."

Jackie frowned, wondering if she was ever going to get her man to take the leap. What a different type of guy he was! She'd have to prod him some more. "Ben, let's get a room at one of the bed and breakfasts here. They're beautiful, and then we can spend all day tomorrow here, too."

Looking down at his feet self-consciously, he said, "Jackie, if we get a room I'm not sure I could control myself."

She thought, that's exactly the point, you lunkhead! In a pouty voice she said, "I told

you two months ago not to make me wait too long, Ben. It's been long enough."

He mumbled, "Okay, Jackie. I just didn't want to rush you."

Rush me! Here's this gorgeous mountain of a man, combat veteran and police officer, scuffing his feet and acting like a teenager on his first date. He truly was a country boy.

They stayed overnight at a Bed & Breakfast just outside of Julian. It was an amazing place. Private hot tub, fireplace, old fashioned four poster featherbed. They spent quite a while exploring each other, tentatively at first, then more and more confident and comfortable. They enjoyed just looking at each other's bodies, after imagining it for so long. Finally they made love for the first time, then again, then they lost track.

Their second day in Julian was probably as fun and interesting as the first, but neither one of them could focus on things. They were both reliving in their minds the incredible night they just had. They looked at each other differently now, and people passing them on the street looked at them differently, too. A blind man could see it - they were in love.

This is not happening! Olsen and Jackie were gone the whole weekend! I was willing to give my girl a little slack, let her figure out Olsen is all wrong for her, that I'm the only one who really loves her, but this is too much. It stops now.

Chapter Seven

Ben walked into his Monday morning pre-shift briefing a few minutes before 6:00 AM. Teo Liwag, Berto Salazar, and Brenda Stockwell were already there. Ben started to say good morning to everyone when Teo spoke up, "Yo! Hey! Somebody got lucky over the weekend."

Brenda said wistfully, "Oh, Ben! I thought you were saving yourself for me. Just remember, I'll still be here when you get tired of her, big guy."

The shy, quiet farmer's son flushed red. He couldn't believe it! Was it that obvious?

Brenda and Teo continued to razz him until Berto spoke up. "Hey guys, Ben's dating Sarge's sister, so you best knock it off." They all fell silent just in time, as Sergeant Selby and Paul Woodruff walked in together.

The Monday briefing was always a bit longer than the others since the squad had to catch up on what had occurred in the city over the weekend. At the end of the briefing Selby said, "One of the task force guys needs a wall stop this morning. Ben, have you ever done a wall stop?"

"No, sir, I'm not familiar with the term."

The sergeant explained, "One of our guys on the regional narcotics task force called and told me they expect a target car to come north across the border this morning. Their source says it will have a load of Mexican black tar heroin. In order to protect the source they want a patrol cop to make a routine traffic stop on the car, so it will appear to the driver to be just bad luck. Once you have the car stopped you either get permission to search or find a legal reason to search the car, and hopefully find the dope and arrest the driver. At that point the task force guys will take over. There's no paperwork for you, they'll take care of everything. They'll call when the car comes across the border. If you're available when they call I'm going to assign you the call for training purposes."

He was excited at the prospect. "Yes, sir, I'll be ready."

The sergeant went on, "The stop will likely be on the freeway. Try to get the car to pull off at an exit. And don't ask for a cover unit unless you feel like you really need one. They want to keep the stop as low key as possible."

"Yes, sir."

The squad went in service. Ben immediately soaked up several cold crime report calls. Just before lunch his cell phone rang. "Olsen? This is Dean Schmidt with the narcotics task force. Sergeant Selby gave me your number. Are you clear to make a stop for us?"

"Yes, sir, I'm in the Paradise Valley Hospital parking garage working on paper."

"Sir, huh? Selby told me you were new. It's Ben, right? OK, our target's northbound on Interstate 805. Should be passing through National City in about ten minutes. Get up on the freeway at Plaza Blvd. and park on the right shoulder. We've got two tails on the target, which is a dark green Cadillac Escalade. I'll give you a heads up when it's about to pass you. We've already found probable cause for the stop - the car has tinted front windows."

He called dispatch on his cell phone and told them what he would be doing. Sergeant Selby had warned him to avoid mentioning anything over the radio since the Mexican drug cartels sometimes monitored police radios.

He had just gotten into position on the freeway ramp shoulder when Schmidt called to tell him the car was one minute away, in the number three lane. He saw the car coming in his rear view mirror and as it passed by he pulled out behind it. A few moments later he was in the number three lane behind the car and turned on his police lights and siren. The Escalade yielded to the right and stopped on the right shoulder. Ben got on his loudspeaker and told the driver to drive on the shoulder to the 43rd street exit just up ahead. He had to repeat himself several times due to the freeway noise, but the driver eventually complied.

He radioed dispatch he was on a traffic stop at 43rd Street and Palm Avenue, then got out of his car to contact the driver. He was a well-dressed Mexican man who spoke good English. He gave Ben his Mexican driver's license, Mexican vehicle registration, and Mexican insurance form. Ben had no idea if any of the documents were legitimate and there was no way to check on their validity. The Mexican government did not use computerized records and there was no protocol in place to contact them for a traffic stop anyway.

The driver gave him permission to search the car. He first frisked the driver, then had him sit him in the back seat of his patrol car for safety. He was careful to explain to the driver why he did that and to make sure the driver knew he was not under arrest. Although he searched the car thoroughly he was unable to find anything. He thought things were going very well up to that point, but no one had told what to do if he couldn't find the dope. He was about to call Schmidt on his cell phone when a San Diego PD K-9 unit rolled up behind him. The officer got out of his car with his dog and winked at Ben. To the Mexican driver it would appear Ben had requested a canine to search the car, though in reality he was taken completely by surprise.

Within a minute the dog alerted on the spare tire. The tire was fully inflated and looked perfectly normal. The SDPD officer removed the tire stem with a pair of needle nose pliers and deflated it. He was then able to pry the tire slightly away from the rim. Inside, Ben could see packages wrapped in heavy cellophane. He informed the driver he was under arrest for transporting narcotics and received a shrug of the shoulders in return.

Ben was told by cell phone to take the driver to the National City police station where he would be met by narcotics task force officers. Task force officers would also take care of impounding the Escalade and the dope. Once at the station he put his prisoner in a holding cell and his part was done. "Wow, that was easy," he thought.

He was told later there were four kilos of pure heroin in the tire. He also learned the task force, using federal forfeiture laws, would be able to permanently keep the brand new Escalade. The nearly nine pounds of heroin had a street value of about $100,000. He was pumped up.

Later, he was getting ready to clear from yet another cold crime report call when Berto Salazar pulled up behind him. "Hey, Ben, how'd that wall stop go?"

He excitedly told Berto the whole story, and how he felt like he had done some real good today, helping to get nine pounds of heroin off the streets. "That's good, Ben. It sounds like you did well. I don't want to burst your bubble, but the dope is just small time. The cartel probably had three or four other load cars all go across at the same time. We got one, but the rest got through. It may even have been the cartel themselves who intentionally tipped off our guys to this car, so we would focus on this one while the others with bigger loads sail on by. A few pounds of dope and a car are merely the cost of doing business for them, and the driver's just a sacrificial pawn in the chess game. We're pretty good players, but the cartels are grand masters. We don't really stand a chance."

The next day, late in the morning, Ben was again parked in the Paradise Valley Hospital parking structure, trying to dig out from under his mountain of paperwork, when the radio came to life. "220 John with 221 John and 225 Adam to cover on an assault with a deadly weapon in the 300 block of East Division Street. Two gunshot victims down in the street. San Diego PD is also responding. Fire and medics will be staging."

Ben was already rolling lights and siren to the call before the dispatcher even finished talking. Anytime dispatch assigned three units to the same call it meant they had reason to believe there was significant danger to the officers. San Diego PD was also responding because East Division Street formed part of the northern boundary between the city of San Diego and the city of National City. The north side of the street was San Diego and the south side was National City.

As Ben arrived from the east Brenda Stockwell rolled up from the west. There were two young Hispanic males in the street. One of them was lying in a pool of blood and the other one was on his knees, with blood running down his chest and back from a head wound. A crowd of people was gathering on the sidewalks and lawns on both sides of the street.

Brenda went to assess the condition of the male laying in the street and Ben ran to the guy on his knees. As he got close Ben saw the young gangster had taken a bullet to the head. It looked like the round had gone through his right eye and exited out the back of his head. How was he not dead? Despite his wound, when the teenager saw Ben he got to his feet and took a swing at him! He stepped back out of the way, but the badly wounded thug came after him, swearing in Spanish. Ben grabbed him with both hands by the elbows and tried to hold him away from his uniform, since he was a bloody mess. He continued to scream at Ben and thrashed around for a few more seconds, then his knees buckled. Ben lowered him gently to the ground. More cops from both National City and San Diego were arriving. Someone radioed it was clear for paramedics and they rolled in from their nearby staging area. When the paramedics got to Ben's guy he walked over to Brenda to ask her what she wanted him to do. As the beat officer she was in charge of the scene, even though Corporal Salazar was present.

She told him to string crime scene tape a full block east and west of the scene. When he completed that he saw Brenda and Berto arguing with a San Diego PD sergeant. He went up to Brenda and asked what he should do next. She pulled him aside, out of hearing of Berto and the SDPD sergeant, who were now almost shouting at each other.

"Just a sec, Ben." She got on the radio and asked Sergeant Selby to come to the scene. He replied he was already enroute and should be there in a minute or two.

Turning back to him, she said, "Okay, for now just stand by. Some witnesses are saying the shooting happened on the north side of the street and others are saying it happened on the south side. If it happened on the north side the whole case belongs to San Diego. If it happened on the south side it's all ours. The SDPD sergeant says it's ours because the two victims are National City gangsters, they were down on our side of the street when we found them, and the witnesses are unreliable."

Ben was incredulous. This was a major crime scene, with two victims and potentially dozens of witnesses. Although both victims were still alive, it could easily become a double homicide. Instead of arguing about whose jurisdiction it was the two police departments should be working together to solve this terrible crime.

Sergeant Selby arrived and walked over to Berto. Without needing to be briefed he knew in an instant what the argument was about. This was nothing new to him. In fact, it was fairly routine. Berto spoke briefly with the sergeant and then left him to work it out with his SDPD counterpart. He came over to Brenda and Ben and told them to try to find blood trails or shell casings on the north side where some of the witnesses said the shooting happened. Brenda located two shell casings in the gutter on the north side, and told Sergeant Selby about them, then she went back to look for additional evidence. The argument between Selby and the SDPD sergeant grew more heated, with both men yelling and pointing at something in the street. A few minutes later Berto found two more shell casings on the front lawn of a house on the north side. He told Ben and Brenda to look closely for blood drops in the center of the street. Brenda finally found a few small droplets of blood about six feet from the north curb. Berto informed Sergeant Selby, and the argument between him and the SDPD sergeant ended.

Selby waved over his officers and told them the case belonged to SDPD. Berto could go back in service but Ben and Brenda were to stay until the SDPD detectives arrived to brief them on what they saw when they arrived on scene.

Berto left and Ben asked Sergeant Selby what the argument was all about.

Selby was obviously still irritated. "The witnesses' stories were all over the place, as usual. San Diego didn't want the case. It seemed clear to me the shooting happened on their side, then the victims ran over to our side where they collapsed. It was Shelltown gangsters who shot the National City bangers. Division Street marks the dividing line between their turf. San Diego PD is almost twenty times bigger than our department. They have more detectives than we have cops, period, and this bozo is trying to dump their case off on us. When Brenda found the first shell casings in the north side gutter I thought that was it, SDPD would do the right thing. But no, now the guy's arguing the shooters must have been standing on our side of the street and their semi-auto pistols threw the shell casings back over to the north side. Unbelievable! Luckily, Berto found those shell casings on the front lawn over there, and then the blood drops on the north side sealed it. Good job, guys."

Ben still could not get over the two departments arguing over jurisdiction. "Sarge, this could turn into a double homicide. Who cares whose case it is? Isn't the important thing to solve it?"

"Ben, the fact it might become a double homicide makes it even more important to determine jurisdiction. A double murder could raise our homicide stats through the roof. The city council would be seriously pissed off. Hey, I heard you were fighting with one of the victims. What happened?"

"I rolled up at the same time Brenda did. We each checked out one of the victims. My guy had a gunshot wound through his head, yet when I got close to him he stood up and started fighting with me. I don't think he really knew who I was or what he was doing, he was just going on adrenaline. Still, I couldn't believe it. The kid takes a bullet completely through his head and he's up and fighting! I've never seen anything like that in my life."

Brenda laughed and said derisively, "You're a rookie, Ben. You haven't seen much of anything yet."

Sergeant Selby snorted, and said, "Actually, I'm sure when Ben was in the…"

"Sarge!" Ben interrupted, and pointed over at a group of SDPD officers. "I think they're asking for you again over there. Oh, no, I guess not."

Selby realized Ben had interrupted him because he had slipped up and was about to tell Brenda of his Marine Corps service. "Anyway, Ben, all the shell casings were nine millimeters. It's a favorite with the gang bangers because Hollywood glamorized it as a gangster gun. I see you're carrying the department issued 9mm Beretta. Now that you've seen how little stopping power the nine has you might consider an upgrade."

Near the end of shift that day Sergeant Selby called Ben on his cell phone. "Ben, you'll have to stay on overtime today until graveyards go in service. The swing shift is going to be short one man. Nobody on our squad wants the overtime so you've got it."

Ben replied, "Sure, Sarge. No problem. I've still got reports to complete anyway."

The swing shift came on duty and Ben stayed out in the field, parked in a hidey spot trying to get his paperwork done. A few hours into his overtime most of the swing shift guys were busy on calls and then dispatch radioed, "434 John with 221 John to cover on a disturbance at The Happy Time Bar, 2015 Cleveland Avenue. Two Hispanic males fighting. No weapons seen."

By the time he arrived at the bar Juanita Circulado, the swing shift beat 4 officer, was already there, and the fight was long over. Everyone had gone back to drinking. The bartender had no idea who had called the police and claimed no one had been fighting. They were leaving the bar when someone stumbled into Juanita, then started loudly cursing at her, drawing the attention of several nearby patrons. "What is your problem, buddy?" she asked.

The guy mumbled something nasty about women cops. Juanita said, "Why don't you go back to your seat before you get arrested?"

The drunk slurred out, "Why don't you suck my dick?" causing the onlookers to hoot and holler. Some even applauded.

In the blink of an eye Juanita spun the guy around, slammed him up against the wall, and had him in handcuffs. "OK pal, you win the prize. You get to go to jail." She took him to her car and stuffed him in the back, then radioed dispatch. "434 John, one in custody for drunk and disorderly."

The dispatcher replied, "10-4. Break. Dispatch needs units to clear and respond to an assault with a deadly weapon at Pepper Park. The victim has been stabbed and the suspect is still on scene."

Juanita said quickly, "Ben, that's my beat, and it sounds like a shit sandwich. We're so busy I shouldn't have arrested that guy, but he pissed me off and a lot of the customers heard him disrespect me. I couldn't show my face in there again if I let him get away with it. I don't want you stuck here all night on overtime. How about you take my prisoner? He's a simple drunk and disorderly arrest, and I'll respond to the stabbing."

It made good sense to him. "Okay. Thanks Juanita." He took her prisoner out of her car and put him in his own. She told dispatch she was responding as primary officer to the stabbing and Ben had her prisoner. 433 John also cleared his call to go to the stabbing. Ben drove to the station with his prisoner, who was extremely intoxicated.

At the station he took the drunk's wallet, keys, ink pens, loose change, and everything else out of his pockets and put them on the table in the prisoner processing room, near the property and evidence locker. All his personal property would be sealed in a plastic bag, which Ben would hand deliver to the jail staff. He left the prisoner in the backseat cage area of his patrol car while he went to take a leak. Once back, he removed the guy from his car and took him to the processing room. There, he removed all the money from his wallet, counted it, and noted the amount on the property inventory sheet. He sealed everything up using a heat sealer and told the arrestee to sign for his property. "All your stuff is in the bag. Wallet, keys, pens, and $245.55 cash."

The Hispanic man said, "Are you crazy? I had 800 bucks in my wallet." He was slurring his words so badly Ben could hardly understand him.

Ben said, "Look buddy, we're really busy tonight and I don't have time to play games. I counted your money twice. It's $245. Sign for it."

The man was indignant. "No way. I know how much money I had. You're trying to rip me off."

Irritated, Ben tore open the bag and counted out the money again, this time in front of the guy. "There, $245.55. Now will you sign for it?"

Incensed, the man said, "I ain't signing for shit. You must be out of your fucking mind thinking you can steal my money. I want to see your supervisor."

Sighing, Ben got on the station telephone and paged the swing shift sergeant to come to the prisoner processing room. Stanley Howard, the weekday swing shift sergeant, showed up. He and Ben had met a few times previously.

"Hey, Sarge. The prisoner wants to make a complaint. He claims I stole his money."

Sergeant Howard was in no mood to argue with a drunk. All the units were busy on calls and he was needed in the field to assist them. "What's your problem, pal?"

The prisoner slurred, "I had 800 bucks in my wallet. I cashed a check earlier today, so I was loaded. He stole my money."

Sergeant Howard said, "You're loaded all right. You're drunk out of your mind. Way too drunk to remember how much money you had. If you had $800, you drank it up, gave it away, or lost it playing dice at the bar, because there's only $245.55 there now."

The guy said, "I was only there an hour and I had three or four drinks. I wasn't playing dice. He stole my money."

"Okay, I'll make a note of your complaint. After you sober up if you still want to make a formal complaint come back here tomorrow. Take him to jail, Officer Olsen."

I took a big risk tonight, but Jackie is worth it. I ripped off $500 from that drunk's wallet while Olsen was in the shitter. Hopefully when the asshole sobers up he'll remember his money is missing and make a formal complaint about it. It doesn't take much to fire a probationary employee like Olsen.

Thursday morning, as the pre-shift briefing ended Sergeant Selby told Ben to remain behind as the other officers filed out. "What's up, Sarge?"

"Ben, the prisoner you had Tuesday night on overtime came back last night after he got off work. He met with Sergeant Howard and filed a formal complaint against you. Let's go to my office and talk about it."

In his office, Selby said, "This is a serious accusation, Ben. I have to decide if it warrants an internal affairs investigation or not. You have the right to have a union representative with you now. Do you want one?"

Ben was relaxed, knowing he had done nothing wrong. "No, Sarge. This is just some drunk who can't remember where he spent his money. I'm fine."

"Okay, then. Unfortunately, it's a little more complicated than you might think. The guy is convinced you stole his money and he has some documentation to back up his claim. He got off work at the shipyard at 6:00 PM. Here is a copy of a receipt showing he cashed his shipyard paycheck at a check cashing place in our city at 6:35 PM on Tuesday. The check was in the amount of $814. 75. He said he had four dollars in his wallet when he cashed the check. The check cashing place charged him $8.15 to cash the check. After he cashed the check he says he went to the AM/PM gas station and bought $50.00 worth of gas. He was told we can easily verify that by looking at the store's videotapes and he was happy to hear that, so I believe him. That leaves him with $760. He says he went from the gas station to the bar, where he bought three drinks for four dollars each. Each time he left a one dollar tip. Sergeant Howard spoke to the bartender. The guy is a regular there and the bartender knows him. He told Sergeant Howard that three drinks sounds right. Then Juanita arrested him at 8:09 PM. That jives with him being there about an hour, as he says."

Ben was becoming concerned now. "Sarge, three drinks can't be right. The guy was totally trashed when we arrested him. He was slurring his words so badly I could barely understand him. Sergeant Howard can back me up on that."

Selby nodded in agreement. "Sergeant Howard noted the same thing in his comments on the complaint form, Ben. The problem is the guy also showed the sergeant a doctor's note. He was taking a prescription cough medicine that contained codeine. The interaction between the codeine and the alcohol could easily explain why he was slurring his words and appeared to be so intoxicated. He claims he received eight one hundred dollar bills at the check cashing place and broke one at the AM/PM. There were two in his property at the jail. He says you stole the other five hundreds."

Ben was stymied by the logic of it. "All right, Sarge. The guy's story seems to make sense, but I have no idea where his $500 might have gone. I certainly didn't steal it. Where do we go from here?"

Taking a more formal tone, the supervisor said, "We're done for now. Maybe somebody dipped into his wallet at the bar. It's happened before. Without any proof or an admission from you we've gone as far as we can go. I'm going to document the incident in your performance record, Officer Olsen, and inform internal affairs. They can choose to pursue it or not."

Ben was annoyed and felt helpless. He had done nothing wrong and yet he was being punished. Raising his voice in anger he said, "So just because some drunken idiot loses his money I get a write up in my jacket?"

"Watch your tone with me, Officer Olsen. That's the way it goes sometimes, and you just have to suck it up. It won't count for much unless we see a pattern in the future, and then it would be given more weight. Every officer gets one of these sooner or later, it's the nature of the job."

Ben was in a sour mood all day due to the false accusation against him. It made him look forward more than ever to spending the weekend with Jackie.

As it turned out, they spent a wonderful weekend together. Jackie surprised him by announcing on Saturday afternoon she had two tickets to the San Diego Chargers game the next day. What made it particularly special for Ben was the fact the Chargers were playing the Green Bay Packers! Of course he was a rabid Packers fan. It wasn't possible to grow up in Wisconsin and be otherwise. Barron was hundreds of miles away from Lambeau Field in Green Bay, and tickets were impossible to get anyway, so he had never seen the Packers play in person. Jackie was amazing!

The game was fun and exciting. Green Bay won it late in the fourth quarter. Ben was decked out in all his Green Bay apparel, including a foam cheese head hat, and he shouted himself hoarse rooting for his beloved Packers. There were a surprisingly large number of Green Bay fans at the stadium, nearly all of them sporting various Packers clothing and paraphenalia. Jackie had on her Chargers sweatshirt and wore lightning bolt earrings. They good naturedly ribbed and razzed each other on virtually every play. Their seats were awful, in one end zone, but so close to the field they could hear the players grunting and swearing when they were down at their end. When the players were near the other end zone they could only guess as to what was happening and then watch the replays on the jumbo screen TV on the scoreboard. Despite that, they both greatly enjoyed the game. Ben was glad the Packers won but really all he cared about was that he and Jackie were together.

All right, I guess it was too much to hope for that they would fire Olsen over an unproven allegation from a drunken idiot. Especially with Selby conducting the investigation. Maybe I'll get lucky and that moron Yang will get involved, but I can't count on it. Farmer Ben needs to go sooner rather than later. I can't stand the thought of him putting his dirty hands on my precious Jackie.

Chapter Eight

Ben was parked in a hidey spot churning out more cold crime reports. Beat 1 was given to the most junior cop on the squad for good reason - it was way more work than the other beats. He didn't mind at all. He was a police officer, and lived and worked in San Diego County. He could have been a turkey farmer in Barron, Wisconsin. Here it was 65 degrees and sunny in November. The temperature wouldn't hit 65 again in Barron until next May. And best of all, he was dating the greatest woman in the world. Yes, sir, life was good!

He finished his reports and was driving to the station to submit them. The traffic was so heavy on the usual routes he diverted over to E.18th Street. He would shoot down 18th Street to National City Boulevard and then turn north to get to the police station. It was a longer route but much faster in the midday traffic. As he drove down 18th Street dispatch radioed, "224 John with 223 John to cover on a suspicious person at the National City Market, 384 E.18th Street. White male adult wearing black pants, white shirt, with long hair and a ball cap. Possible narcotics sales."

"224 John 10-4."

"223 John 10-4"

Ben realized the National City Market was only two blocks ahead of him. He was not assigned to the call and it was not on his beat, but he was practically on top of it. He slowed way down and rolled up to where he could see the parking lot of the market. A male matching the description of the suspicious person made a hand to hand transfer with another white male. Ben got out of his car and started sneaking up on the two men, using the trees and fence line along the sidewalk as cover. When he was directly across the street he stopped to observe them and wait for the other patrol units to arrive. Suddenly his portable radio burst loudly to life, "224 John on scene." Paul Woodruff, the beat 4 officer, was reporting he was here, but Ben could not see him. He silently cursed himself for not remembering to turn down the volume on his radio before sneaking up on the suspects. The two guys heard the radio and immediately sprinted away in opposite directions. Ben ran after the person with the long hair and ball cap and used his portable radio. "221 John in foot pursuit northbound D Avenue from East 18th Street. The suspect is the person from the National City Market."

The dispatcher had to be surprised by Ben's report, since he had not reported he was on scene, he wasn't assigned to the call, and it wasn't his beat. Despite that, she calmly replied, "221 John 10-4. 224 John do you copy ?"

"224 John 10-4. I'm at 18th and National City Boulevard." He was four blocks away.

Ben radioed, "221 John crossing 17th Street still northbound. I think he's headed for Kimball Park."

Woodruff acknowledged and drove to E.16th Street. He was rolling up to D Avenue when he saw the suspect with Ben close behind him. The guy saw Woodruff's patrol car in front of him and slowed down, apparently trying to decide where to run to. It was all the break Ben needed. He caught the man from behind and drove him to the ground face down with a hard football tackle. The suspect struggled underneath him as Ben tried to pin his arms down. He got control of his right arm but the dope dealer's left hand was beneath his body. As he tried to get the man's left hand under control Woodruff ran up and delivered a hard kick to the guy's left thigh. "Show me your hands now! Hands. Show me your hands!" Woodruff yelled.

The suspect continued to struggle and kept his left hand beneath his body. Woodruff forcefully dropped both his knees onto the suspect's lower back and legs and rammed the end of his police baton into the man's side. He let out a loud "Ooof!" and stopped struggling. Woodruff pulled the guy's left hand behind his back and Ben handcuffed his wrists together.

Both officers got off the suspect and rolled him over to his right side. A small silver revolver lay beneath his body. Ben lifted him to his feet. Teo Liwag, the other officer assigned to the call, rolled up. Paul flashed him four fingers and Liwag radioed, "223 John, the units are code four at 16th and D Avenue, one in custody."

Ben searched the dope dealer and found a plastic bag with twenty three individually wrapped rocks of crystal methamphetamine. He felt good and was rather proud of himself. He had chased the dealer two blocks and caught him in possession of meth ready for sale and a concealed handgun. Both were felonies and the gun and dope together would carry a minimum sentence of five years in prison. Teo's car was closest, so Ben put the prisoner in his car for the moment, then returned to his squad mates. He stuck out his hand to shake with Woodruff. "Nice job, Paul. You got to me right in the nick of time."

The veteran officer ignored his outstretched hand and said heatedly, "Fuck you, rookie! You better not ever jump one of my calls again."

Ben was stumped. "What are you talking about? I was driving by on the way to the station and saw the suspect. He took off and I ran after him."

Woodruff angrily replied, "Yeah, right, and I believe in the Easter bunny. You jumped my call, asshole. You weren't assigned and you're way off your beat. You took a nice felony bust away from me. I could've used the stats."

Ben said, "You can take the credit, Paul. I don't care about that."

"That's not the way it works, boot. You caught him, you clean him. That's the rule. You get credit for the bust but you get all the paperwork, too. I ain't doing shit to help you."

In a soft voice Teo said, "You still have to write a report on your use of force, Paul."

Woodruff's face grew red with rage. "Shit! Fucking rookie takes my collar and I still have to write paper. I save your life and you screw me in return. Nice. Make sure that goes in your report, dickhead." He stomped away.

Teo said, "Come on, Ben. Get in my car and I'll drive you and your prisoner back to your car."

As they drove to Ben's car he said, "What's Woodruff's problem?"

The Filipino cop replied, "Ben, you did jump his call. Why didn't you report you were near the scene before you got there? Then you could have taken the cover for me and there wouldn't be an issue. I was pretty far away when the call came out. Some guys are hot to make felony arrests. The stats look good and it helps at promotion time. And maybe he did save your life. It looked to me like you were having a hard time getting that guy under control. If he got to his gun…"

Ben said, "You might be right about that, Teo." He thought a minute and said, "In fact, you might be right about all of it."

"There's a rule on the street, Ben. You run from the cops, you get beat down. The scumbags all know that. You need to learn it. If they run, they're going to fight when you catch them. They almost never just give up. Don't wait for them to stab you or shoot you. When you catch them, take them down hard and fast and knock the fight out of them before they can hurt you. Nobody will ever fault you for that. The most important thing is to go home in one piece at the end of your shift."

The next day he was just finishing up his reports when he heard dispatch assign Paul Woodruff and Teo Liwag to a violent mentally ill man. Ben started rolling their way just in case they needed help. Mindful of Woodruff being angry with him, he stopped at the edge of his beat and waited. After a few minutes they radioed they were code four with one in custody, and Teo radioed he was back in service. Ben decided to swing by the scene and see if he could make amends with Woodruff.

When he arrived, the beat 4 officer was interviewing a witness to the mentally ill person's bizarre behavior. It would bolster his case that the man was dangerous and should be carefully evaluated at the hospital. The man was seated in the backseat prisoner area of his patrol car, with his hands handcuffed behind his back. He was screaming, trying to get Woodruff's attention.

Ben walked up. "Hey, Paul, I came by to talk to you about yesterday."

He gave Ben a nasty look. "Yeah well, I'm busy. You want to make yourself useful see what that idiot is yelling about. And roll down the back window a bit, it's hot in the car."

Ben went to Woodruff's car and started the engine, then rolled a rear window down all the way so he could talk to the mentally ill man and let him cool off a bit. It was one of the older patrol cars and did not have a set of window bars over the back windows. As soon as the window went down the guy stopped yelling, but then he spoke so softly Ben couldn't hear him. He stood closer to the window so he could hear the man, but still couldn't understand what he was mumbling. Whatever it was, it seemed urgent, so he bent down closer to hear him. In an amazingly quick movement, the guy swiveled on the rear seat, flopped backwards and fired both his feet out the window into Ben's face, knocking him backwards. Both the suspect and Woodruff were roaring with laughter as Ben rubbed his sore face.

Whirling on his fellow cop, Ben said, "You son of a… You knew he was going to do that!"

Woodruff was still laughing. "Yeah, I could have predicted it, and you should have, too. You need to pay more attention to things, rookie. We were dispatched to a violent mentally ill man. I told you to roll the window down a bit and you rolled it down all the way. He suckered you in close and you fell for it. Serves you right. The guy's a nut, so we can't charge him with assaulting an officer, it'll never fly. Chalk it up to a cheap lesson learned and get the hell off my beat."

Ben had his first court appearance the next day. It was for a preliminary hearing on a domestic violence case he and Zobriskie had done when Ben was in phase four of field training. His subpoena said he had to report to the district attorney's office at the south bay courthouse in Chula Vista at 8:00 AM. Since Ben was scheduled to be working day shift that morning, a graveyard officer was held over on overtime to replace him in the field while he was in court. He went to court in uniform, driving a patrol car.

He arrived to find George already there, in a suit and tie. Since he worked graveyard shift, all of his court appearances were on overtime and he went there in civilian clothes. Ben said hello and asked George what he should do. The old vet showed him where to check in with the DA's clerk and then they sat down in the officers' lounge.

Ben got some coffee and offered to get some for his former training officer. "Nah, I'm hoping to be in bed soon."

"What do you mean?" Ben asked. "I thought these things take hours, if not all day."

George replied, "This is just a preliminary hearing, Ben. The defendant's not in jail, he's out on bail, so there's no urgency to hear the case. Most likely it will just get continued to another day."

Ben wanted to ask a whole bunch of questions but before he could the assistant district attorney who was prosecuting the case showed up. He looked at them and said, "Are you guys the officers for the Morales case?"

They both said yes. The distracted and overworked prosecuting attorney said, "The case is continued. I'll resubpoena you both when the time comes. Thanks for being here," then he walked rapidly away.

George was up and walking out the door before Ben realized they had been dismissed. "Hey, George, that's it?"

"Yup."

"So what happens now?"

"You go back to work and get in service so the graveyard guy can go home. I go home and go to bed, with four hours of overtime in my pocket."

"Four hours of overtime? You were only here for fifteen minutes."

"Yup. Union rules, my friend. Four hours minimum overtime pay for any court appearance. If they're gonna take away my beauty sleep they got to pay the man. You be safe, Ben."

As soon as he crossed the city line from Chula Vista into National City he reported he was in service and the held over graveyard officer was sent home. Since his shift had ended at 7:00 AM and it was now 8:30 AM the graveyard cop would get an hour and a half overtime. Five and a half hours of overtime paid to two officers for nothing more than their being inconvenienced. A wonderful deal for the police officers. Not so good for the taxpayers. No wonder the city bean counters were always complaining.

Ben and Jackie spent the weekend together. It was becoming a regular routine for them. On Saturday they went to the Children's Pool in La Jolla. They had been back there several times since their first date. Jackie just loved the place. On Sunday they went to Seaport Village and strolled around the waterfront shops hand in hand and arm in arm, like a couple of Midwestern tourists. In some ways that was still a reasonably accurate description of Ben.

Because she asked, he told Jackie about his week at work. He told her of the foot pursuit and arrest of the meth dealer and the argument that ensued with Paul Woodruff. He did not mention the dealer had a gun. Jackie took his side, of course, but Ben was conflicted about his own actions. He told Jackie he would handle it differently if something similar came up again. Jackie thought Woodruff was predisposed to not cut Ben any slack because Woodruff was a friend of Hopkins.

Jackie's brother Rod and Ben both had to work on Thanksgiving Day, it being a Thursday and their regularly scheduled work day. Because she insisted, Ben was going to their house for Thanksgiving dinner on the day after Thanksgiving. He was very apprehensive about it. He and Sergeant Selby got along okay at work but they maintained a professional relationship and did not socialize at all off duty. In fact, Ben did not socialize with any cops off duty. By his nature he was slow to make friends, and most of the cops followed the unwritten rule that veterans didn't socialize with probationary employees.

The days before Thanksgiving were pretty easy and the calls for service were light. Thanksgiving Day turned out to be the roughest day of the week for Ben's day shift squad. Every cop drove from call to call virtually from the minute they went in service. Most of the radio calls were family squabbles. All of them seemed to be fueled by alcohol. The fire department and paramedics were run ragged by non-stop calls of people choking, seizures, heart attacks, alcohol poisoning, kitchen fires, and of course, victims of domestic violence. The squad even had a call of sexual assault. A distant second cousin was groped by her drunken cousin. The family tried to cover it up but the woman insisted her cousin be arrested, and so he was.

Ben responded with fire and paramedics to a call of a burn victim who had been badly scalded by the grease from a huge turkey frying vat that had overturned. The paramedics said it was poor odds the guy would survive. The smell was nauseating and Ben had scenes of Iraq flashing through his mind, which greatly disturbed him. He had occasional bad dreams of his time in Iraq but was otherwise unbothered by his service. At least that's what he kept telling himself. The unforgettable smell of cooked human flesh triggered some images from the war he would rather not have remembered.

Both Ben and Rod worked late on Thanksgiving Day, staying to finish their reports. Ben's reports were getting better and better and each new one he submitted required less editing and discussion with his sergeant. Finally they each went home, with both of them wishing Jackie had not insisted on their all having dinner together the next day.

He rang their doorbell right on time, of course. He arrived fifteen minutes early, then after parking his car, he sat in it and waited until it was time to go in. It was just his way. Jackie greeted him with a big hug and kiss. He guardedly looked around, but her half-brother was nowhere in sight. She giggled at his discomfort. She led him by the hand into the kitchen, and there was Rod, in an apron, cooking. OK, Ben thought, so much for making assumptions. They said hello and he put down the pumpkin pie and bottle of wine he had brought. Rod told him there was beer in the refrigerator and to help himself. He seldom drank beer, but he didn't want to appear rude, so he reached in and got a bottle of Budweiser. Jackie sat down at the kitchen table and motioned for him to join her there. They all talked in the kitchen while Rod tended to the side dishes and occasionally checked on the turkey in the oven.

It was not at all what Ben had envisioned. He figured Jackie would be cooking in the kitchen while he and Rod sat in front of the TV set watching football. As he relaxed and watched the interaction between Jackie and Rod, he realized how close they really were. Their relationship was much more akin to father - daughter than brother - sister. He understood now why Rod so zealously protected her.

Dinner was far better than he had anticipated. Rod was an excellent cook, and like all good cooks, he enjoyed the cooking as much as the eating. By unspoken agreement they did not talk at all about police work. Jackie was the center of attention, and she loved it. At the end of the day the two men shook hands warmly and Jackie walked Ben to his car, where they made plans to get together Sunday. Saturday was for Jackie and Rod. She told Ben she was so caught up with him she had been neglecting her brother and she needed to spend some time with him.

In early December Jackie told Ben she and Rod were going to Atlanta for the Christmas - New Year's holiday period to visit with their mother. Jackie would be on Christmas break from college and Rod had been granted vacation time. Ben was immensely disappointed. He had been looking forward to Christmas with her and been agonizing over what presents to buy. As the most junior officer in the whole police department he didn't have a prayer of getting vacation time over Christmas. Christmas Eve was on a Wednesday, Christmas on a Thursday. New Year's Eve was on a Wednesday, and New Year's Day a Thursday, so his squad had to work every one of those days. Oh well, he had spent Christmas in much worse situations, so he shouldn't complain. He decided to put the time away from Jackie to good use and earn some extra money working overtime. Many officers were looking for someone to take a shift or two for them so they could have more time off during the holidays. Might as well make them happy and make some extra money in the bargain.

Working his regular day shift, Ben was dispatched to a report of a suspicious, unoccupied vehicle. Per the computer call screen, the car had been parked there for days and the reporting party thought it might be stolen. No license plate info was given. He rolled up a few car lengths behind the beat up old car and parked, then ran the license plate on his dashboard computer. It showed no record for the plate. That was not at all unusual in National City. People often rescued cars and license plates from the junk yard and the DMV computer would show no record of the plate if it had been junked long ago.

He approached the car carefully to see if it was occupied. Sometimes people would be asleep or even having sex in cars that were reported as unoccupied to dispatch. Sure enough, there was a scruffy looking man slumped low in the front seat. Ben radioed the plate info and told dispatch the car was occupied, and a cover unit was assigned.

Taking no chances, Ben drew his gun and kept it low, behind his leg. He rapped on the side of the car and loudly called out, "National City police! Show me your hands!"

The man very slowly raised his hands into the air. In his left hand he held an open badge case. Ben told the driver to roll down the window and hand the badge out, and he complied wordlessly. After examining the FBI badge and ID card he handed it back to the agent as he radioed code four and cancelled the cover unit.

The irritated fed said, "Thanks for blowing my cover, pal. I guess I can go get some lunch now."

Ben was miffed, too. "You blew your own cover. If you had checked in with our dispatch as required I wouldn't be standing here now."

The FBI agent said, "It doesn't matter anyway, he wasn't going to show. It was a long shot."

"Who were you looking for? Which house are you watching?" Ben asked.

"It's a federal matter. Sorry."

This is unbelievable, Ben thought. Even after 9/11 the feds still won't talk to other agencies. Did they learn nothing? "Whatever. I'm outta here," he said.

"Hey, wait. I've got something for you. Here." The agent handed Ben a piece of paper with a name and date of birth on it.

"What's this for?" Ben asked.

"I saw that guy here yesterday and took his picture. We ID'd him and he's got a felony warrant for assault with a deadly weapon. He was here again this morning. Thought you might want the info."

Ben said, "So this guy with a felony warrant for a violent crime was standing in front of you and you didn't arrest him because…"

"Hey, ADW is a state crime, not federal, and I didn't want to blow the surveillance."

Berto was the acting squad sergeant while Rod and Jackie were in Atlanta. Christmas week was far busier than Ben had expected. He realized the Christmas holidays were probably going to be a lot like Thanksgiving Day for the police and fire departments.

Brenda Stockwell was driving her patrol car down E.4th Street when she saw a couple of Hispanic gangsters in a new Chevy Tahoe pass by her in the opposite direction. She decided to road test them. A "road test" was copspeak for trying to scare a driver with a guilty conscience into fleeing by making an aggressive maneuver towards them. Once in a blue moon it actually worked. Most of the time it didn't, but it was always fun, at least for the cop. After the Tahoe passed her she flipped a quick U-turn and accelerated rapidly until she was up on their bumper. She was watching the driver's face closely in his rear view mirror. She wanted to see the "Oh shit" look in his eyes, then she would back off, turn off and disappear laughing. She got the look she expected, but the driver flooring it was an unexpected bonus.

"222 John in vehicle pursuit eastbound east 4th Street from C Avenue. White Chevy Tahoe, California plate 2FLT842."

Upon hearing her radio call, all the clear units in the city started towards the pursuit. Brenda regularly reported her direction, speed, traffic conditions, violations of traffic laws, and a description of both people in the car.

"223 John I'm number two. I'll call it." Teo Liwag had joined the pursuit behind Brenda. As the number two car, he would take over calling the pursuit information so Brenda in the lead car could simply concentrate on driving and staying with the suspects. Police were always at a huge disadvantage in vehicle pursuits. The criminals recklessly disregarded all traffic laws, had no concern for public safety, and great incentive to get away at all costs. The police had to always keep public safety in mind first, and balance that against whatever offense the suspects may have committed. The end result was more often than not the fleeing driver got away.

The suspects chose to stay on the city streets instead of heading for the freeway. As an experienced police officer, Brenda knew this meant they were most likely National City gangsters. When criminals flee from the police they tend to go to places they know well, to neighborhoods where people will help them and hide them. A couple of National City gangsters who fled into San Diego might end up lost and if they evaded the police and stopped in the wrong neighborhood they might end up dead at the hands of a rival gang.

The pursuit wound its way through the city and Ben finally got lucky and caught up to them. He joined up and radioed, "221 John I'm number three."

National City policy allowed no more than three patrol cars in a pursuit. Any remaining units could now only loosely parallel the pursuit to be near at hand if there was a crash or a foot bail, or to jump in if one of the pursuing units dropped out for some reason.

The chase took them up near Lincoln Acres, a small, unincorporated part of San Diego County that existed within National City, but was not actually part of it. It was technically the county sheriff's jurisdiction. As the Tahoe rounded a sharp corner it slowed and the passenger side door opened. Brenda radioed, "Standby for foot bail. The passenger's gonna bail."

Moments later the passenger leapt out of the moving car and rolled onto the street. He had a backpack with him. As Brenda and Teo drove on past, the gangster got to his feet and started running. Ben saw in his rear view mirror a sheriff's deputy was driving up fast behind him. He radioed, "221 John I'm stopping for the foot bail at Granger and 20th Street. There's a sheriff's car joining the pursuit as number three."

He stopped his car and ran after the young Hispanic man, who was running through yards and climbing over wooden fences. Ben tried to get on the radio to inform dispatch of his direction and location, but it was jammed up with the vehicle pursuit traffic. On his third attempt to get on the radio he finally succeeded. "221 John southbound on foot through backyards from Granger and 20th."

Dispatch replied, "221 John switch to channel 2. 223 John stay on channel 1 for the vehicle pursuit."

He switched over to channel 2. Ben was now talking with a different dispatcher as the two dispatchers tried to follow and coordinate the vehicle pursuit and the foot pursuit simultaneously. He could no longer hear what was happening with the vehicle pursuit, nor could those officers hear him.

He had channel 2 all to himself. He could still see the suspect up ahead of him. Young, but fat, the gangster was having trouble getting over the many fences, and his long head start was rapidly dwindling. Dispatch asked Ben for an update. He realized with a shock he no longer knew exactly where he was. He was still not thoroughly familiar with beat 3 and even less so with Lincoln Acres, and he had been running through backyards. He had not seen a street sign in over two minutes. He radioed his direction and estimated distance traveled from Granger and 20th. Paul Woodruff and Berto Salazar, the only units left in the city, were racing in his general direction, if only they could find him.

After another minute of chasing him, and several more fences, he caught up to the suspect. Ben had been yelling himself hoarse, "National City police, stop! Get on the ground! Police, stop!" All to no avail, of course.

The hardened street kid heard Ben's voice close behind him and stopped. He turned to face the cop, in a fighting stance. Ben remembered what Teo had told him - "If they run, they fight. Don't wait to be stabbed or shot."

Without breaking stride he slammed the suspect hard into the trunk of a large tree. The teen lost his backpack and fell down. Ben took out his police baton and said, "Face the ground and put your hands behind your back."

The young man ignored the orders and sprang to his feet. Ben hit him solidly several times in the legs with his baton, knocking him back to the ground. He radioed he was fighting the suspect in a backyard somewhere near La Siesta Way and E.24th Street. He hoped he was even close about his location. The kid got up again and was hammered back to the ground with more baton strikes. When he was still on the ground, Ben hit him twice in the ribs. It seemed to take the fight out of him and he lay still. He secured his baton and got out his handcuffs. He had one handcuff on the gangster when a very fat Hispanic woman ran out of the house whose yard they were in and started screaming at him.

"Get off of my brother you son of a bitch! Stop beating him!"

Ben told her to back off and not interfere. She ran straight at him and he realized too late she was not going to stop. She slammed into him with her whole 250 pounds, knocking him off her brother and onto the ground, the fat woman now on top of Ben. He was able to get to his portable radio and yelled, "Cover now! Cover now!"

"Cover Now" was an officer's urgent plea for help. It meant he was unable to control the situation himself and was in serious danger. As he struggled with the large woman he heard both Woodruff and Salazar asking for his exact location. They still couldn't find him.

Ben felt a large object beneath him and realized he had rolled on top of the suspect's backpack. He was finally able to get some leverage and partially raise himself up with the huge woman on top of him, when her brother came over and delivered a devastating kick to his head. He went kind of hazy and fell flat on the ground, on the verge of blacking out. The gangster kicked him viciously again, which had the perverse effect of rejuvenating Ben. The woman got up off of him and said, "Get the backpack and let's get in the house."

Her brother bent down to get the backpack from beneath Ben, who took the opportunity to land a very satisfying right hook to his jaw, sending him sprawling. As Ben struggled to his feet the sister kicked him squarely in the balls. He went down like a ton of bricks, gasping for air.

The brother came over and started kicking him in the upper body and head. Still reeling from the blow to his groin, all he could do was curl up and try to shield his face with his arms. When he felt someone trying to remove his gun from its holster, he realized he was in mortal danger. The thug said, "That's it. Get his gun and kill him. Kill the motherfucker."

The woman continued to tug at Ben's gun while her brother rained kicks on him. Having survived three combat tours in Iraq, he was determined not to die here in California. He managed to get his pepper spray from his belt and hosed down the sister, who fell away screaming in pain. He faintly heard, "National City police! Stop and get on the ground!"

It was Paul Woodruff, climbing over the fence into the yard. The brother gave Ben one more kick, snatched the backpack, and grabbed his sister by the arm. "Come on, we've got to get into the house." They took off into the house together as Woodruff ran up to Ben.

He dragged a semi-conscious Ben behind the tree so they had some cover between them and the house, in case the suspects started shooting. Then he radioed their exact location to dispatch, and moments later Berto was with them. Several sheriff's deputies arrived and surrounded the house. Berto and Woodruff helped Ben out to the street.

The suspects did not respond to repeated shouts to come out of the house and a standoff developed. Ben was leaning against the trunk of a patrol car. His left eye was swollen shut, his face was badly bruised, and a hematoma on the side of his head had grown to the size of a tennis ball. He turned suddenly to one side and threw up. A sheriff's sergeant and a man in a suit and tie walked up to Ben. The sergeant told Ben an ambulance was on the way for him, then he introduced the man in the suit. "This is Special Agent Johnson of the Drug Enforcement Administration."

The federal agent said, "One of the National City cops told me you're a rookie. I guess that's why you let that girl kick your ass."

Still woozy, Ben just looked at him, wondering why the DEA was here.

"My team has been set up next door, surveilling this house for four months. We were hoping you'd take the brother into custody and not burn the house for us, but then the sister came out and kicked the shit out of you. Now our whole operation is blown."

Confused, Ben said, "Wait a minute. You were watching me fight those two people and you just sat there next door and didn't come to help me?"

The agent said testily, "I told you, asshole, this is a major operation. We've got tens of thousands of dollars and four months of time invested. I wasn't going to take the chance of exposing my team. It's not like this was a gunfight."

Ben was thoroughly disgusted and appalled. He could have died while this scumbag sat there and watched! Without further thought he swung his fist from the waist with his whole 235 pounds behind it, connecting solidly with the agent's jaw and knocking him completely off his feet. After a few moments on the ground the federal narc tried to stand up, but he hurt so badly he settled for sitting there. "You're done, shitbag," he mumbled. Something was wrong with his jaw and he couldn't speak normally. "It's a felony to strike a federal officer. I'll have your badge and you'll be lucky to not end up in federal prison. Fuck that hurts!"

Berto came over and started arguing with the DEA agent. Ben leaned back against the car, holding his aching head in both hands. The ambulance arrived and a paramedic came over. He examined Ben and said to Berto, "This officer has a concussion and needs to be transported to the hospital." He looked at the DEA agent, whose jaw was swelling up rapidly. "Did you get hit, too?"

"Yeah, by this dipshit here. And he's gonna pay for it."

The paramedic replied, "I kind of doubt that. He's got a serious concussion. He's not oriented. He thinks today is Saturday and it took him three times to tell me his name. He's not responsible for anything he says or does in that condition and I'll testify to that if I need to."

In the back of the ambulance Ben smiled and extended his hand to the paramedic, who shook it firmly. "I'm Benjamin Lloyd Olsen, and today is Tuesday. I'm oriented just fine. What was that all about?"

"Dennis Clay. Glad to meet you. Fuck those feds, man! They come into our city all the time, never cooperate with anyone, and they think their shit don't stink. And you do have a concussion."

Ben spent the night in the hospital and was given the next two days off due to his injuries. That would take him to his regular days off, so he found himself with five days off in a row.

After he was released from the hospital on Christmas Eve, he didn't know what to do. He now had Christmas Eve and Christmas Day off, but Jackie was in Atlanta and he didn't feel well enough to do much of anything. He decided to track down Nacho and see how the grievously wounded, homeless army vet was doing.

Jackie and Rod were enjoying the Christmas holiday with their mother and her live-in boyfriend. Over dinner one evening, she told her mother about Ben. She went on in great detail about his growing up in small town Wisconsin and his service in the Marine Corps. After some time her mother's boyfriend said, "Hey, I just realized, this guy is a white boy, isn't he? There ain't no blacks in his neck of the woods, they're all blonde haired Swedes."

Jackie said, "Actually, his family is Norwegian, but yes, he is white. So what?"

The older man shrugged. "So nothing. It just seems kind of odd you're telling us everything about him but his shoe size and you forgot to mention he's white."

Rod spoke up. "Jackie and I had a long talk about this, Mom. I wasn't too keen on it myself, but I'm starting to come around. Ben is a good guy. He's been assigned to my squad and he is as hardworking and honest as they come."

Jackie's mother said nothing for several minutes, just went on eating. When she had gathered her thoughts she said, "Jackie, your Ben sounds like a wonderful man. But you and him aren't going to live in wonderland, you're going to live in the real world with the rest of us. There's folks out there who will make life harder for you. You know that. And if God wills it and you and Ben bless me with some grandchildren, they're going to have the hardest time of all. You need to think about that real carefully before you get in over your head."

Jackie said, "I don't think we're at that point yet, Momma. We might get there one day, though. I know what you're saying and I'll think carefully about it."

Her mother laughed gently. "Child, you can say you'll think on it but I know better. When the time comes to decide, your heart will make the decision, not your head. In the end, a girl always goes with her heart. And maybe that's the way God meant it to be."

Chapter Nine

After being released from the hospital on Christmas Eve Ben drove to National City to look for Nacho. The young, homeless army veteran had made quite an impression on him. There was something about him he couldn't quite define. He supposed part of it was pity, but in reality it was also an unwarranted feeling of guilt. Guilt that he had survived the war intact, while so many others had come home mangled, like Nacho, or in flag draped coffins. He wanted to find the former soldier and give him something for Christmas, or at least talk to him for a while. Nobody should have to spend Christmas alone.

He went to the large homeless encampment near Plaza Bonita mall. There were about a dozen homeless people there, in tents, cardboard boxes, and just huddled beneath blankets. It reminded him of some of the slum areas in Iraq. He parked his car and walked up to a shapeless pile of blankets. "Nacho, wake up, man."

A voice from beneath the blankets said, "I ain't sleeping, Ell Tee. Just laying here thinking about things." He threw back the blankets and got a look at Ben's face and head.

"Damn, LT! Somebody sure beat the snot outta you. He in jail?"

He was still shocked by Nacho's grotesquely misshapen head, but he tried to hide it. "It was a she and a he. And that's a good question. I wish I knew the answer. It's a long story for another time, maybe. Nacho, you're freaking me out again. Why are you calling me LT?"

"You was, wasn't ya? An LT? Over there."

"Yeah, I was. Who told you that?"

"You told me. In my head. Like I said before, sometimes I just know things. Maybe you startin' to know some things, too."

Ben said, "I know you need to get yourself cleaned up, and I want to help you. Don't you have any family around here? Somewhere you could go for Christmas?"

He replied, "Nah, there's nobody, LT."

"OK, Nacho. How about I buy you some lunch and we can talk some more?"

"Sounds good, LT. Thanks."

"Why don't you call me Ben? I think we're going to be spending a lot of time together."

"OK, Ben. You didn't strike me as one of them hoity-toity officers. Besides, a jarhead lieutenant ranks below an army PFC anyway. Hehehe."

Chuckling, Ben said, "Is that what you were in the army, a PFC?"

"Yeah. I grew up here in National City. My parents came up all the way from Colombia to find work. I was just a baby when they snuck across the Rio Grande. I like to think they floated me across in a wicker basket, like the baby Jesus, but that's just me dreaming.

"They ended up here in National City. I went to Ira Harbison Elementary School and then Granger Junior High. Things were okay. We were poor, but we got by. When I was fifteen years old my father got caught in an immigration raid where he worked. Somebody warned us La Migra was coming to our house next, to get the rest of the family. My mother decided rather than try to make it here without my father the whole family would go back to Colombia. Colombia! It may as well have been the moon to me. I was an American kid, a California boy. I told my mom we should stay and fight to keep Dad here. Then she told me she was illegal, and so was I. I had no idea! I had a birth certificate and a social security number, both fakes. My younger brother and sister were born here, so they were American citizens. They could stay here with some other family, some make believe cousins or something, but we had to go back. It wasn't right, Ben. Nobody should be allowed to break up a family like that.

"I couldn't go to live in Colombia, no matter what my mother decided, so I packed a bag and took off. I headed for Arizona and lived on the street there for a while. Then I moved over to Texas. I lied about my age and worked like a dog under the table on construction jobs. It was a rough time for me. I was sick of living day to day and job to job. When I turned eighteen I went to an army recruiter and joined up. They didn't look too hard at my birth certificate, or they just didn't care. We were fighting two wars and they needed bodies."

Ben said, "What a sad story, Nacho. I want to hear about your army service, too, but let's get lunch."

They got into Ben's car and started driving. "Nacho, no offense, but you smell really bad. We've got to get you showered and cleaned up before we eat lunch someplace decent. They'll never let you into a restaurant like this."

"Sure Ben, just drop me by my country club and I'll go freshen up. Get a clue, will you? You think I like smelling like this?"

"OK, I'm sorry. We'll swing by my place and you can shower there. Then we'll go and get you some new clothes. It'll be my Christmas present to you."

The proud young Hispanic man said, "I don't need your charity, and I don't need new clothes, just clean ones. I have some money. We can go to a thrift store and I'll buy some clothes there."

That impressed Ben. "Fair enough, buddy. Fair enough."

Nacho smelled so bad, despite the late December chill they drove with the windows down. As he pulled into the driveway of his rental home in Pacific Beach he fleetingly wondered if he was doing the right thing. He hardly knew this guy, who was clearly an alcoholic. What else might he be? Would he need to watch him carefully while they were inside his house?

Just as quickly as that thought went through his mind an intense feeling of shame overcame him. They had fought virtually side by side in Iraq. Although they never knew each other over there, Ben had no doubt each would have given his life for the other. Nacho had shown no indication of dishonesty. In fact, he had refused Ben's offer of money to buy clothing. He was a disabled war veteran. How dare Ben think so poorly of him. This was the very least he could do for someone who had given so much for his country.

After showering, Nacho put on a pair of Ben's running shorts and one of his old T-shirts. They were huge on Nacho's small frame, but he couldn't put on the filthy clothes he arrived in. He threw them in the trash.

At the local Goodwill store he bought two complete sets of clothing. He put one set on in the store's dressing room, being sure to first tell the clerk he was going to buy them and wear them out of the store, so there would be no misunderstanding. He returned the running shorts and T-shirt to Ben. An oversized floppy hat and a pair of flip flops completed his wardrobe. The hat hid his deformity and he looked like a typical casually dressed southern Californian. Now they were ready for lunch.

They ate at a Soup Plantation restaurant which featured an all you can eat buffet. Ben picked it because he assumed Nacho would make a pig of himself. He was wrong. He ate sparingly while it was Ben who made a spectacle of himself, gorging on everything.

"Nacho, tell me about your army service."

"Well, after boot camp I went to a few weeks of infantry training. Most the guys were trying hard to get specialty training in electronics or aviation, armor, anything but infantry. I didn't care. The army was giving me three hots and a cot and that was good enough for me. Then they sent me back to Texas. I was assigned to the 2nd Battalion, 7th Cavalry at Fort Hood. Garryowen. I can't get the unit song out of my head. It wasn't long before we deployed to Iraq. I don't have to tell you about it, you lived it, too. Near the end of the battle for Fallujah my squad got ambushed by some Hajiis with rocket propelled grenade launchers. One of the rockets exploded near me and I took a big hunk of shrapnel right through my helmet. The next thing I remember was waking up in Brooke Army Medical Center in San Antonio. They told me I went from the battlefield to a field hospital in country, then to Germany for a month, and finally to Brooke. I believe them, but I don't remember any of it.

"They removed about 25% of my brain in a half a dozen surgeries. The brain is an amazing organ. Sometimes when you lose part of your brain the remaining parts teach themselves to do all the things the missing parts used to do. The doctors know this happens but they don't know why or how. My brain seems to have adapted very well, but ever since the surgeries all of my senses are messed up. Sometimes I see smells. Some sounds have smells, too. Letters and numbers always have certain colors to me, no matter what color they really are. Sometimes I see my pain as bolts of yellow or even red if it's really intense pain. The docs at Brooke said it's called Synesthesia. It's a rare but documented medical condition some people are born with and other people get from brain injury. They don't consider it to be a big deal, and when it's caused by brain trauma it usually fades away with time, as the brain adapts to its new condition.

"They discharged me from Brooke but wanted me to come back twice a month for follow up tests. After I got out of the hospital I started to know things I shouldn't know. Sometimes it's weak and sometimes it's so strong it hurts my head. I could also see other peoples' pain as colors, not just my own pain. I told the docs all about it when I went back for my first couple of follow ups. They said what I was describing was impossible. They readmitted me for more testing and when they couldn't find anything different they decided I had mental problems, post-traumatic stress, whatever. It was all horseshit. I know what I see, and I know what I know. The docs got so freaked out they were going to commit me to a mental hospital. I gave up trying to tell them the truth and just lied to make them happy. It worked, and they discharged me again.

"With most people I get a feeling - I sort of know if they're good folks or bad folks. Most people are both, and they kind of let their two halves fight each other. Some people are so good they seem to shine, and others are so bad they seem to have a black cloud around them. You are one of the shiniest people I have ever seen, Ben. That's why I'm talking to you. You're the first person I've told about this since the docs said I was nuts. I know you won't make fun of what I'm saying or think I'm crazy

"At times I hear people thinking inside my head. Sometimes it's clear, but usually it's all jumbled up and hard to understand. When it's very strong it hurts my head. I started drinking to make it go away, and that works most of the time. It got so I was drunk all the time, just to keep the noise down in my head. I get a disability retirement check every month from the army so I have money if I don't drink it all away, but most of the time I do.

"I have to tell you, though, Ben. You smell real bad of turkeys. That's a new one on me. And every time I think of your turkey smell I hear the name Jennie-O. It's like you're screaming the name in your head, I hear it so clearly. What did that woman do to you to make you hate her so much?"

Ben was fascinated by what Nacho was saying, but when he heard that he had to laugh. "Jennie-O isn't a woman, Nacho. It's a large company in my home town. They raise turkeys. If it wasn't for Jennie-O, Barron,

Wisconsin would dry up and blow away. Everyone in Barron works for Jennie-O one way or another. I swore I would never work for them and be stuck in Barron for my whole life, so I left there after high school and eventually ended up in Fallujah just like you. I guess we've got that in common."

He went on, "I believe you're sincere about everything you told me, Nacho. I'm going to look up Synesthesia on the internet later, and I'm sure it's real, just as you say. But there must be another explanation for what you know about me. Maybe you overheard some cops talking about me when you were arrested before, and you don't remember it because you were drunk. Maybe you recognized me as a fellow combat vet. Sometimes I can tell that about a person myself. Vets who have seen a lot of combat get a certain look about them other vets can see, because they've been there themselves. It's got to be something like that."

Nacho smiled. "I know you believe me, Ben. You just won't admit it to yourself yet. Let me ask you a question - How did you know where to find me today?"

"What do you mean? You're homeless, so I went to a homeless camp."

Shaking his head in disagreement, he said, "There're homeless camps all over town, and lots of homeless people stay to themselves. I don't usually stay at the encampments, they're too dangerous. I just ended up there last night. I wasn't there the day before. Where else did you look for me?"

Ben was puzzled. "Well, nowhere. That was my first stop. I got lucky, that's all."

Nacho snorted. "Oh yeah? There were at least a dozen tents there, and cardboard shelters, and guys under newspapers and blankets. How many of those did you check before you found me?"

Ben was stunned. "None! I hadn't thought about it until just now. I walked right up and started talking to you even though you were buried under that pile of blankets. I knew you were in there. How could I know that?"

"It's like I told you then, Ben - maybe you're starting to know things, too."

He actually considered the possibility, then dismissed it. "No, I don't think so. This is all so hard to believe, but I don't know how else you could know the things you know. Maybe somehow you led me to you, Nacho. That feels more right to me."

"I guess it could be, Ben. I guess anything could be."

"You're very well spoken, Nacho. I hope you don't take that wrong, I mean it as a compliment. You said you left school when you ran away from home at age fifteen."

He chuckled. "I sure didn't learn much when I was in school. It seemed to me the teachers just wanted to get through the day with no drama, and learning was secondary. I can't blame them, since so many of the students in National City were little wannabe gangsters.

"My parents were first generation immigrants. They wanted badly to make good in America, and they wanted even more for me and my brother and sister to succeed. They forbid us to speak Spanish outside the house and insisted we speak only proper Spanish inside the house. No "Spanglish" for us. Every night we had to do all of our homework for school before we could watch TV, and our mother made us read books, too. As the oldest child, I was expected to teach my brother and sister proper English and help them with their homework if they needed it. I guess in a way you could say I was home schooled. Even after I ran away I still read books."

After lunch, Ben was driving around, wondering where to go next. He was very concerned about Nacho's drinking. He was trying to decide how to diplomatically bring up the subject when Nacho said, "Yeah, Ben, I'm an alky. We can talk about it."

Geez, Ben thought. This keeps getting spookier. Did he just hear me think that? Nacho, say "spookier" if you hear me thinking. But his passenger was looking out the window and remained silent.

He drove back to his house. He couldn't think of anywhere else to go. They talked there for a long time, and he finally broached the subject of Nacho's drinking. "You're too young to spend the rest of your life drowning in a bottle. If you'll make an effort to stop drinking I'll help you in any way I can. You can shower here whenever you need to. You can keep some clothes and other personal belongings here so they won't get stolen. I'll give you a reference if you need one when you go to look for a job. Oh, gosh, you're an illegal alien. I'll find out what we need to do to get you some kind of legal status. What do you say?"

Nacho laughed. "Ben, you had me at 'you can shower here.' I don't want to waste my life, either. I should be dead and God kept me alive for a reason. I'll start going to AA meetings and see what they have to say. And you don't have to worry about my legal status. The army discovered I was illegal over in Iraq. They have a program that allows some aliens a path to citizenship in return for combat service. I became a citizen in Brooke Army Medical Center."

Ben replied, "That's excellent, Nacho. I'd like to attend a few AA meetings with you, if that's OK. I've never been to one. We can go to the first one right now."

He found an Alcoholics Anonymous meeting center in the phone book that was only two blocks from his house, and when he called he was told a meeting was scheduled to start soon. They walked there. Ben thought the place would be deserted on Christmas Eve but it was jam packed. He was also surprised to see most of the people there were well dressed and appeared to be regular, middle class folks.

The meeting started with a non-denominational prayer. Ben believed in God but he had not been to church in years. He did not join in the prayer, but he saw Nacho did. After giving a short talk, the meeting facilitator asked for people to stand and speak. One after another people got to their feet and told something about themselves. They all started with the same line: "My name is ___ and I'm an alcoholic. I've been sober for ___ days." One man stood up and said he had been sober for seven years. He said he seldom attends meetings anymore but felt the need to go on this Christmas Eve. Finally there was a pause, and Nacho stood up. "My name is Ygnacio Evangelista and I'm an alcoholic. I've been sober for one day. This is my first meeting." As he sat down the room exploded with people saying hello to him and congratulating him on his decision to get sober.

At the end of the meeting the facilitator introduced himself to Nacho. He gave him a business card with his cell phone number and told him he could call him anytime for any reason. "I'll be your friend when you need a friend, Ygnacio. Don't hesitate to call me."

Nacho thanked him but said if he felt he needed it he would call his friend Ben. The shy Wisconsin farmer felt a burst of pride and happiness. Nacho considered him a friend!

The facilitator said to Ben, "Are you an alcoholic?"

He replied, "No, I'm not. I just came to be with him."

"Well, that's very good of you, but when Ygnacio needs help he would do best to call me. I've been where he is. It's part of our program. One alcoholic buddies up with another. In the end, it helps us both." Nacho kept the card.

They walked back to Ben's house. He had not decorated his house with Christmas stuff nor did he have a Christmas tree. With Jackie in Atlanta he didn't see the point of it, and he had planned on working through the holiday period. He turned on the TV hoping to find a basketball game to watch. He flipped through the channels to TBS. Instead of a basketball game the old Christmas movie "Miracle on 34th Street" was just starting. Ben had loved the movie as a kid. Nacho had never seen it before, so they got comfortable and settled down to watch, Ben in his favorite chair and Nacho on the couch. Ben became engrossed in the movie, and when it ended he saw Nacho had fallen asleep. He was about to wake him up, but then what? Drive him back to National City and dump him out on the street? On Christmas Eve? He found a blanket for him, shut off the lights and went to bed.

The next morning he awoke to the ringing of his cell phone. It was Jackie calling from her mother's house in Atlanta to wish him a merry Christmas. They spoke for almost an hour. Jackie assumed he was on duty, since he had been scheduled to work. He didn't tell her he was at home, nor did he mention Nacho, or tell her of his getting injured in a fight.

After speaking to her he called his family in Barron. They were gathered for their traditional Christmas dinner and he spoke at length with his parents and two brothers.

Nacho and Ben enjoyed Christmas together. They attended another AA meeting, and it was even more crowded than the first one. Back at his house they watched some NBA games on TV and Nacho again spent the night on the couch. On Friday morning he thanked Ben for everything and told him he wanted some time alone. Ben offered to drive him back to National City but Nacho said he was going to spend the day in Pacific Beach.

He returned to the house on Sunday afternoon. Ben did not ask him where he slept for the past two nights. He had a couple of shopping bags of clothing he had bought at the Goodwill store, which he left in a closet. He also put some personal toiletries in Ben's bathroom and used his shower. They watched the Charger's game on TV together. After the game, Nacho asked if he could use Ben's address on his employment applications. He said he was going job hunting

Monday morning. Ben agreed, and offered to let him sleep at his house again. He declined, but said he would be back now and then to shower and visit.

After he left, Ben thought to himself even though he missed Jackie it had been a pretty good Christmas after all.

Chapter Ten

Ben reported to work Monday morning after his five days off. He felt fine. His black eye was pretty much back to normal and the big goose egg on his head was gone. Berto led the pre-shift briefing as the acting sergeant with Rod still in Atlanta until New Year's.

After they were caught up on what had happened over the weekend, Berto told Ben the squad had debriefed the big vehicle pursuit/foot chase last week. He summarized for Ben. "Brenda and Teo and a sheriff's deputy chased the Tahoe all the way down close to the Mexican border. The driver bailed out in San Ysidro and got away. The car turned out to be a stolen that had not yet been reported. There was a loaded sawed off 12 gauge on the front seat."

He went on, "The brother and sister you fought with refused to come out of their house. SWAT was called and after a pretty long standoff they went in with tear gas and flash bangs. Six people inside were arrested, including the two you fought with. The brother actually tried to play things off. He claimed he had been inside all day watching TV. Pretty tough sell since he still had your handcuffs on one wrist! The crime scene unit swept the house but all they found were traces of cocaine, scales for weighing dope, and a bunch of packaging. The suspects had hours to flush all their stuff. Interestingly, according to the DEA the sister is the big honcho in all of this. The whole family works for a Mexican cartel. Their house was a major warehouse and distribution center."

Berto was about to continue when the dayshift lieutenant walked into the briefing room. "I wanted to give everyone the latest word on your bucket from last week. Are you all done, Berto?"

"Yes, sir, go ahead. I was just filling Ben in on that. He's pretty much up to speed now."

"Good. Ben, the agent you clocked is the number two DEA guy in San Diego County. A pretty big frog in this pond. He immediately filed a complaint against you and tried to have you arrested as well. You broke his jaw, by the way. Two things saved your bacon. One, the doctors and paramedics all said due to your severe concussion you were not consciously aware of what was happening, and therefore not responsible for your actions. In layman's terms it's called a 'gray out.' You're walking and talking but you're not really there. It's a common occurrence with concussions. Two, the DEA surveillance team had a parabolic microphone set up to hear conversations inside and outside the house. The sounds of your fight were caught on tape. The tape shows you called for cover now and it also recorded the brother telling the sister to get your gun and kill you. The surveillance team members heard it all and were going to assist you but they were ordered not to interfere by their boss, the guy you punched. Since you were in mortal danger that was a violation of DEA policy."

"So, the complaint has been withdrawn and you're in the clear. Not only that, but it looks like the DEA guy is going to receive a reprimand."

The whole squad broke into applause and hollering. Even Woodruff joined in. There was no love lost between local cops and the feds.

The squad hit the streets. Ben was dispatched to a few cold crime reports. Burglars don't take time off for the holidays. In fact, holidays are prime time for burglaries. He was enjoying some coffee in his car when dispatch radioed, "221 John, assist 240 Yellow on a report of a dead dog in the alley north of the 2100 block of E.11th Street." 240 Yellow was the call sign for the animal control officer, Isabel Molina. Ben had met her before but never been dispatched to a call with her. He wondered what it was about.

When he arrived Isabel was waiting for him near her truck. "Hi Ben. Thanks for covering me. I've had some problems in the past with the people who live off this alley. I just wanted an officer to stand by while I scoop up the dog. It'll only take a minute."

They walked into the alley. Isabel said, "The reporting party said it's by the dumpster. I think I see it."

As they neared the dumpster Ben could see part of one leg of the dog sticking out from under a bunch of crumpled up newspapers. He stopped to let Isabel pick it up. She bent over to get the dog and suddenly screamed out, "Madre de Dios! Es un bebe!" She staggered backwards.

"Ben, it's a baby! A baby!"

He looked. Now that Isabel had removed some of the newspaper he could clearly see it was a human infant. He was about to radio dispatch when Isabel yelled, "It's alive, it's moving!"

One of the baby's arms was moving back and forth. Ben rushed in and brushed aside the remaining newspapers so he could pick up the tiny infant. Beneath the papers was a large rat, gnawing away at the dead baby's arm. With one more pull the rat separated the arm from the baby's body and trotted off with it. Isabel was screaming hysterically. Ben fell to his knees *and dove for cover as another rocket propelled grenade exploded nearby. A heavy machine gun was hammering away at his platoon from a third story window.*

"Gunny, we've got to get a LAAW on that machine gun. It's chewing us to pieces. Where's Jenkins?"

"Jenkins is down, LT. I don't know where his tube is."

"How about Washington?"

"He's behind cover on the other side of the alley. He doesn't have the angle to take a shot. You're hit, Lieutenant."

He was bleeding from multiple shrapnel wounds, and blood was running into one of his eyes. "I'm OK, Gunny. We need to get some air support. Get the radioman up here."

Ben radioed to field headquarters, "Charlie Six, this is Charlie Three. We are pinned down in an alley by heavy weapons fire. Request urgent close air support, over."

"Roger, Three. All of our gunships are already engaged. I'll try to get a fast mover for you. Standby." A fast mover was a jet aircraft. The Marines much preferred helicopter gunships for close air support but Ben would take whatever he could get.

"Charlie Three, your bird is Navy Swordsman 02. He'll contact you on this net. Standby."

After what seemed like an eternity the radio crackled, "Charlie Three this is Swordsman 02. I have your grid coordinates and I am one minute out. Say your status, over."

Ben replied, "We are pinned down by a heavy machine gun northeast of my position. It's in a third story window in the southwest corner of a three story building, friendlies close, over."

"Swordsman 02, roger. My first pass will be for targeting only. Out."

The U.S. Navy F/A-18 aircraft screamed overhead and disappeared just as quickly. A few moments later the pilot radioed, "Charlie Three this is Swordsman 02. I have your target and am coming in hot. Tell your boys to keep their heads down, it's gonna get loud."

Ben did not see the jet again, but he caught a fleeting glimpse of the precision guided 500 pound bomb as it flew through the wall next to the third story window with the machine gun nest. He ducked his head and was rocked by the tremendous pressure wave. The noise was incredible. When he looked up the last few pieces of concrete were tumbling into a pile. There was no more gunfire from the building because the building itself was just a smoking heap of rubble. The upper floors had collapsed down to the ground.

"All right, Gunny, let's get our wounded taken care of and recon that building for survivors."

They made their way carefully through the wreckage of the building. The devastation was beyond description. Body parts were strewn in the *alley. They found no survivors. As they were leaving a Marine called out, "Gunny, LT, I got something over here."*

They walked over to the Marine. There on the ground in the rubble was a tiny arm, probably from a three or four year old child. Ben fell to his knees in shock. The Marine said, "There must have been a family hiding on the first or second floor."

Through his tears, Ben said, "Oh Lord, what have I done? I killed a child!"

He awoke in a hospital bed, completely disoriented. He thought at first he was in a field hospital in Iraq, then little by little his mind returned to the present day. He pushed the call button and a nurse came in. The woman said, "Oh good, I can see from your eyes you're back with us now. Let me get the doctor."

The doctor told Ben he had lost consciousness in the alley where he and Isabel had found the dead baby, and not come around until just now. "Well, actually you weren't completely unconscious. You were ambulatory. Your body was working but your head was not. You suffered another 'gray out.' It's kind of unusual since your concussion happened six days ago, but it's not unheard of. There are a lot of things about the brain we still don't understand. Apparently your concussion was more serious than we thought. We're going to keep you in the hospital a few days and run some tests, and let you get some rest."

Ben was chagrined. He knew this was not a residual effect from his concussion. He didn't think he even had a concussion in the first place. The sight of that dead baby had caused him to flash back to a similar scene in Fallujah. He had suffered a severe episode of Post-Traumatic Stress Disorder, and if he told the doctors about it he would surely lose his job as a police officer.

Chapter Eleven

On his second day in the hospital Ben felt fine and was bored. He was hoping to be discharged soon. Every test so far was negative. He was flipping through TV channels when Nacho walked in.

Ben was pleased and surprised, and cheerfully greeted him. "Hey, Nacho! Good to see you, man. How did you know I was here? Ah, wait, don't answer that. The doctors already think my brain is scrambled. If somebody overhears us talking about that spooky stuff they'll never let me out of here."

Nacho laughed and said, "Been there, done that."

Ben laughed at the irony of the situation. "So, what's new?"

"Well, I'm still sober. Haven't had a drink in seven days now. I feel real good, but it's getting kind of noisy." He pointed to his head.

Nacho filled him in on his job search and living situation. "No luck finding a job yet. I'm going to the AA meetings regularly, and I'm staying at a mission in Pacific Beach. It's OK, but kind of a rough crowd. I sort of miss National City. At least there I knew most of the street people."

Ben said, "The docs are gonna keep me here at least one more day. They still think I might have a relapse."

"There ain't nothing wrong with you, Ben. I can see you're as healthy as a horse."

"Thank you for the diagnosis, doctor," he said, chuckling.

"You're laughing, but you know I'm right. You hearing me? I *see* that you're healthy."

Ben got serious. "Yeah, you're right. I wish I could go home. Hey Nacho, here's my house key. You must be needing some clean clothes and a shower. Just leave the key under a rock near the front door when you leave. Better yet, make yourself a copy first. That way, you can come and go as you please."

He was touched by Ben's gesture of friendship and trust. "You sure you want to do that, Ben?"

"Yup. Just make sure you lock up when you leave the house. It's not the best neighborhood in the world."

He was discharged the next day and told he could report to work the following Monday unless he experienced any new symptoms. As he was preparing to leave a nurse walked in. "Maybe you don't remember me. I was your nurse when you were admitted."

She was a pretty woman in her early thirties. Ben said, "No, I'm sorry, I don't. But thank you for taking care of me. Everyone here on the staff was very pleasant and professional."

She said, "I'm a nurse in the Navy Reserve. I did a year of active duty in a field hospital in Afghanistan. You were a Marine, weren't you?"

Ben said, "Yes, I was. How did you know?"

"When they brought you in here you were mumbling a bunch of gibberish. I couldn't understand much but I heard the word 'Gunny' a few times. Then when I undressed you I saw your shrapnel scars. I must have seen a million of those wounds over there. It seemed pretty obvious after that."

"Well, thanks again for taking care of me."

She handed him a business card and said, "If you ever need to talk."

He put the card in his pocket and thanked her again. When he got home he found his house key under a rock near the front door. Once inside, as he was changing his clothes, he took all the stuff out of his pockets and looked at the card for the first time. He had assumed it was the nurse's business card. Instead, it was a card for Veterans

Village of San Diego, a Post-Traumatic Stress Disorder support group.

Jackie and Rod flew into San Diego late on Saturday afternoon. When she was all settled in she called Ben and they made plans to get together Sunday. On Sunday morning he picked her up and they ate breakfast at a family restaurant. Over breakfast she told him all the details of her trip to Atlanta. When she was finished she asked him about his holidays. "I know you had signed up for a lot of overtime, Ben. How did that go?"

Choosing his words carefully, he said, "Jackie, we're just about done with breakfast. I've got a couple of long stories to tell you. Why don't we get out of here and go somewhere we can talk?"

Jackie didn't like the sound of that, but she said, "OK, how about the Children's Pool? It's a warm enough day, and it shouldn't be crowded this time of year."

She tried to get Ben to open up on the drive over, but he deflected all her questions and only made small talk. She became more and more worried something very unpleasant was about to unfold. Once they were settled down at the Children's Pool she said, "All right, Ben, out with it. I could tell by the tone of your voice it's not gonna be good." Her voice quavering, she said, "Please don't tell me you're dumping me."

Astonished she would even think such a thing, Ben hugged her hard. "Oh, honey. I'm never going to dump you. I'm crazy about you!"

He proceeded to tell her all about the car chase and foot pursuit of the Mexican cartel suspects. He didn't leave anything out, but tried to downplay the danger he had been in. She listened raptly and was infuriated when he related what the DEA agent had said and done, and then laughed gleefully and clapped her hands when he told her of punching him in the jaw. He saw the concern flash across her face as she realized the implications of that, so he quickly told her what the lieutenant had said.

"Ben, all this happened before Christmas, but you never mentioned it when we talked on Christmas morning. I thought you were at work on Christmas but you were at home recovering, weren't you? And you spent a night in the hospital and didn't say anything about it. What's the matter with you?" She was genuinely angry.

"If I told you about it you would have just gotten worried about nothing. I didn't want to spoil your Christmas with your mother."

She was calming down some. "OK, Ben. But promise me if something like this ever happens again you'll…"

He interrupted her. "Well, actually, Jackie, it already did happen again."

"What! Ben Olsen, I swear, you are infuriating sometimes! What happened?"

He told her of his second hospital stay and what had really caused it, including all the details of finding a child's limb in Iraq after he had ordered the air strike on the building. Instead of becoming angrier she hugged him fiercely. Tearfully, she said, "Oh, Ben. That is the most horrible story I have ever heard. That poor baby. And Isabel. And you. And the child in Iraq. Oh God, the whole thing is just so… there are no words to describe it."

They hugged each other for a long time, each gaining strength and comfort from the other. When he sensed Jackie had recovered sufficiently, he told her he had more news to discuss with her. "What, space aliens landed in your backyard and abducted you?"

"No, next year's squad assignments are out. I've been assigned to the weekend graveyard shift." She groaned. It meant they would see a lot less of each other. He decided to tell her about Nacho another time.

Chapter Twelve

Ben was at home on a Wednesday evening when Nacho knocked on the door. He let him in and said, "Why don't you just use your key?"

Nacho said, "I didn't want to maybe walk in on you and your girlfriend."

Ben smiled. "Yeah, that would take the cake. Jackie doesn't even know you exist, man. I had so much news to talk to her about and she was so upset by everything I never got around to telling her about you."

Nacho smiled and said, "I've got some news myself, Ben. I found a job."

They slapped high fives and Ben said, "Sweet! Gimme the 411."

Nacho cracked up laughing. "Ben, you're a farmer from Wisconsin. That's OK, but when you try to talk ghetto slang you just sound like a stupid farmer from Wisconsin."

Ben laughed at himself. "OK, I hear you. Tell me about your job."

"I'm just a stock boy at a Safeway here in Pacific Beach. It's only minimum wage, but it's full time. The manager who hired me actually said he was honored to help a disabled veteran. How about that?"

"Congratulations, Nacho. And I can tell you're staying sober. How's the noise in your head?"

"I'm learning to deal with the noise. Usually I can ignore it but sometimes somebody's thoughts are so strong they overwhelm me. It's like an obnoxious person is talking softly and then suddenly starts yelling."

"You'll handle it, Nacho. "Adapt and overcome." That's what we used to say in the Marines. Did you say that in the army?"

"Nah. We used to say "Kick ass and take names, and if something goes wrong, blame the Marines. Hehehehe."

Friday night Ben went into work early. He didn't want to be late for the first pre-shift briefing on his new graveyard shift squad. He was back to working Fri-Sat-Sun-Mon, 9:00 PM to 7:00 AM. He would be living on coffee for a while.

The good news was Alberto Salazar was the squad corporal. Ben liked and respected him. Their sergeant, Stanley Howard, had a reputation as a no-nonsense, fair supervisor. Lelani Kekela was the female officer assigned to the squad. Berto said she was a good cop, and that was good enough for Ben.

The bad news was Wayne Hopkins and his friend Scott McFadden were also on the squad. Both of them kept volunteering for the graveyard shift. Some guys liked it for the cops and robbers part of it. Others liked it because there were often long periods of inactivity. If you worked it out with a buddy you could park together in a hidey spot and sleep in shifts.

He was driving home from work on Saturday morning when his cell phone rang. It was Jackie. "Hey, Ben, I've got some good news. Want to meet for breakfast?"

He said, "Sure. But I won't last long after that. It's going to take me a few weeks to get accustomed to working these graveyard hours."

Over breakfast, she told Ben she had managed to change two of her classes at SDSU. As a result, she had no classes on Wednesdays and only an 8:00 AM class on Thursdays. That meant they could spend all day together on Wednesdays and all day on Thursdays once Jackie got out of class at 9:30 AM.

Ben was elated. "That's wonderful, Jackie! Thank you!"

"I did it for me as much as for you, Ben. I still have to work part time but my hours are pretty flexible."

They talked about her classes and his new squad. Jackie thought Hopkins would ease up on him since he would be on his squad and working with him for the next twelve months. Ben hoped that was true but somehow he doubted it.

Jackie was in such a cheerful mood he decided it was a good time to tell her about Nacho. He told her how they had met, how Nacho's family had been deported when he was a teenager, and his army service in Fallujah at the same time Ben was there. She was saddened to hear about his horrible brain injury. Ben made no mention of his strange mental abilities.

He went on to tell her about Nacho's alcoholism, how he had been sober for almost two weeks now, and had just started a full time job. She seemed genuinely happy he and Nacho had met and were becoming friends.

Ben was pleased she was taking this so well. "I had him over to my house on Christmas Eve. He spent the night on the couch and we spent Christmas together as well."

"He spent the night on your couch?"

"Actually he spent Christmas night there as well."

Red flags were going up for her. She started to say something, then changed her mind. "Oh well, I guess there was no harm, and it was Christmas, after all."

Ben sensed she was not going to like this, but he was in too deep to stop now. "He comes over a few times a week to shower. He keeps some clothes and other stuff at the house, too. I gave him a key."

The red flags became full-fledged alarm bells. "What!? You gave him a key to your house? Are you out of your mind, Ben?"

He tried to calm her down. "He's good guy, Jackie, and he deserves a break. He gave up a lot for our country and it's only right he get some kindness in return. I would think you'd be a little more compassionate towards him."

She was steaming. "Ben, let me make sure I understand this. You're letting a brain damaged, alcoholic homeless man you arrested a few weeks ago stay at your house, with his own key? And you want to know why I'm not okay with that?"

Now Ben was angry, raising his voice and talking rapidly. "He's not drinking anymore and he's going to AA regularly. He's got a full time job. And he's not really brain damaged. OK, scratch that, he is brain damaged but he's highly functional and nearly normal. And don't forget, he got the way he is because he volunteered to fight for America. He's a hero, Jackie. He's a good guy who's had some tough breaks and he needs some help. I want to help him."

Jackie had never seen him so worked up about something. "Ben, I've known you for six months now. You're a great guy and I really, really like you, but this is crazy. You want to help everybody, but you can't. You can't save the whole world, Ben, nobody can. Some people don't want to be saved, and some people are beyond saving. You just have to live your life and let them live theirs."

Taking a deep breath to calm himself down, he said, "Jackie, I know I can't save the whole world, but Nacho is special. It's like the story of the all the starfish dying on the beach at low tide. A man is tossing them back into the water one by one. Another guy comes up to him and says, 'Why bother? There are thousands of them on the beach dying and you can only save a few of them. You can't make any difference.'

"The first man picks up another starfish and says, 'It makes a difference to this one,' and he tosses it back in the water. Maybe Nacho is my starfish. He deserves a chance."

Jackie's heart melted. "Oh, Ben. You really are a boy scout. Rod says they call you that at work. Maybe that's why I'm falling in love with you."

He was caught flatfooted. "Wait a minute. Did you just say you're falling in love with me?"

She was a little embarrassed now at having revealed so much to Ben. "I was caught up in the heat of the moment. I thought I said *I think* I'm falling in love with you."

He was thrilled, and he couldn't help but tease her a little bit. "No, I'm pretty sure I heard you say you're falling in love with me."

She let out a big sigh, pretending to be exasperated. "OK Ben, we can talk about it another time. I know you need to get some sleep, but first let's figure out when I can meet your starfish."

Chapter Thirteen

On a Monday morning after his shift was over, Ben went up to the administrative offices on the third floor of the police department to sign some paperwork. In a hallway he had to flatten himself against the wall to let a big bellied man in shirt and tie get by. He knew the guy was a cop because he was wearing a gun in a shoulder holster and he had his badge clipped to his belt. As they passed, he could smell alcohol on the man's breath.

Monday night, "Friday" for Ben's squad, was very slow, with almost no calls for service. He and Berto met for coffee at a 7-11. After chit chatting about the usual stuff, Ben asked him, "What would happen to a cop who got caught drinking on duty?"

"Why, you thinking of knocking back a few beers after this coffee?"

Ben laughed. "Come on, Berto. I'm serious."

"Of course you're serious, Ben. You're the most serious guy I know. Obviously, none of your training officers gave you the 'lighten up' training session." Now Berto was laughing.

Ben just looked at him stone faced until Berto stopped laughing and sighed. "All right, Ben. Knowing you, this is not just a hypothetical question that popped into your head, is it?"

"Let's say it is, for now."

"In theory, the cop would be fired. Can't have some drunk driving around in a police car with a gun. Too much liability for the city. Zero tolerance."

"How about if it wasn't a street cop?"

Nodding his head in sudden understanding, Berto said, "Ah. You went topside this morning, didn't you? You met Boom."

"Boom?"

Berto said, "Let's keep this hypothetical. I'll tell you a fairy tale. Once upon a time back in the last century we had a really nasty robbery crew working San Diego and Chula Vista. Three guys with guns knocking over 7-11s, AM/PMs, and doughnut shops between 3:00 and 4:00 AM. They killed a guy in Chula Vista, shot a customer once in San Diego, and almost always pistol whipped the clerks. Then they decided to rob our AM/PM. One of our graveyard sergeants rolled right up on it as it was going down. Some say it was pure luck, others credit good police instinct. He parked his patrol car right in front of the doors before he saw what was happening. He radioed it in, grabbed the 12 gauge shotgun and jumped out behind the trunk of the car.

"The first two crooks came out the doors with guns in hand and the sergeant blew them away. The store surveillance tape showed both guys drawing down on the sarge. The third guy came out the doors and the sarge blew him away, too. The clerk said the third guy was walking out with his hands up. The first two buckshot rounds not only nailed the robbers, they blew out all the glass windows and doors, and a pellet caught the surveillance camera, too. So, the sarge's last shot wasn't on tape. The clerk had been pistol whipped and had blood in his eyes, so internal affairs called it a good shoot.

"The sarge was a big time hero, but things went downhill from there. He started getting citizen complaints about rudeness and he crunched up his patrol car right in the PD parking lot. There were rumors of him drinking on duty, but nobody really wanted to prove it. He wasn't retirement age yet but they had to do something, so they promoted him to Lieutenant so he could ride a desk until retirement. Word is he carries an empty gun now.

"Right after the shooting the guys started calling him Doctor Doom. That later morphed into Boom Doom, and now everyone just calls him Boom."

Ben asked, "When is he eligible for retirement?"

Berto chuckled. "That's the thing. He was eligible about five years ago but he's one of those guys who just won't give up his badge and gun. He'll probably still be here when you retire, Ben."

"But this is all just a story, right?" Ben asked.

"Yup. A fairy tale. You never heard it from me. You could probably find something about it on a Google search, but you know lots of stuff on the internet is just urban legend."

Wednesday was a big day for Ben. He had been looking forward to it and dreading it at the same time. It was the day Jackie would meet Nacho. In anticipation of the big moment, Nacho had spent the night on Ben's couch. On Wednesday morning he showered and changed into his best, freshly laundered clothes. And just for Jackie, he bought a new hat. He had a shapeless, battered floppy hat he wore every day, and it hid his deformed head. For Jackie, he bought a "new" snap brim fedora at the Goodwill store. The hat, $80 when sold new, was $12 at the Goodwill. He bought it on a 50% off Tuesday special and got an additional 25% disabled veteran's discount, so the hat set him back four and a half bucks. Ben thought it made him look like Michael Jackson, but Nacho thought it was just plain cool.

"Come on, tell me what you really think," Nacho asked.

"You be stylin', homie," Ben replied, but he spoiled it by cracking up laughing.

Nacho was laughing, too. "Man, I told you about trying to talk ghetto slang. It just ain't you. You know the old saying, 'You can take the boy out of the farm, but you can't take the farm out of the boy.'"

"All right, Nacho. You look good. Seriously. In a Tom Landry sort of way," and he cracked up again.

Jackie arrived a few minutes early, as she usually did. She too had taken the time to dress unusually well. She also had her hair done and a manicure before coming over. She knew Nacho was important to Ben, and she wanted to make a good impression. Nacho knew Ben was deeply in love with Jackie, even if he had not yet admitted it to himself. For that reason it was important to him Jackie accept him, if not actually like him.

As it turned out, they both had been fretting over nothing. They hit it off immediately. Ben was the happiest of them all.

Later that night, Jackie and Ben had dinner together at an upscale restaurant in San Diego's gas lamp district. It was pricey, but Ben had a few extra bucks from some overtime he had worked. During dinner, Jackie spoke effusively about Nacho. He had clearly charmed her.

"Ben, I have to say I was wrong about Nacho. He's a very nice person. I'm kind of ashamed now that I thought badly of him before I even met him. Isn't that the very definition of prejudice? And me a black woman. I should know better."

Ben said, "He really is an unusual man. His personal story is so compelling. Most people never would have survived his wounds, let alone tried to live a regular life afterwards. He says God saved him for a reason."

"Is he a very religious person?" she asked.

"Not as far as I know," said Ben. "He's a lot like me in that regard. I believe in God but I don't go to church. I don't know how a person could experience the things I have and not believe in God. Too many things have happened to me to think otherwise, but I never thought there was anything special about church. Look at what religion has done to these radical Islamists. They have perverted their faith to the point where they feel justified in killing innocent people. I live my life doing what I believe is right, or just, or fair - pick your own word to describe it. I don't follow the teachings of any particular church, I follow my heart."

She smiled and said, "Sometimes you sound an awful lot like my mother, Ben."

He waited for her to elaborate but she did not. He felt the time was right to tell her about Nacho's unusual mental abilities. As he tried to think of a way to ease into it she said, "What did you think of Nacho's new hat, Ben? I love the fact he bought it just for me."

Ben laughed. "I guess it's okay. I'm not much on telling stylish from foolish. Give me a pair of blue jeans and a work shirt and I'm good to go. I told him it made him look like Michael Jackson or Tom Landry."

Jackie smiled. "I think it was adorable. And wearing it he reminded me of the character named Powder in that old science fiction movie. You know, the one where Powder was struck by lightning and develops strange mental powers."

Ben had a mouthful of food and nearly choked. When he finally finished coughing he had tears in his eyes. "Powder. Yeah, I remember the movie. Pretty cool."

Jackie said, "It's good for the soul to watch a fantasy or sci-fi movie once in a while. It lets you escape from your everyday reality. Not that I believe in any of that stuff. I gave it up along with Santa Claus and the Easter bunny."

"You never know, Jackie. Some things in this world just can't be explained."

"Oh, Ben. You are the most down to earth person I know. It's one of the things I like most about you. You're not going to go all Zen on me, are you?"

He decided he would tell her about Nacho another time.

Chapter Fourteen

Ben was dispatched to a theft call at a cell phone store. Tara Morris, a weekend swing shift officer, was assigned as his cover unit. The store stayed open late on Saturday nights and the theft had occurred just before the 10 PM closing time. He radioed to Tara he would contact the store owner and she should patrol the area around the store looking for the suspect.

The store owner told him a black male teenager had asked to see a $200 cell phone. When the owner handed him the phone he turned and ran out of the store with it. In answer to Ben's questions, the owner said the thief pushed open the front door with his shoulder coming and going, and he did not touch the glass display case or anything else in the store. Ben explained since the phone was valued at less than $400 and no force was used, the crime was a simple misdemeanor theft. Based upon the owner's statement, there was no point in trying to get fingerprints since the suspect didn't touch anything except the phone. He offered to take a crime report but explained the detective division only investigated felonies, so there would be no follow up investigation of this crime.

Realizing having the police take a crime report would be a waste of time, the owner told Ben to forget about it. It wasn't the first time it had happened to him and it probably wouldn't be the last. He chalked it up to the cost of doing business in the city.

Ben informed dispatch the victim did not desire a crime report. Tara radioed there was no sign of the suspect in the area, and both units went back in service.

The next afternoon a police officer entered the phone store and spoke with the owner. The cop explained unless the phone thief was caught he or his buddies would return again and again to steal phones.

"I know. That wasn't the first time. What can I do about it?" he asked. "The other cop said the detectives would not investigate."

"That's true, unless you were robbed. Then it's a felony and they have to take the case."

The owner said, "But the other cop explained that. It wasn't a robbery, just a shoplift."

The cop gave him a knowing look. "I'm trying to help you out, here. Maybe the suspect shoved you when he turned to run. Isn't that what happened? That makes it a robbery. Are you sure he didn't touch the display case or the door? There'd be fingerprints. Weren't you afraid he would hurt you? That supports a robbery charge. You need to get the detectives involved here. The word will get around the street and the thieves will go somewhere else where there's less heat."

Dejectedly, the shop owner said, "That sounds good, and I want these guys to leave me alone, but it's too late now. I already said what happened. I can't just change my story."

The officer was insistent. "Look, the cop who responded last night is a rookie fuck up. Call the station tomorrow and demand to know why no report was taken. Tell them it was a robbery. Say you told the cop but he didn't believe you. They'll send another patrolman out to take a report and then the detectives will get on it. Just leave me out of it."

Monday night after the pre-shift briefing Sergeant Howard asked Ben to meet him at his office.

"Ben, you responded to a theft call at a phone store Saturday night, right?"

"Yes, sir."

"What was your disposition of the call?"

"It was a simple theft with no evidence, Sarge. I offered to take a crime report but the owner said no after I told him the detectives wouldn't look at a misdemeanor case. Did he call to complain about that?"

"Yes, he did, Ben. Cisneros from the day shift went out there and took a report. The owner told him the suspect shoved him before he ran away, and he pushed the door open with his hand. Cisneros listed it as a robbery and found a bunch of prints on the door."

Ben couldn't believe it. "Sarge, the guy completely changed his story from what he told me. I specifically asked him if any force had been used or if the suspect touched anything. He said no. You know there's going to be tons of prints on the door. Every customer who goes in or out probably pushes it open with their hand."

"The prints are not a big deal, Ben. The owner told Cisneros you blew him off when he said he was shoved. Per policy you should have taken a report."

Ben was angry. "This is ridiculous. I'll go back out there and speak to the owner and straighten this out."

"His store is closed now, Ben. And I'm ordering you not to speak to the owner. The day shift sergeant spoke with him and he's convinced the guy is telling the truth. I'm giving you a written reprimand for failure to follow procedure. You should have taken a report and dusted for fingerprints."

He was nearly speechless. "This isn't right, Sarge."

"Ben, you need to get your act together. This isn't the first time someone complained about you. I took the complaint from the prisoner who said you stole his money, remember? And there was the time you didn't impound the marijuana. You're a probationary employee. You aren't going to get another chance."

Ben saw Jackie several times on his days off, and they spent some time with Nacho as well. Nacho was doing fine at his job and staying clean. Ben told them about the phone store theft that somehow changed into a robbery. He was convinced Hopkins or one of his buddies had it in for him and was trying to get him fired. Jackie disagreed, saying Hopkins had left him alone since the new year.

Nacho said, "Maybe he's just keeping a low profile and decided to work behind the scenes."

"That's precisely what I was thinking," said Ben. Did Nacho read his mind? It was kind of eerie being around him sometimes.

Jackie said, "This is a lot different than some rookie hazing prank. They could have fired you for this."

"Bingo. Hopkins told me I'd never make it off probation. Maybe he's just trying to tip the odds in his favor. The guy hates me. He's everything I will never be as a police officer. And I still think he and McFadden are doing something more on shift than just taking turns sleeping. Those guys have worked graveyard shift together for four years now. They've got something going on."

Jackie left to go to her part time job, and Nacho had to get ready to go to work, too. Before he left, he said, "Hey Ben, you ever see anyone get fragged over in Iraq?"

"You mean a Marine intentionally blowing up one of his own officers?"

"Yup. That's exactly what I mean. Guys in my unit said it happens."

Ben said, "Nope. Never saw it. Never heard of it happening, either. I think it's a myth. Why?"

"For something you never saw and never heard about you sure do think about it a lot."

Ben said grimly, "Yeah, Nacho, I guess I do."

Goddamnit! All he got was a written reprimand? Why won't they fire this asshole? How does he keep hanging on to his job? No matter what I do he somehow skates out of it. Is Selby protecting him for Jackie's sake? It's the only possible explanation. I can't hurt Selby, he's too senior and too sharp, but

Olsen is still on probation. I can hurt him. Oh yeah, I can hurt him real bad.

Chapter Fifteen

Ben settled into a routine at work and there were no more unusual incidents. Hopkins and McFadden ignored him, but that was better than them actively hassling him.

In April, Nacho told him he had saved enough money and felt secure enough in his job that he was going to start looking for his own apartment. He had been sober for over 100 days and was still attending AA meetings.

"That's a big step, Nacho. You know you're welcome to stay here. I can bring in another bed if you're tired of the couch."

"No, you've been great, Ben. I owe you a lot, but it's time for me to get my own place. It's not like we'll never see each other. We're still best friends, right?"

Ben said, "Well, yeah, but I'll deny it if one of my old Marine buddies stops by. Hah!"

They talked about the best neighborhoods for him to find an apartment. Then he asked how Jackie was doing. "She's amazing, Nacho. She's on track to graduate in June. She's already filling out job applications for elementary school teaching positions. And I'll be getting off probation in June also. Assuming she doesn't hate me by then I'm going to ask her to marry me. That's for your ears only, of course."

Nacho was beaming. "That's wonderful, Ben. She's a great person. She doesn't glow as much as you do, but she's way better than most."

Ben said, "You're still seeing that in people? And still hearing thoughts, too?"

"The auras are clearer now than ever. And the thoughts are louder and clearer, too. I used to drink to make them go away. It never made them disappear, but it sure dulled the noise. Now that I'm completely sober I feel like a near sighted person who put on glasses for the first time. Let me tell you what happened to me at work."

He went on, "Sometimes I'd see a customer with a dark gray aura around them. As I concentrated on them I got the feeling they were going to shoplift something, so I kept an eye on them. Sure enough, they'd sneak some toothpaste or food under their jacket and walk out of the store. I know stealing is wrong, but these folks looked desperate and it wasn't like they were robbing the cashier or taking hundreds of dollars' worth of stuff, so I didn't tell anyone. I've been pretty desperate a time or two myself. A couple of times when I saw someone really starting to load up on stuff I went over to them and told them to put it all back or I'd call the security guys, and they did.

"So, one day this guy comes in the store. He's got this jet black aura around him. Just looking at him made me feel dirty and queasy. Of course, to everyone else he's just another shopper. I thought at first he was going to rob the store, but as I concentrated on him I knew that wasn't it. He wasn't going to do anything in the store, he was just shopping. But his head was filled with horrible images of children. It sickened me. He was some kind of child molester, Ben. And he was terrified of the police. That came through loud and clear, too. This guy was so evil I couldn't just let him walk out of the store. I went to one of our security guys and made up a story about the guy shoplifting. Two security guys approached him and identified themselves. The guy freaked out, punched one in the face and tried to run away. They tackled him and got him into handcuffs. They were puzzled when he didn't have any merchandise hidden on him, but they called the cops to charge the guy with assault and battery. The cops came and, as they always do, they ran a warrant check on him. He had a felony arrest warrant for child rape in Louisiana! That's why he tried to run."

On his next days off, Ben and Jackie were deciding where to spend the day. "How about we go fishing today instead of to the beach?" Ben asked. "Didn't you tell me you used to fish as a little girl?"

Jackie replied, "I did. My uncle Eddie took me out a couple of times to some lake. We spent a few hours in a boat and caught a bunch of fish. It was a lot of fun. But I was looking forward to just lying on the beach reading, Ben."

He smiled. "Perfect! We'll go carp fishing to Santee lakes. It's beautiful out there. Carp fishing isn't like regular fishing. There's no boat, first of all. I'll set up everything and do all the work while you lay there on a blanket and read a book, just like at the beach. The only time your reading will be interrupted is when we catch a fish."

She wrinkled up her face in disgust. "Carp? Are you serious? Uncle Eddie called them trash fish. If we caught one he always killed it and threw it away. He said they're not good to eat."

"A lot of fishermen feel that way, but I think they're wrong. Carp fishing is a national sport in England and hugely popular throughout Europe. I spent a lot of time carp fishing back in Barron. I have all the specialized gear, and these fish are so big we'll need it. And we're not going to eat them, just have the fun of catching them and then release them to grow even bigger. You'll see, it'll be fun."

Jackie was not enthused. "I don't know, Ben. I don't want to get all fishy smelling and waste a good beach day."

"How about this? We'll go carp fishing and all you have to do is fight the fish. I'll be the only one to get my hands dirty. And to seal the deal, if you don't catch the biggest fish of your life I'll take you to dinner at the restaurant of your choice tonight."

She laughed. "All right, sucker! You've got a deal. I caught a five pound bass with my uncle one time, and I've got a picture somewhere to prove it."

Ben chuckled. "No problem. I believe you. I'll pack the car and we'll head out. How about throwing some sandwiches and drinks in a cooler?"

At Santee lakes, they set up on the shore and settled in. Jackie could not believe the size of the fishing rods Ben had. They were twelve feet long and rested atop something Ben called a "rod pod," which had bite alarms built into it. Once the baits were cast out the rods went into the pod and then there was nothing to do until a bite alarm sounded.

It was a beautiful sunny day and Jackie had been engrossed in her book for hours. The alarms remained quiet and there was no sign of fish anywhere. In fact, there were no other fishermen, and she decided they were wasting their time. She was looking forward to a gourmet dinner at the Marine Room, an expensive restaurant in La Jolla. That would teach him!

Ben was disappointed in the fishing, but he could tell Jackie was enjoying the day anyway. It was an idyllic setting. He decided it was the perfect time to tell her about Nacho's paranormal abilities.

"Jackie, could you put down your book for a minute? There's something important I want to talk to you about."

They were lying next to each other on the blanket. *Yes! This is it!* she thought. *Ben is going to ask me to marry him!* She put down her book and tried to keep her voice normal. "OK, Ben. Go ahead."

He said, "Well, I've been trying to talk to you about this for some time now, but it never seemed like the right time."

Her head was spinning. *Yes! Yes! Say it!*

"Jackie, I..." BEEEEPP! BEEEEEEEEEPPP! BEEEEEEEEEEEEEEEEEEEEP!

"It's the bite alarm!" yelled Ben, jumping to his feet.

"What?" Jackie was flustered. The bite alarm was screaming so loud she couldn't think.

"The bite alarm! Grab the rod, Jackie! It's a fish!"

She got up, still trying to recover her senses. She pulled the rod out of the pod and engaged the reel, which had been freewheeling, with the line disappearing rapidly into the lake. The moment she engaged the reel the line grew taut and the big fishing rod doubled over in a huge arc. "Oh my God," she groaned.

The line continued to peel off the reel despite the pressure of the rod. This was a big, strong fish. "Ben, help me! I can't stop this thing."

Ben was beaming, and he was thrilled for her. "Just keep holding on. The fish will get tired and stop. When it does, start to reel it in. When he pulls, you hold. When he stops, you reel."

Ten minutes later, she was sweating and the fish was nowhere near the shore. In fact, they still hadn't seen it. "Ben, this started out as fun but now it's just plain work. Why don't you take the rod? I'm exhausted."

He said, "Hang in there, Jackie. He's tired now, more than you are. Each run gets shorter and shorter. One or two more runs and we'll have him in the net."

She was gaining back a lot of line when the big fish rolled on the surface of the lake. "Oh my God, Ben! What was that?"

He laughed. "That's your fish, Jackie."

She couldn't believe it. "It's longer than my leg!"

A few minutes later the fish lay quietly in the net. Ben removed it from the net and unhooked it. Then he weighed the fish on a digital scale. "22 pounds 4 ounces, sweetheart. I think that tops your five pound bass."

She was ecstatic. "That's bigger than the saltwater fish we see down at the docks! From this tiny lake. Nobody will ever believe me."

"Don't worry, we'll take plenty of pictures. Do you want to hold the fish?"

"No, but I'll squat down by it for the photos. I don't want to get my hands dirty."

But as she posed near the fish she couldn't help but stroke the beautiful golden hued creature's smooth side. After taking the photos Ben gently put the fish back in the water. Holding it by the tail, he massaged it with his other hand. The fish made no attempt to swim away. After more than a minute it suddenly flexed its massive tail and shot away into the deep water. Despite his dirty clothes and fishy smell, Jackie gave him a big hug. The bait had hooked the fish, and the fish had hooked Jackie. He knew they would go carp fishing again.

Chapter Sixteen

At 10:00 AM on a Tuesday morning the phone rang, waking him from a solid sleep. "Ben, it's Tom."

He had been asleep for less than two hours, exhausted from his last graveyard shift. "Tom?"

"Your brother Tom, Ben. Wake up. Something's happened."

He sat up in bed quickly. Tom knew the hours he worked. He would never have called at this time unless it was serious. "What is it, Tom?"

"I'll just tell you straight out. It's Dad, Ben. He's been diagnosed with cancer. He's going to have surgery in two days. Can you come home?"

He was dumbfounded. His Dad has cancer? He never got sick. He was a farmer. How does a farmer get cancer?

"Ben! Are you there?" Tom shouted into the phone.

"Yes. Yes! I'm awake now. I'll talk to my sergeant about emergency leave right away. They might want some documentation. I'll have to let you know. Tell me about Dad."

Tom said, "He has colon cancer. It's very serious, Ben. Stage 3. They say he has a fifty/fifty chance of five year survival after the surgery, if the surgery is successful. Then he has to have chemotherapy. Mom is a wreck. You need to come home."

"Okay, Tom. I'll make the arrangements and call you back."

He got out of bed and started the coffeemaker. He was going to need it. He knew Jackie was in class, so he called her cell phone and left a voice mail message to call him on his cell immediately. She would know something was wrong just from that, but he could never leave news like this on voice mail.

He thought to call Sergeant Howard, but he realized he would be sound asleep. Instead he called the dayshift sergeant, told him about his father, and asked him how to proceed. The sergeant told him no documentation would be needed. If the department couldn't trust their officers to be truthful about something like this then they wouldn't be employed very long. He told Ben he would inform Sergeant Howard later in the afternoon. He needed to come into the PD and fill out a vacation request, which would be immediately approved by the dayshift lieutenant. He could make airline reservations now and arrange to fly home as soon as possible.

Jackie was shocked to hear the news, of course, and she offered to go with him to Barron. He appreciated the offer but it would hurt her to miss classes, and they both agreed it would be an awkward time for his family to meet her.

Nacho did not own a cell phone. He was still sleeping on Ben's couch most nights, not yet having found a place of his own. He left a detailed note for him on the kitchen table.

Ben had gone home to visit his family periodically while he was attending San Diego State, and also on the rare occasions he was granted leave from his Marine Corps unit. It had been about a year since he last visited. He had been given one week's vacation from the police department. With his regular three days off on each end of his four day work week that gave him ten days off.

He got on an airplane and was back at his family's farm near midnight. He slept for nearly twelve hours. His whole family was waiting for him at the kitchen table. Like most farm households, the kitchen table was the family gathering place.

After the discussion of his 60 year old father's cancer diagnosis had finally petered out, Ben got caught up on everything that had happened since he had last been home.

For a small farm family in a tiny town, there were a seemingly endless number of things to talk about. He had nearly forgotten how fast news travels in Barron. Secrets didn't stay secret for very long. When it was his turn, he brought his family up to date on his life in San Diego County, and his work as a police officer. For his mother's sake, he left out any mention of danger or his problems at work. He talked at length of his relationship with Jackie and hinted strongly she would soon be a member of the family. His mother was ecstatic about the prospect of grandchildren, and she took the opportunity to again scold her two older children for failing so far to get married and give her some grandchildren. Ben's brothers took it in stride. They had been hearing it for years now.

Mindful that gossip in Barron traveled faster than the speed of light, he chose not to tell his family of Jackie's race. He rationalized his decision by convincing himself he was protecting his family from the vicious gossipers, but the reality was he didn't know how his family would take the news. He didn't want to possibly stir up a nasty argument on the eve of his father's hospitalization.

The surgery went well and there were no complications. After a few days in the hospital his father was sent home to recuperate, then he would start a chemotherapy regimen. After that, it was just a matter of closely monitoring the area for any return of the cancer. Considering the circumstances, Ben had a good visit with his family. He returned to San Diego on a Thursday afternoon, to start his work week the next night.

He called Jackie when he got in. She was at work. He had called her daily from Wisconsin, so she was up to speed on everything. They agreed to get together on Wednesday, as usual. He saw his kitchen table note to Nacho was gone, but there was nothing from him in return, and he had not contacted Ben by phone when he was in Wisconsin.

Chapter Seventeen

Just before six in the morning on Saturday Ben arrested a man for domestic violence. He was not fond of any criminals, but he had a particular dislike for men who physically abused women or children. It took all of his self-restraint to not use a little extra force in making domestic violence arrests. He had to admit to himself he actually hoped the suspects would resist arrest so he would be justified in thumping them.

The man sitting across the table was especially nettling to Ben. He had come home drunk at 5:30 AM, to find his wife ironing his work shirt. He was supposed to start his shift at 6:00 AM. Upon walking through the door he had demanded sex and breakfast. When his wife refused they argued, then he split her forehead open with the hot clothes iron. Ben had found him hiding behind a dumpster in the alley near the house. Much to his disappointment, the rather small Hispanic man was intimidated by his large size and had surrendered without a struggle.

During the arrest processing, he let the suspect know exactly what he thought of him. He told him real men did not beat women, and only a very weak, insecure man would use a weapon on his wife as he had done. Ben knew a lot more about the Hispanic culture than he did when he first started out, but he either forgot or did not care there is no greater insult than to question an Hispanic male's manhood.

He finished the processing and paged his sergeant over the station telephone. Sergeants had to review and sign all arrest paperwork before the prisoner could be taken to the county jail. The supervisor said he was on his way down to the prisoner processing area for an end of shift inspection, so he would sign the arrest paperwork there.

When the sergeant arrived the prisoner became animated. Like many people who have been arrested several times, he recognized the sergeant as a supervisor, and he knew how to game the system. "Hey, boss. I want to make a complaint against this officer. He's racially prejudiced."

Ben was immediately worried. He had not had any performance related problems or complaints since he was reprimanded for not taking the phone store report. His sergeant had warned him then he probably wouldn't get another chance if something else came up while he was still on probation. Even an unfounded complaint like this one might be enough to get him fired. And he had been needling the guy pretty hard.

"What's your complaint, pal?" the sergeant growled out.

"This cop is racist. He called me a wetback and a motherfucking beaner."

Ben started to protest but the old cop raised his hand to quiet him. "Tell me again exactly what he said to you."

"He called me a wetback. And a beaner. He said, "I'm tired of you motherfucking beaners beating your wives." That's exactly what he said to me."

Sergeant Howard laughed loudly. "Yeah, right. You picked the wrong cop to lay that one on, pal. Officer Olsen is the only officer on the force who never swears, ever. Maybe the only one in the whole state of California. Take him to jail, Ben."

Normally, so close to the end of the graveyard shift the suspect would have been left in a holding cell at the police station until the dayshift went in service, and then a dayshift officer would take him to jail. That way the city would not have to pay the graveyard officer overtime. This morning, though, Ben had already been told he would have to work until noon due to one of the dayshift officers calling in sick.

He drove his prisoner to the county jail in downtown San Diego. They had not spoken a word to each other the entire trip. Ben was still fuming about the guy's attempt to get him in trouble by fabricating a story for the sergeant.

As the jail deputies were finishing their processing the prisoner asked him, "You really never swear? Never?"

Ben was disgusted with the guy and turned and walked away.

The guy shook his head in disbelief. "Shit. Anybody who never swears must be a fucking pussy. I should have kicked your ass in that alley."

Back in the city he found a hidey spot and tried to catch up on his paperwork. Dispatch would follow the unwritten rule of not sending an officer on involuntary overtime to a call unless it was absolutely necessary. A few minutes later a patrol car parked alongside his, facing the opposite way so the two drivers could talk face to face without getting out of their cars. It was Eddie Keaton.

"Hey Ben, sorry you had to hold over past your shift. Cisneros is out sick."

He smiled. Eddie was a good cop and Ben liked him. "Nothing serious, I hope."

Eddie said, "He's got an infection in his left arm. Scraped his elbow fighting some Chud and two days later it blew up like an overstuffed sausage and turned a weird color."

Ben recalled Chud was a slang name some cops gave to people who were always getting arrested. "Geez, he got all that from a scraped elbow?"

"Yeah, it's filthy around here. And it's just the natural law."

Ben was puzzled. "Natural law? I don't get it."

Eddie chuckled. "We call it the natural law of the ghetto. A Chud gets shot six times in the chest and lives to brag about it to his homies. A cop gets shot in the toe, it ricochets up his leg, pops his femoral artery and he bleeds to death. Natural law."

Ben thought back to the gangster shot through the eye who fought with him. "You might have something there, Eddie."

Chapter Eighteen

On Wednesday morning Jackie went over to Ben's house for breakfast. After a brief hug and kiss she asked, "Is Nacho here?"

"No, he's not. In fact..." Ben was unable to finish because Jackie was kissing him deeply.

When she was finally finished he smiled and said, "Wow! Maybe I should go away and come back more often."

"Don't you dare! I missed you terribly, Ben. How is your Dad doing?"

"He's OK. The surgery seems to have been successful. The chemo is going to be pretty rough on him, they say. He's a tough old guy, he'll handle it and be back to running the farm in no time."

With a mischievous smile she asked, "What would you like to do today? How about we just stay here and get seriously reacquainted? Is Nacho working all day?"

He frowned. "I wanted to ask you about him. I was starting to when you, uh, distracted me. I haven't heard from him since I left for Barron, and there's no sign he's been here in quite some time. Have you talked with him lately?"

Jackie said, "Nope. Didn't you tell me he was looking for a place of his own before you left? Maybe he found one."

"I don't think so. His bathroom stuff and all of his clothes are still here. I'm worried, Jackie. I'm going over to Safeway to see if he's at work."

"I'll go with you, Ben. Now you've got me worried."

The phone rang as they were going out the door. Ben grabbed it. "Hello?... Yes, it is... No, he's not here... Who's calling?... I'm his roommate. We were just going over there to see if he was at work... What? What?... All right, I understand. Yes, I'll tell him when I see him. Thank you. Good bye."

He put the phone down and looked at Jackie. She could tell by his face something was very wrong. "What is it, Ben?"

"That was the manager at Safeway. Nacho hasn't been to work in over a week. He just didn't show up one day. The manager was calling to say his last paycheck is available to be picked up. He's been fired."

Ben did the easiest thing first. He called dispatch, gave them Nacho's full name and date of birth, and had them run a query. He was not in jail and had not been arrested since Ben arrested him the previous year. Then they called every hospital in San Diego County. He was not at any of them. Finally, Ben called the county morgue. Nacho's name was not listed. They had two John Does, but based upon the physical descriptions neither one could have been him.

Jackie knew how much Nacho meant to Ben. She could see the worry and sadness in his face. "Ben, it may not be what you think. He has a traumatic brain injury. Maybe he's had some type of medical setback and it caused him to forget his…" Her voice trailed off when she realized what a horrible thing she was saying. "What I meant was maybe he…"

He interrupted her. "Jackie, I know what you're trying to do, and I appreciate it. But we have to face the obvious - he must have fallen off the wagon. He's probably passed out in a cardboard box somewhere."

They spent the rest of the day at Ben's house, consoling each other and hoping the phone would ring or Nacho would walk through the door. In an effort to cheer him up and distract him, Jackie asked Ben for every detail of his visit home.

He filled her in on all the latest news in the lives of his brothers and parents, then went on to tell her of his carp fishing exploits at the Yellow River. After he told her some juicy bits of small town gossip he finally ran out of things to say.

She said, "Well, while the story of Jurgen and Betty Clausen's spat down at Fliegel's Tire Store was fascinating, I was really hoping you'd tell me what your family thought when you told them about me."

He smiled. "They probably think you're Saint Jacqueline. I told them about all the things we do together, the places we go, the fun we have. My brothers think I'm the luckiest guy in the world, maybe because I told them I was. I told my mom we were getting pretty serious. She's pushing hard for grandchildren. My father can't believe I found an old fashioned girl so far from Barron. They're all looking forward to meeting you."

She frowned. "Ben, please don't play dumb with me. What did they say when you told them I was black?"

He hunched his shoulders, crossed and uncrossed his legs, and looked everywhere except at her. "Uh, Jackie, well…"

"You didn't tell them did you? How could you not tell them?

"Jackie, please don't misunderstand. My parents and brothers are good people. They're not prejudiced at all. I know they'll love you. It's just that Barron is a small town in northern Wisconsin. I think there's only one black family in the whole town, and maybe two other black men. They don't socialize with anyone, they're farmers and they stay to themselves, just like most farmers. I just…" He shook his head.

She was angry now. "The blacks don't socialize with anyone. They stay to themselves. I get it. Everybody there is fine with black people, as long as they keep to themselves, but an interracial couple is a whole 'nother story, isn't it? And Lord knows you wouldn't want to feed the gossip mongers down at the Rexall's Drugstore. I'm very, very disappointed in you, Ben."

He looked like a whipped puppy. "I'm sorry, Jackie. Everything you said is true."

"I'm going home now, Ben. I need some time to think. Please don't call me unless you have news of Nacho."

Chapter Nineteen

He spent his next two days off looking for his friend. He searched all the homeless hangouts in Pacific Beach, then he searched National City. There was no sign of him. On Friday he went into work early and wrote a bulletin for all officers to be on the lookout for him. The bulletin would be read at pre-shift briefings for all the shifts. Officers commonly wrote bulletins when they were searching for people or vehicles. In the space on the bulletin form that said "probable cause for arrest" Ben wrote, "No PC to arrest. Do not detain. If sighted call Officer Ben Olsen 24 hours a day at 619-204-4321."

Saturday morning he was unloading his patrol car at the end of his shift. Dayshift had finished briefing and been in service about half an hour when his cell phone rang. "Hey Olsen, you're looking for a Hispanic male adult 5'7" 130 pounds, with half his head missing?"

Ben did not recognize the voice, but he felt his heart speed up. "Yes! Yes I am."

"Oh. Sorry. I saw a 6'1" 200 pound black guy with half his head missing. Couldn't have been your man. Plus, he was dead from a shotgun blast. Then there was a 5'2" white guy with half an ear over by the National City Market. Oh yeah, and last year I saw a fat woman with three tits at the carnival freak show. HaHaHaHaHa!

Ben snapped his phone shut as the laughter continued. It immediately rang again. "You won't be laughing when I pound you into the ground," he spat out angrily.

"Ben, it's Eddie Keaton. You OK?"

He blew out a big breath. "Yeah, Eddie. Sorry about that. I thought you were somebody else."

"I saw your guy yesterday behind Smitty's Liquor. He was passed out with a couple of other homeless."

He felt a rush of excitement followed immediately by a feeling of dread. "Are you sure he was just passed out, Eddie?"

There was irritation in Eddie's voice. "Ben. Gimme a break, would you? I've been doing this a whole lot longer than you have. I nudged all of them to be sure they were alive. I always do."

"I'm sorry, Eddie. Nacho is a friend of mine. He straightened himself out and just recently fell off the wagon. I'm off duty and I'll be heading over that way in five minutes. Thank you very much."

"Don't bother, Ben. I'm calling from there. They're all gone."

Over the next few weeks he continued to look for Nacho without success. He regularly violated procedure by leaving his beat to search other parts of the city. Fortunately he had never been caught out of position for a radio call. He even tried mentally calling out to Nacho for hours each day, repeating his name over and over in his head like a mantra. He felt kind of foolish doing it, but he was desperate. Finally, he resigned himself to the fact he was gone. He hoped he had gone back to Texas but in his bleaker moments he feared his friend was dead.

Jackie had gotten over her anger at Ben and they were back in their routine of spending Wednesdays and Thursdays together. It was early June. She was into finals week at San Diego State and eagerly looking forward to graduation. He was only a few weeks away from his one year anniversary of hiring, when he would officially be off probation and no longer a rookie. It should have been the happiest of times for them, but the loss of Nacho had left a void in their lives.

Ben was watching the traffic light at the intersection of E.4th Street and Highland Avenue. It was 1:30 AM. The city had been quiet all shift and he was caught up on his paperwork. Since the bars had just closed he was hoping to find a drunk driver. A Honda Civic approached the intersection northbound on Highland Avenue and blew right through the red light at 30 MPH. He hit his police lights and siren and the driver pulled over into the car wash parking lot at 2nd and Highland.

He reported he was on a traffic stop and Lelani Kekela radioed she was enroute to cover him. He contacted the driver and two things became immediately clear to him: the driver was not drunk, and he didn't speak a word of English. Ben's Spanish was getting a lot better but he wasn't yet able to get by on his own. He asked dispatch for a Spanish translator. Berto replied he was enroute and Lelani cancelled her cover.

Ben managed to tell the driver a Spanish speaking officer was on the way. As they waited for Berto he noticed the driver was getting nervous. When Berto arrived Ben immediately told him the driver was hinky and to be careful. Salazar had the driver get out of the car and frisked him, then he explained why Ben had stopped him. After a minute of conversation, Berto told Ben the driver was nervous because he did not have a driver's license, and both cops relaxed.

Per state law the car would be impounded and the driver issued a citation. Berto explained this to the driver, who became nervous again. Salazar tried to reassure him he could claim the car from the tow yard as long as a licensed driver was with him. After a lengthy exchange in Spanish, the corporal said to Ben, "He just told me his two cousins are in the trunk. He smuggled them across the border, and he's afraid they might die in there while the car is at the tow yard."

Ben opened the trunk, revealing two young Mexican men. They stepped out and meekly followed Berto's instructions. Mexican citizens who are not criminals are terrified of the police. Salazar had the two stowaways and the driver sit on the curb. Ben notified dispatch and asked them to call the border patrol, then he went back to completing the driver's ticket. Dispatch informed them the border patrol would not be available for several hours. Per policy, they ran a warrant check on the two illegal immigrants. When they came back clean Berto told them they were free to go. With the confusion obvious on their faces, and not believing their good luck, the two hurried away into the night.

 Ben had thoroughly searched the car and found nothing. He was closing the trunk when a small crack in the bottom rear of it caught his attention. He widened the crack a bit with his knife and shined his flashlight into it. The light was reflecting off something shiny. He enlarged the hole further and realized he was looking at a package wrapped in heavy cellophane. He got Berto's attention and hand signaled for him to handcuff the driver. When that was done he showed him what he had found. Berto jabbed at the rear wall of the trunk with his police baton and it cracked along its base. A few more whacks and he was able to pry the false rear wall completely free. Inside were dozens of tightly stacked packages wrapped in cellophane. He made a small cut in one with his knife and white powder fell out. "Jackpot! You hit the mother lode, Ben. There's gotta be fifty pounds of cocaine here. Each of those packages is probably a kilo. Nice job."

 They photographed the drugs in place before removing them. Berto had underestimated the amount by half. Ben removed fifty separate one kilo packages and transferred them to his patrol car. He informed dispatch of what they had found and asked for another officer to stand by the car until the tow truck arrived. Berto drove the driver to the police station and Ben followed. At the station Berto processed the prisoner while Ben impounded the cocaine. He used a test kit to confirm it was coke, then he weighed each package and did the math. 110 pounds of cocaine! After weighing it he filled out the evidence receipt and locked the fifty kilos into an evidence locker, where it would stay until the evidence clerks found it and put it into deep storage on Monday morning.

On Monday afternoon his home phone rang and woke him from a sound sleep. It was Sergeant Yang from internal affairs. In his typically brusque manner, he said, "Officer Olsen, report to my office at 3:00 PM today."

"Sarge, I'm on my off time. I was sound asleep. What's going on? Can it wait until I come on shift at 9:00 PM tonight?"

"Olsen, I'll tell you what's going on when you get here. I'm well aware of your duty hours. You'll be paid overtime, don't worry. Just be here." He hung up the phone.

Ben was standing outside of Sergeant Yang's office at 2:45 PM. A few minutes later the door opened and he was surprised to see Corporal Salazar walk out. "Berto! What's going on?" Ben asked.

He just shook his head and walked away. From inside the office Sergeant Yang said, "Officer Olsen, step inside and close the door."

"Officer Olsen, I am conducting a formal internal affairs investigation. You are the focus of the investigation, not a witness. You have the right to have a police union representative present during this investigation. Who would you like that to be?"

He was stumped. What had he supposedly done now? He could think of nothing. "Can I know what this concerns before I make that decision, Sergeant?"

"It concerns your handling of narcotics evidence two nights ago. There are some discrepancies."

Gosh, he thought. Why can't IA ever speak like regular cops? "Can you tell me what I'm being accused of?"

"Not without a union rep present or your waiver of his presence."

"OK, I'll sign the waiver." He might not be a veteran cop but he sure felt like he was a veteran of IA investigations.

After he signed the waiver Sergeant Yang said, "Officer Olsen, how much cocaine did you impound the other night?"

"Fifty kilos, each kilo individually wrapped."

"Did Corporal Salazar assist you in impounding it?"

"No, sir. I tested it, weighed it, and photographed it myself. Berto was busy processing the prisoner. He only spoke Spanish so it seemed like the easiest way to do things."

"Did Corporal Salazar handle the cocaine at any time?"

"No, sir. Wait. At the scene of the traffic stop he punctured one package with his knife so we could see what was inside. That was it. I unloaded all the packages from the suspect's car and put them in my patrol car. I did all the evidence handling at the station, too. To my knowledge Corporal Salazar never touched it."

"Tell me again how many kilos you impounded."

"Fifty kilos. I weighed each package separately and counted them several different times. I converted the kilos to pounds and I remember the math was easy with the round numbers - 110 pounds.

Yang said, "And that's what your evidence sheet says. Fifty kilos. The problem is there are only forty nine kilos in evidence. One package is missing."

Ben was perplexed. "I don't get it, Sarge. Are you accusing me of miscounting or stealing?"

"You didn't miscount, Olsen. There were fifty kilos in the pictures you took. All laid out in neat little rows and easy to count."

"So you think I stole a kilo. Why would I log in fifty and then take one package? If I wanted to steal one I would have logged in forty nine and taken the other one home, with nobody the wiser."

"Is that where it is? At your house?"

Exasperated, he said, "No, it's not at my house because I didn't steal anything!"

Yang said, "Actually, Ben, I'm thinking Salazar took a package when you weren't looking. Maybe he thought as a rookie you wouldn't do a very good job of documenting it all."

Ben was emphatic. "No way. Berto didn't get near the dope once we left the street. He was in the prisoner processing room the whole time I was in the evidence processing area."

"Well, that only leaves you then, doesn't it? Maybe you thought the evidence clerks wouldn't bother to count every package before they locked it all up. Why don't you just tell me the truth, Ben, and get it over with? You know we're going to find out how things went down. Save yourself the trouble."

"Sergeant, I did not steal anything, period. I impounded fifty kilos and put all fifty packages into the evidence locker and locked it. If something went missing it went missing from the evidence locker."

"That's not possible, Ben. No one has access to the evidence locker except the clerks, and they strictly followed all their procedures this morning, including always having two people present. I'm going to give you one more opportunity to tell me what happened."

"I told you what happened," Ben said flatly.

The sergeant grimaced. "OK. I was hoping you'd make this easy on yourself. You're suspended until further notice. Contact your union rep for legal representation."

He jumped up. "Whoa, Sarge! This is a mistake, that's all, or a set up maybe. You know Hopkins and his crew have it in for me. I'm still on probation for another couple of weeks. If you suspend me I'll just be fired. They won't even bother with an investigation. Give me some time to find out what happened."

Sergeant Yang was shaking his head. "You said those marijuana joints you dropped were a mistake, and I believed you. Now we've got another 'mistake' involving dope, on top of the $500 that went missing from your prisoner. It all points to a classic drug user, Olsen, stealing money to feed your habit. Look, you wouldn't be the first cop to get hooked on drugs. Hell, maybe it started for you back in Iraq. Perhaps you could go to the VA and get a disability pension out of this. Make it easier on yourself and just admit it now."

Ben was furious. "Sarge, you're not hearing me! I did not do this! I never did dope in my life. I never did any of the things you're accusing me of. I'll take a polygraph test to prove it. I'll take a urine test. I did not do this!"

"Your union rep will never allow you to take a polygraph or a piss test. You know that, so stop jerking me around."

"I don't have a union rep and I don't want one. Give me the tests right now."

"All right, Olsen. I let you off easy before. I'll call your bluff this time. I'm a certified polygraph examiner. Sign the waivers and I'll strap you into the polygraph machine right after you pee in a bottle."

After he gave the urine sample he was hooked up to the polygraph machine. Sergeant Yang was very thorough in his questioning. He took him through the entire incident that resulted in the big dope arrest, then he asked about the marijuana joints Ben had dropped in the locker room. After that it was questions about the prisoner's missing money, and lastly the phone store owner's complaint of Ben not wanting to take a robbery report.

When he was finally through with all of it Yang said, "OK, let's talk about Hopkins now."

Ben started removing the sensors from his upper arms and chest. "No. We're done. This is about me, not Hopkins. I'll take care of him on my own. If you want Hopkins you'll have to get him yourself."

Sergeant Yang wasn't happy about that, but since Ben was taking the whole test voluntarily there was nothing he could do. "All right. I need a few hours to review your test results. Go hit the gym or something, but don't leave the building."

Ben went to the gym and exhausted himself lifting weights. The moment he stopped his mind started whirling with a thousand questions, so he just kept pumping iron. Finally he heard his name over the station paging system.

After showering he reported to Sergeant Yang's office. "Sit down, Olsen. You failed the polygraph."

"What!?" He flew out of his chair. "That's impossible! Everything I told you was absolutely true. Your machine must be screwy. Let's do the test again."

"OK, OK, calm down. Sit down. Jesus. You passed the test. I always tell people they failed just to see their reaction, especially in cases where the results are ambiguous. You passed with flying colors, Olsen. No sign of deception at all, so either you're a pathological liar or you're telling the truth."

He went on, "I'm going to go way out on a limb here and not suspend you. We'll keep investigating this whole thing while we wait for your urinalysis results. They take about two weeks. Until then, you are not to discuss this case with anyone."

Chapter Twenty

He made it through his shift that night, but his mind was elsewhere. Who could be doing these things to him, and why? Hopkins and his crew didn't like him, they made that abundantly clear, but would they risk their own careers to destroy his? If not them, then who?

Perhaps this was just a mistake on the part of the evidence people and not a frame up. Maybe someone working in the evidence room stole the dope. He realized he was grasping at straws. Yang had already assured him there was no mistake and the evidence room employees had strictly followed their procedures. It had to be a frame up.

Near the end of his shift Ben had an idea about who might be behind the frame ups, and he decided to talk to Jackie about it right away.

He got home from work at 8:00 AM and called her. She was in finals week and had an exam in two hours. She was not happy he disturbed her last minute cramming. When he explained what had happened her tone immediately changed. "Oh, Ben. I am so sorry. I thought all that stuff was behind us. You're so close to getting off probation."

"Jackie, as much as Hopkins and his friends dislike me, it's hard for me to believe they would risk their careers to get me fired. Whoever did this is looking at prison time, and a prison sentence for a cop is a death sentence. With that in mind, I had an idea of who might be motivated enough to risk all of that to hurt me, and why."

"Go ahead, Ben, though I have a feeling I'm not going to like this."

He laid it out for her. "I think it can only be one of your ex-boyfriends in the department. Someone who is still in love with you, and sees me as a threat. You said one of the cops you dated became very demanding and controlling and you broke it off with him. I think he's the guy behind all of this."

Jackie said, "His name was Ken Damone, but it can't be him. He doesn't even work at the PD anymore. It was such a blow to his inflated ego when I broke up with him he left the National City PD. Rod told me he works up in Sacramento now for their department. Honestly, I think Rod probably helped to push him out of National City. He can't be behind this."

Ben was disappointed. He thought he had it all figured out. "How about the other cops you dated? Who were they?"

She was silent a long time. Then she said, "I don't think I should tell you, Ben. I never had more than two dates with either one and we parted friends. You might be working with them for the next thirty years, and I don't want two dates a few years ago to spoil your relationship with them."

He was irate. "My career is on the line, Jackie! Please. You just have to trust me to act like an adult about this."

"All right Ben. I had two dates with Vern Jefferson more than two years ago and two with Josh Williams about eighteen months ago. They're both good guys, and they treated me well. We just didn't hit it off."

Now he was truly stumped. "I've met those guys but I don't know them at all. You're certain they couldn't be behind these events?"

"As certain as one person can be about another. It's got to be someone else, Ben."

Jackie was busy studying for and taking final exams, so she and Ben spent very little time together over his days off. He racked his brain trying to figure out who might be behind his problems, but after three days of pondering it he still had no idea.

I knew if I was patient a golden opportunity would come around, and it did. It was so easy to steal some of that dope. They would have fired anyone else, but I suspected Olsen might somehow squirm out of the trap I set for him. That's okay, I took out some insurance. Golden opportunity, indeed. That piece of shit leads a charmed life, but his luck has run out.

Chapter Twenty One

Ben spent the next ten days in a fog. He was so paranoid he was hardly able to sleep. At work he was constantly looking over his shoulder at the cops around him, carefully scrutinizing each one, seeking some sign they were the one he was looking for.

Jackie did well on all her final exams and term papers and graduated with honors. Ben and Rod both attended her graduation ceremony, and they all had dinner together afterwards. After two days of basking in the glory of finally having her college degree she mailed off more applications for teaching positions.

On a Tuesday morning, Ben had changed into civilian clothes and was getting ready to leave the station after his shift, when he heard his name over the paging system. He was told to report to Captain Ambito's office on the third floor.

When he entered the captain's office he saw Sergeant Yang was also there. He was elated. This could only mean they had discovered who was behind everything.

"Officer Olsen reporting as ordered, sir."

Without preamble the captain said, "Mister Olsen, the results of your urine test are in. It came back positive for methamphetamine. In accordance with our zero tolerance policy you are terminated effective immediately. Since you were a probationary employee you have no right of appeal."

Ben was flabbergasted. He tried to speak and found he could not. Finally he was able to croak out a denial and to ask for a retest.

The captain was solemn. "As I said, Mister Olsen, you have no right of appeal. The decision is final. You are no longer a police officer. Turn in your badge, gun, police ID, and all city issued equipment before you leave the building this morning. Your termination was based upon the urinalysis results. If our investigation into the theft of cocaine uncovers sufficient evidence you committed the crime, a warrant will be issued for your arrest. You're dismissed."

He turned in his equipment and left the National City Police Department in complete humiliation.

Finally! Farm boy played a good game, but he lost. Now Jackie will drop him like a hot rock. She would never stay with a disgraced ex-cop doper. After all this she'll need someone to comfort her, and I'll be there waiting. Once she's back in my arms I will never let her go again. Never!

Ben drove straight to Jackie's house. He knew Rod was at work and had already heard the news. Everyone had already heard the news. NCPD was as bad as Barron when it came to gossip.

When she answered the door Jackie could tell by the look on his face something awful had happened. Before he could say a word she hugged him fiercely. "Oh, Ben. Whatever it is, we'll get through it together. Is there news of Nacho?"

"Jackie, I've been fired. My urinalysis came back positive for drugs."

"Oh! How is that possible? I know you aren't using any drugs. There has to be some mistake."

He said, "Of course I'm not using drugs. I never have and never will. Somebody must have doctored the test. It's the only thing I can think of."

"We'll have the sample retested then. Hire a lawyer. We'll fight this, Ben."

"We can't fight it, Jackie. That's the thing. I was a probationary employee. There is no right of appeal. Legally, they don't even need a reason to fire me. It's enough for them I was causing an administrative burden. 'Sorry, it just didn't work out.' That's all they have to tell a lawyer. I'm through."

"Oh, Ben. I'm so sorry. I know being a police officer meant a lot to you."

"It did, but you mean a lot more to me, sweetheart. Do you still want to be with a disgraced ex-cop?"

She threw her arms around him and squeezed him hard. "Ben Olsen, I love you, not that uniform. As far as I'm concerned nothing has changed."

Ben thought his heart would leap out of his chest he was so happy. "Thank you, Jackie. I love you so much." They barely made it to her bed before they started their lovemaking. When they lay resting she asked, "What will you do, Ben? What other type of work are you interested in?"

His mood turned glum. "I'm not really qualified for anything. I don't have any civilian job skills or training. Nobody will hire a fired cop anyway. No law enforcement agency will touch me. Even the Marine Corps won't take me back after this."

They were silent a long time. Finally, Jackie said quietly, "Let's go to live in Barron."

He did not respond. "Ben, did you hear me?"

"What? Yes, I'm sorry. It's generous of you, and I love you even more for it, but you don't know what you're saying. You've never been there. It's a tiny little farm town with almost no black people. They may not even accept us. I can't work at Jennie-O. I just won't, even if they would hire me. You've lived in a big city all your life. You'd be bored out of your mind there. All your friends and your brother are here. It just wouldn't work."

She smiled and said, "Are you finished? I can teach school in Barron or somewhere nearby just as well as I can in San Diego. You don't have to work at Jennie-O, you can take over your father's farm. You told me yourself your family was hoping you would do that. I can fly back to San Diego whenever I feel the need to see Rod and my friends, and I'll make new friends in Barron. You've told me a million times what good people live there. They'll accept us, I know they will. I think it's the only option we have, Ben. If you can't find a job here we couldn't afford to live in San Diego and raise a family on my salary alone."

"Raise a family?"

"Yes, Ben. I'm pregnant."

Jackie's brother Rod took the news of her moving to Barron with Ben surprisingly well. He said he would continue to investigate on his own to try to find out who had framed him. He refused to believe Ben had stolen money, stolen the cocaine and used drugs. Jackie chose not to tell him about her pregnancy until she was further along and they were settled in Barron.

Her mother also took the news well. In fact, she was not even surprised. "I knew he was your man since you visited us at Christmas," she said. "Every time you talked about him your face lit up. Mothers know these things."

The word got around the police department, too. Most of the cops didn't care. After all, they hardly knew Ben. A few cops, like Berto Salazar and George Zobriskie genuinely liked Ben and they knew somebody had screwed him somehow. One cop was enraged.

No!
Nooooooooooooooooooooooooooooooooooooooo!!!!!
This cannot be happening! I will not allow it. Jackie is mine. Mine! There's only one solution to this. Ben Olsen must die.

Chapter Twenty Two

Ben was driving to a Penske Truck rental store to see about renting a small moving truck when his cell phone rang. "Ben, it's Tara Morris from the PD. I was sorry to hear about your problems at work. I didn't know you real well but you never struck me as the type of guy who would do the things they say you did. I stumbled across something on duty last night. I found out who set you up, and I can prove it."

Ben was so shocked he pulled off the road and parked his car. "Tara, that's fantastic news! Are you at the PD now? I can be there in twenty minutes."

"No, I'm not on duty. And it's not safe to meet at the PD, he might see us. You have to see this for yourself, Ben. Meet me behind the National City bowling alley. I'm on the way there now."

He was thrilled. "OK, Tara, I'm already in my car and on the way, but I can't wait until I get there. Who framed me?"

She said, "It's Allen Gerhardt. Word got back to his wife after you reported him for having sex with the 7-11 clerk. It destroyed his marriage."

Ben made it to the back parking lot of the bowling alley in record time. Tara was waiting there for him. He hurried over to her and she said, "This way, Ben. He's got the stuff hidden inside the drainage tunnel."

"What stuff, Tara?"

"It's a whole bunch of things, including the kilo of coke that went missing. You'll see. It'll be obvious once you see it."

They got to the tunnel entrance and he stopped. "Tara, there's nothing here. What's going on?"

"It's inside the tunnel, Ben. Just a few yards in there's a maintenance door on the right hand side. Mike Wilson and I were in here last night looking for a robbery suspect we chased. We didn't find him but I found Gerhardt's secret hiding place. I was afraid to say anything to Wilson. He's a friend of Gerhardt and they're both friends with Hopkins. I didn't know who I could trust so I haven't told anyone but you."

They walked into the tunnel about fifty feet. Ben could see the small maintenance door on the right. "I see the door, Tara. Did you bring a flashlight?"

She turned the flashlight on. "Yes I did, Ben. Just keep walking past the door. I'll tell you when to stop."

"What do you mean walk past the door? You said…" He turned to look at her and saw the semi-automatic pistol in her hand.

She leveled the pistol at his chest. "Just keep walking, Ben. You know I'm on the gun range all the time, and I couldn't possibly miss you from this distance."

They walked a long ways, turning at intersections, going into cross tunnels, then more cross tunnels. At first he tried to keep track of where he was but he quickly became confused and knew he was lost. Realizing he was probably going to die and his body might never be found, in desperation he mentally called out to Nacho. "Nacho, tell Jackie Tara killed me in the tunnels. Tara killed me in the tunnels." Over and over again he repeated the words in his head. Could his thoughts carry all the way to Texas, if that's where Nacho was? Was he even alive?

He wasn't in Texas. Nacho was passed out in one of the drainage tunnels. Something roused him out of his drunken slumber. Ben was in danger! He tried to concentrate on his friend's thoughts, but was too drunk to see them clearly. Ben was in trouble, and somewhere nearby, he got that much, but the rest was indecipherable.

He felt himself drawn towards his friend and started hurrying.

They came to yet another intersection of tunnels and Ben stopped. He had had enough. "This is as far as I go, Tara. Whatever it is you want to do, do it here and get it over with."

"All right, Ben. Do you want to say a prayer before you die?"

"What I want is an explanation. Is Gerhardt paying you to do this? There's still time for us to go to internal affairs and turn him in. You'll be a hero."

She laughed. It was an ugly, menacing sound. "I didn't think it was possible, but you're actually stupider than you look. I can't imagine what Jackie sees in you. Gerhardt has nothing to do with this. I made that up to lure you in here. You stole Jackie from me, and for that you have to die. It's that simple."

He was stunned. "What! I stole Jackie from you? What are you talking about?"

"Jackie and I were lovers for years, you moron. She had a few flings with some other cops - men! Men who know nothing about what it takes to love a woman. Only I could give her that. We had decided to start living together but Jackie panicked. She was worried about how her mother and brother would take the news she was in love with another woman. She said she needed some time to think it over, and then you came along and confused her. You almost spoiled everything. Jackie loves me! She could never love you, or any man.

"I tried hard to get you fired. It's so easy to fire a probie, but you kept worming your way out of trouble. I stole the money from that drunk when you were in the bathroom. I told the phone store owner to call it a robbery. It didn't work. It's like you were made of Teflon. I used to date an evidence clerk and I made a copy of her keys one night after she fell asleep. You wouldn't believe how easy it is to steal stuff from there. Once they log it in everyone forgets about it. I kept checking the arrest logs, hoping you would make a dope arrest. The bosses go ballistic over missing drugs. But I figured Mr. Teflon man would find a way to skate out of that, too, so I had a backup plan. I knew they'd want to piss test you, they always do. I got some dirty urine from a meth freak I busted. Told her it was just part of the arrest procedure. She was so out of it she probably forgot it five minutes later. I kept that piss handy, waiting. The night after you impounded all that coke I went into the evidence locker and stole a kilo. I knew the clerks would inventory it on Monday morning and report one missing. Then when the word got around the station about IA giving you a polygraph test and piss test, I went into the evidence locker again to doctor the urine. It just sits there in a refrigerator until they send it out to the lab for testing. Easy enough to siphon out some of yours and inject some dirty stuff into it with a tiny needle.

"You didn't need to die, Ben. I just wanted you to get fired so Jackie would come to her senses and come back to me. But you poisoned her mind somehow. You're pure evil. Only a monster like you could keep her from coming back to me. When I heard she was going with you back to Wisconsin you left me no choice - I had to kill you."

Ben's mind was reeling. Tara was obviously insane, and obsessed with Jackie. How could Jackie not have told him about her years long love affair with this woman? Was she that ashamed of it? If he had known about it he would have focused on Tara and been able to expose her. Certainly he would never have agreed to go into the tunnels with her. Jackie's shame may have cost Ben his life.

Nacho was close. The adrenaline pumping into his system was sobering him up and he could sense Ben more clearly. He was very close, just around the bend, at the next intersection. And there was someone with him. The feeling of malevolence was so strong it hit him like a mule kick. Ben was in mortal danger.

Tara pointed the gun at his head. "So now you know the truth, Ben. You can see how foolish you were to think you could take her away from me. You never had a chance. Like all men, you were stupid, clumsy, and arrogant. I..."

He lunged at her and she pulled the trigger. At the same instant an unopened can of malt liquor sailed out of the darkness and slammed into the side of her head. The sound of the shot in the tunnels was deafening. Tara fell to the ground, unconscious, her flashlight skittering away.

Nacho retrieved the flashlight and shined it on Ben's prone form. He was bleeding badly from a bullet wound to his neck. "Ben! Ben!"

He looked up at Nacho and smiled weakly. His lips moved but no sound came out. "Ben, we've got to get you to a hospital. You have to try to walk. It's not too far to an exit."

Nacho pressed his beloved floppy hat into the wound on his best friend's neck. "Come on, jarhead! That little nick wouldn't stop an army trooper. Don't go all Marine Corps pussy on me. Direct pressure on the wound, Ben. You know the routine. Get up and follow me. Let's go!"

Ben got to his feet and with Nacho cajoling and half carrying him they started out of the tunnel. He couldn't handle Ben and carry the big flashlight, so he laid it on the floor of the tunnel, the powerful beam illuminating their path. They made some distance but he could feel his badly wounded buddy getting weaker with each step. Finally Ben could go no more and collapsed. With no pressure on his wound the blood again flowed freely.

Nacho began dragging Ben through the tunnel. He was a small man and Ben was 235 pounds of dead weight. He was nearly hysterical with fear and frustration. "Ben! Stay awake! Stay with me. I'll get you there. This is why, Ben. This is why God saved me in Iraq. Why he gave me this head, why he sent me down in these tunnels, drunk, to wait for you. Don't you see? You can't spoil God's plan. You can't! You've got to stay alive."

They reached the end of the tunnel, which opened near a 7-11 store. He took off his shirt and pressed it into Ben's wound, staunching the flow of blood, then began screaming for help. A woman looked down at them from the parking lot above and saw the blood pooling around Ben's head. Nacho told her to call 911 and tell them there was an officer down. "Police officer shot! Officer down!" He had been in a drunken stupor for weeks and had no idea Ben had been fired.

11-99 is the rarest of all police radio codes. It is only used when a police officer is in the most extreme, life or death circumstances. When the NCPD dispatcher announced 11-99 over the mutual aid radio circuit every law enforcement officer, firefighter and paramedic for miles around dropped whatever they were doing and responded with lights and siren. Dispatch quickly polled all the NCPD officers on duty and determined they were all accounted for. It was not unusual for other agencies and especially federal agencies to operate in National City without informing dispatch as required, so the dispatchers assumed it was an officer from another agency. The first National City units on scene saw it was Ben and the 11-99 was cancelled. All the other National City units continued to the scene, however, and paramedics took him away. Nacho told them what he could and a search team was sent into the tunnels. He described the suspect only as "an evil woman with a deep black aura." Ben's mental message about Tara had not gotten through to him. The cops took in his misshapen head, filthy clothes, and the stink of alcohol, and gave no credence to anything he said. The search team followed the blood trail and quickly found Nacho's blood soaked hat. Farther down the tunnel, at an intersection, they discovered the full malt liquor can Nacho said he had thrown. The blood trail ended there. They also found a nine millimeter shell casing. There was no sign of Tara.

Eddie Keaton was among the officers responding. He remembered Ben telling him Nacho was his friend, so rather than take him to the police station to be interviewed in depth he took him to the hospital, so he could be there for Ben.

Ben was unconsciousness and had lost a lot of blood by the time he arrived at the hospital. The bullet had nicked his carotid artery and passed through his neck. He had been in surgery for over twenty minutes when they arrived.

Eddie was frustrated. "Come on, Nacho. You were right there. You've got to have a better description than this stupid black aura thing."

He replied, "It's dark in those tunnels. She had a flashlight in one hand and a gun in the other. I could see the gun because it was in the cone of light, but I couldn't see her face. I heard her talking so I know it was a woman. After I hit her with the can I grabbed the flashlight and was so focused on Ben I never even looked at her. She was out, though. She went down hard and didn't move."

Eddie was determined to squeeze more information out of this strange Hispanic man. "OK. A woman. That's a start. You said you saw the gun, so you must have seen the hand holding the gun, right?"

"Well, of course I did."

"What was her skin color?"

"She was black! It was a black woman!"

"Good. Now we're getting somewhere. How about her height and weight? Age?"

"Sorry. No idea on her weight. She sounded young but not like a teenager. Adult. She was holding the light up near her head. I could tell because the gun hand was about a foot lower. She was maybe my height, about 5'7."

"Can you describe the gun?"

"Beretta M9 nine millimeter."

"Whoa. You seem pretty sure of yourself. Do you know guns?"

"I carried that pistol as a side arm in the army."

"OK. How about the flashlight?"

"It was a magnum Streamlight. I left it in the tunnel."

"How do you know it was that brand?"

"Are you kidding? I've been arrested at least twenty times. All you cops carry them."

If life was a comic book a light bulb would have clicked on over Eddie's head.

"Yes, we do, Nacho. And in National City we're issued the Beretta FS nine millimeter. It's probably identical to the military pistol, just a different model designation. And cops are trained to hold the light as you described, the butt end on their shoulder, so they can swing it down and whack someone if things go sideways. I need to make a phone call."

Eddie was on the phone as Ben was coming out of surgery. The nine millimeter bullet had gone through the side of his neck cleanly, barely nicking the carotid artery. Once the bleeding was stopped he was in little danger.

"Sergeant Yang, it's Eddie Keaton. I'm over at the hospital on the Olsen shooting. I want to run something by you. Olsen's friend was a witness to the shooting in the tunnels. He's a homeless alky and has some brain damage. I know it sounds odd, but he still seemed very credible to me. He described the shooter as a young black woman of average height. She was carrying a nine millimeter Beretta and a Streamlight magnum flashlight. He knows the gun from the army and says he knows the flashlight because he's been arrested a lot. Our guys found a nine millimeter shell casing on the scene so it backs up his story on the gun. You know where I'm going with this?"

Yang replied, "Yes I do. Olsen swore to me a cop was framing him for the dope, but the piss test was the nail in his coffin. Still, it won't be hard to check out. We only have two black female cops, Shawntelle Lockwood and Tara Morris. Both of them are young and average height. Thanks, Eddie. I'll let you know what I find."

A few minutes later his cell phone rang, annoying a nurse who was walking by. Cell phones were supposed to be turned to silent mode in the hospital. "Eddie, it's Sergeant Yang. Shawntelle Lockwood says she's been home all day with her children. School's out so they're all home. Easy enough to check, so I think she's in the clear. Tara Morris's swing shift started thirty minutes ago. She didn't show up for work and she's not answering her cell phone. I've got units on the way to her house."

The full can of Schlitz malt liquor had hit Tara on her right temple, knocking her cold. She was almost certain she saw her shot strike Olsen in the head as she lost consciousness. When she awoke a few minutes later Olsen and whoever had thrown the can were gone. She saw her flashlight still shining down the tunnel and retrieved it. It was obvious from the large pool of blood and the smaller blood trail that Olsen and his rescuer had fled that way. It was pretty sure he was dead, but she couldn't take the chance. Plus, whoever had thrown the can might be able to ID her. Things were spinning out of control. She had to act.

She backtracked to the edge of the tunnel opening where she had come in and carefully checked all around. Seeing no sign of the police she got into her car and drove towards Jackie's house. With her plan of killing Ben in the tunnels a bust, she was now just going on instinct. There was only one thought burning through her feverish mind: get Jackie.

She arrived at Jackie's house at 3:30 PM, vaguely aware her shift had started and she had missed briefing. She knocked on the door several times with no answer. In a near panic she began pounding on the door. A woman working in her garden next door walked over and asked her what was wrong. Tara showed her NCPD ID card and badge. She told the woman there was an emergency and she had to find Jackie. The neighbor said she was in the backyard, packing some items from the garden shed. Knowing Jackie's brother Rod was a police sergeant she asked, "Is it about Rod? Is he OK?" but Tara was already running around the corner and ignored her. The neighbor asking about Rod had inadvertently given Tara an easy way to fool Jackie.

She found her in the garden shed. "Jackie, I have some news about Rod. Come with me."

She had dreaded this moment ever since Rod became a police officer. She immediately dropped everything and went with her. "What is it, Tara? Just tell me straight out."

"Rod's going to be okay, but he's been shot. He's at the hospital now. I'll take you there."

She had a million questions but Tara said, "Let's not waste time. Get in the car and we'll talk on the way."

Traffic was already starting to jam up for the early afternoon rush hour. They got on Interstate 8 and headed west. "Tara, where are you going? What hospital is he at?"

"Sharp Memorial. He was at juvenile hall when he got shot and it was the closest place. It's right next door."

As they moved along at thirty miles an hour in the thickening rush hour traffic she peppered Tara with questions. They turned north onto Interstate 805. Finally, they came to Mesa College Drive, the exit for the hospital, and drove right past it. "Tara, oh my God, you missed the exit!"

"I'm so sorry, Jackie. I wasn't thinking. I guess I'm pretty upset, too. We'll get the next one."

Ben awoke abruptly. After a moment of disorientation he realized he was in a hospital bed. He tried to call out to someone and found he was unable to speak. His thumb found the nurse call button.

The nurse came into his room, expecting he had triggered the call button by accident. "Oh my. You're awake way earlier than usual. You'll probably drift off to sleep again in a few moments." She saw the panic in his eyes, and misinterpreted the meaning of it. "It's all right! You're in a hospital. You were shot, but you're going to be fine. Get some rest."

He tried to yell out a loud, "No!" but all he managed was a feeble croak. He grabbed the nurse's hand and with his other hand he mimed writing with a pen. She put a pen in his hand and paper beneath it. In barely legible writing he wrote, "Cops now impo" before he ran out of steam. The nurse said, "There's one right outside the door. I'll get him."

A moment later Eddie Keaton and Nacho came into the room. Ben wrote, "Tara" on the pad. Eddie said, "We know, Ben. Tara shot you. Nacho put us onto her. She didn't report for shift and she's not at her house. We found her cell phone there, so we can't track her by that."

He wrote "Jac" but couldn't manage any more. Eddie said, "Jackie? Don't worry. Everyone's been busy trying to track down Tara. Sergeant Selby's been coordinating it all, and he insisted on telling her himself. He's probably calling her now."

Nacho could see the look of fear and frustration in Ben's eyes. He reached out and held his friend's hand. "Tell me, Ben. Slow and clear, like you were talking to a small child."

Eddie started to ask something but Nacho stopped him with a gesture. A moment later he said, "Jackie's in danger. Jackie's in danger. That's all I'm getting."

It was enough for Eddie. He called Sergeant Selby and learned Jackie was not answering the home phone or her cell phone. "Sarge, Ben is awake. He says Jackie is in danger."

Selby replied, "I'll call the San Diego PD and have them go lights and siren to my house, then I'm heading out there myself. Morris is in the wind. There's no sign of her anywhere."

As they approached the next exit Jackie told Tara to get over into the right lane. Instead, she pulled her gun from behind her back with her left hand. She rested the gun on her lap, her left index finger on the trigger, pointing it straight at Jackie. "We're not going to the hospital, Jackie. And this is not about Rod. He's fine."

Jackie was so befuddled the significance of the gun pointed at her didn't even register. "Rod's OK? He wasn't shot? I don't understand."

Tara said, "Your brother's fine. This is about you and me."

Two San Diego PD patrol cars arrived at Jackie's house nearly simultaneously, cutting their lights and siren as they sped up the last half block. They were warily approaching the front door with their guns held loosely at their sides when a voice called out, "There's no one home there. Another cop already got her."

The two SDPD officers went to the neighbor, who was still working in her garden.

"Did you say a police officer picked her up, ma'am?"

"Yes, don't you know that? Oh, I see. You're from San Diego. A National City officer picked her up some time ago. She was in quite a hurry, but she seemed like a nice enough young lady. The girls today could take a lesson from her."

A few minutes later Eddie's cell phone rang. It was Selby. "Tara's got Jackie. I'm on my way to the hospital. We've got to figure out what the hell is going on."

Nacho continued to hold Ben's hand as he slipped in and out of consciousness. Eddie didn't know what to make of it. Nacho told him, "Sometimes I can hear other people's thoughts. I've been drinking a lot so it's not very clear for me. Drinking makes the voices go away, but I'm sobering up and things are getting clearer. I'm hoping a physical connection to Ben will make it even better."

Seeing the obvious skepticism on the cop's face, Nacho stared hard at him. Finally, the strange Hispanic man with the horrifically damaged head said, "Tommy is sick. You're very worried about him."

Those eight simple words hit Eddie like a freight train. When he was recovered enough to speak, he said, "Oh my God. Tommy is my son. He's got the flu."

Nacho said, "Ben wants me to find Jackie. I'm trying, but I've been drinking too much. It's so hard. There're so many voices."

Tara turned west onto state route 52, towards the beaches. Traffic was lighter here and she picked up speed. "You don't love him, Jackie, you're just confused. You and I were the real thing. You could never really love a man, and a man could never love you the way I do."

Jackie was nearly speechless. "You and I were friends, that's all. Just friends."

"Oh, no. We were much more than that. We were lovers. Lovers then, and lovers now. Lovers forever."

"Tara, we were friends once. Good friends. We spent a lot of time together. Then after I broke up with Ken

Damone I made a mistake. You tried to comfort me as more than a friend, and I let it go too far. But nothing happened. We were not lovers. I know I hurt you and I'm sorry. We've hardly spoken to each other since then."

Tara yelled, "It's not true! You don't know what you're saying. We were lovers for years! Olsen has poisoned your mind. He's brainwashed you."

She knew now that Tara was insane. Still, she could not stop herself from saying, "I don't love you, Tara. I never did. I love Ben Olsen."

Instead of exploding in anger as she had expected, the female cop smiled. It was a cold, ugly smile. "Ben Olsen is dead. I shot him through the head."

Nacho suddenly jerked his hand away from Ben and placed both hands over his ears. He bent over in his chair and moaned loudly. "What is it, Nacho? What's wrong?" Eddie asked.

Ben stirred awake. Nacho looked at him and said, "She's crying, Ben. She's so sad. So very, very sad. She thinks you're dead. Tara told her you're dead. Her grief is so strong it's like a knife in my head."

Jackie sobbed uncontrollably for several minutes, then, with great effort, she composed herself. "It changes nothing, Tara. I don't love you and I never will. Just kill me now. Without Ben, I don't want to live anymore."

Tara smiled her ugly, demented smile. "I will kill you, Jackie, and then myself, but not yet. When we get there. Then we'll go to heaven and be together forever."

Suddenly, it occurred to Jackie Tara might be lying about Ben. If so, then she very much wanted to live. And how incredibly selfish of her! She was carrying his baby inside of her. Whether he was dead or alive, she must live for the baby. Ben's baby. "Where are we going?"

"To the Children's Pool. I followed you and Ben there many times. I know it's your favorite place on earth. From there we'll go to heaven together."

They were already west of Interstate 5. She had ten minutes to figure something out.

Jackie's brother came into the hospital room, still in uniform. Ben was conscious for longer periods now and saw him walk in. Seeing he was awake, Rod said, "Ben, we're doing everything we can. There's an all-points bulletin out and an amber alert for the two of them, with Tara's car info. It's just a huge city. They could be anywhere."

Nacho seemed unaware Sergeant Selby had joined them. He moaned loudly, and said, "She's crying again, but she's happy now. She's thinking of you, Ben. Hoping you're still alive. She's thinking of the happiest day of her life. The day you asked her, and she said yes. She said yes and cried then, and she's crying now, remembering it. They're going back to where you asked her."

Ben flailed his free arm and lifted his head off the pillow, struggling to speak. Eddie bent over him, his ear to Ben's lips. He managed to whisper something like, "Chillenpuh."

Eddie didn't get it. "Say it again, Ben, say it again." Ben just slumped down in the bed, slipping back into unconsciousness.

Rod asked, "What did he say, Eddie?"

The frustrated cop shook his head. "I'm not sure. It sounded something like 'chill and puh.' Maybe he's delirious."

To Eddie, Nacho said, "Say it again."

"Chill and puh. Chillin puh."

They all played with the words. Nacho finally got it. "The Children's Pool! That's it! That's where they're going. Ben and Jackie went there all the time. She loves that place. Tara must know about it somehow."

Rod was skeptical, but Eddie was convinced. "Sarge, we've got nothing else. It's worth a shot. Send some SDPD guys over there to check it out."

Selby called the SDPD dispatcher and asked her to send their closest unit to the Children's Pool. A moment later he heard on his radio over the mutual aid net, "Any units in the vicinity of the Children's Pool in La Jolla, regarding a reported kidnapping. Be on the lookout for a 2007 Chevy Malibu, green, California license plate 3CBX475. Suspect is a black female adult, 5'6" 130 pounds. The kidnap victim is also a black female adult, 5'7" 125. Suspect is considered armed and dangerous. Possibly heading to the Children's Pool. SDPD clear."

A minute later Selby's radio came to life again. "Lifeguard 13 to SDPD dispatch. That vehicle just pulled into the parking area at Children's Pool. Driver and passenger match the description, over."

The radio squealed loudly as numerous police units all tried to talk at once, then it cleared. "SDPD 2750 David, 10-4. We're about five minutes from there. All other units stay off the air. Lifeguard 13, do not approach the vehicle. Keep us updated, over."

"Lifeguard 13, 10-4. I believe the suspect is in the driver's seat. She's got a crazy look to her. The woman in the front passenger seat is crying, over."

A long, tense three minutes passed before the radio squawked again. "Say your status, Lifeguard 13."

"No change. The driver's talking, the passenger's crying."

"SDPD 2750 David, we're less than one minute out. Two detectives in an unmarked unit."

"Lifeguard 13. There's a civilian approaching the driver's side door. He's banging on the window! Gun! Gun! They're fighting over the gun. They... shots fired!"

There was an eternity of dead silence from the radio. Selby quietly prayed, "Please God, let Jackie be alive." Ben was awake again. He was highly agitated and making strange gurgling noises.

Then, "SDPD 2750 David, code four, suspect is in custody. Victim is not hurt. I repeat, the victim is not hurt."

Rod, Eddie and Nacho all jumped up and yelled happily. Ben was crying with relief. Suddenly Nacho lurched sideways and stumbled into the wall, holding his head. "Nacho, what is it? What's wrong?" Eddie asked.

"Nothing's wrong." He turned to Ben. "Jackie just found out you're alive, Ben. It almost knocked me over. That woman sure does love you."

Selby went over and sat on Ben's bed. "I think I know what that 'You asked her and she said yes and cried' stuff was all about, but I want to hear it from you, Ben, if you can talk."

Rod was practically Jackie's father. Ben took a deep breath for strength and whispered. His words were slurred, but Rod got the gist of it. "We're going to be married, Sarge. It would be wrong to live together. She was working up the nerve to tell you."

The sergeant snorted. "I'll be damned. 'It would be wrong to live together.' Jesus, Ben, you really are old fashioned. Well, if I have to have a hayseed white boy for a brother-in-law I guess I'm glad he's a boy scout."

Eddie Keaton shook hands with everyone and left. A few moments later Rod's cell phone rang. After listening a minute he said, "Hang on a sec, let me put you on speaker so everyone can hear." To Ben and Nacho he said, "Guys, this is Jim Kershaw, one of our detectives. He just got on scene out in La Jolla. OK, go ahead, Jim, you're on speaker."

"All right, Sarge. I'll start over. Bill Norton and I are on scene. Jackie's fine, and Morris was not hurt either. As soon as another one of our units gets here somebody will drive Jackie to the hospital so she can be with you and Ben. Morris is in San Diego PD custody and they won't give her up to us. They want credit for the arrest and hostage rescue, and they're saying since Jackie was kidnapped from your house in San Diego it's their case. We'll get her back in our custody, though, since it all started in National City when she shot Olsen in the tunnels. She's already demanded a lawyer and clammed up."

Rod asked, "What was the deal with the civilian knocking on the car window? Some good Samaritan trying to be a hero?"

Kershaw laughed. "No. It was just one of those goofy things. The guy was bringing his disabled daughter to see the seals and Morris was parked in a handicapped spot. He didn't see a handicapped license plate or placard on Morris' car so he went up there to read her the riot act. The knocking on the driver's window startled and distracted her and Jackie went for the gun. They grappled over the gun and Morris capped off two rounds through the roof of the car. SDPD rolled up as they were still tussling and ripped Morris out of the car. Not exactly a textbook hostage rescue, but we'll take it."

Thirty minutes later Jackie walked into Ben's hospital room. Rod jumped up at the sight of her and they hugged fiercely, then she noticed Nacho. "Nacho! Oh my God! We thought we would never see you again!" She went over and despite his filthy clothes and horrible smell she hugged him tightly. Then she went to Ben and immediately started crying.

"Oh, Ben. Tara told me you were dead. Shot in the head. It was the worst moment of my life. Then when the detective told me you were alive with a neck wound I was so happy, not about the neck wound but, you know, I mean... Oh God, I've feel like I've been on a roller coaster." The tears came faster.

He held her hand. He could speak only in a hoarse whisper. "Come closer."

He flicked his eyes toward Rod and said very quietly, "Tara told me you were lovers. It doesn't matter. I still love you. We can talk about it later." Again he rolled his eyes toward Rod.

She understood he was telling her not to talk about it in front of her brother. Loud enough for all to hear, she said, "Ben, it's all lies. I already told the detectives everything. It doesn't matter anymore. Tara and I were friends for years. Friends, not lovers. Then I broke up with Ken Damone. He had treated me badly and I was scared and angry. Tara and I talked about it, the way girlfriends do. We hugged a lot and I cried. Then she kissed me on the lips. I don't know, I guess I was emotionally upset and not thinking clearly. I returned her kiss. It was comforting to know someone could still kiss me and be gentle about it. She kissed me again and then she started doing things with her hands and pulling at my clothes. I came to my senses and made her stop. I could tell she was disappointed, but that was not who I am, and I told her so. It's not like we had a big scene or anything. After that we were not very comfortable with each other anymore and drifted apart. That's all there ever was, Ben. Everything else was in her mind. She's insane."

Rod had a funny look on his face. He was trying to digest what Jackie had said. Then, with a shrug of his shoulders he said, "Since we're baring our secrets you should probably know Ben told me the two of you are getting married."

"Ben! How could you? I told you I wanted to tell Rod. And did you tell him..."

Ben interrupted with a hoarse "No."

"Tell me what?" Rod wanted to know.

"Never mind," Jackie said. "A girl's got to have some secrets."

Rod chuckled. "It seems awfully hard to keep secrets around here anymore. It was actually Nacho who let the cat out of the bag on you guys planning to be married. Ben just confirmed it."

Jackie was puzzled. "Nacho? Ben, when did you tell Nacho? He disappeared before you proposed."

Ben had a helpless look on his face, so Rod bailed him out. "I'm still trying to understand it myself, but apparently you told Nacho, Jackie. If I didn't see it for myself I would never believe it."

Jackie was clearly lost. Ben whispered, "I've been trying to tell you for months now, Jackie. Nacho is special. Since he got wound…" He had to stop to catch his breath.

Nacho said, "I'll tell her, Ben, you rest." Turning to Jackie, he explained, "The wound that took part of my brain changed me somehow. I see, hear and feel things differently than normal people. Everything - colors, sounds, people, animals. I see auras. I can see or hear thoughts sometimes. Not all the time, and not with everyone. Sometimes it overwhelms me. Drinking dulls it all, so I drank a lot and turned into an alcoholic. My being drunk almost cost Ben his life, so that's it for me. I'm done drinking."

Jackie was silent for a few moments. "I don't know what to say, Nacho. I've never given any credence to such things. I'll have to think on it a while."

Rod said, "He's too modest to tell you the rest of the story, Jackie, so I'll do it for him, and then maybe you'll change your mind. He saved Ben's life in the drainage tunnels beneath National City. He found him in that maze somehow, and hit Tara with a beer can as she shot Ben. That bullet would have gone through his head otherwise. Tara is a sharpshooter."

She started to say something but Rod stopped her. "Wait, there's more. Nacho got Ben out of the tunnels, dragging him the last hundred feet or so. He's a bonafide hero for that reason alone. And then he found you. With his mind. I was sitting here when he did it. He told us to look for you at the Children's Pool."

She was still skeptical. "I believe you believe what you said, Rod. I just don't know if I do. Nacho, thank you for saving Ben's life, and mine, however you did it. Thank you so much." She walked over and hugged him again.

Rod's cell phone rang. "Yeah, OK. I'm leaving now." He hung up. "They need me back at the PD. Ben, get some rest."

After he left Jackie said, "Nacho, Rod had one of his guys drop my car here. I'll give you a ride over to Ben's house so you can clean up and sleep inside for a change."

He merely nodded. She saw he was studying her. "You getting ready to do some of that mojo on me? I don't think I'm ready for that right now. How about you tell us instead what happened to you and where you were all this time?"

Nacho said, "Just the usual story of an alcoholic. I got careless and cocky. I was sober and feeling great. I had a steady job, just found a decent apartment and was getting ready to move into it. Life was good. Some of the guys at work invited me to a bar with them, and I went along. I intended to just have soft drinks, but then I figured one beer wouldn't hurt. After all, I had been sober for months.

"I forgot one of the cardinal rules of AA: an alcoholic is an alcoholic for life. I woke up in an alley the next morning and bought a bottle for breakfast. I stumbled home to Ben's at some point and found his note about his Dad. Here was my friend in a time of need and where was I? Drunk in an alley. I was so ashamed, but not ashamed enough to sober up. I found my way to National City, where I was more comfortable on the street. I wasn't ready to face Ben and I knew he would be looking for me, so I went into the tunnels to hide. God works in mysterious ways. If I wasn't in the tunnels I couldn't have helped him."

He talked a bit more, but when Jackie saw Ben was soundly sleeping she and Nacho quietly left.

They talked all the way to Ben's house. When she was parked in his driveway she said, "Can you really read minds, Nacho?"

He got out of the car. "I wouldn't call it that, Jackie. Sometimes I just know things. I know about your baby. You think about it constantly. And your aura is brighter. I think that's from the baby."

Jackie was still not convinced, but it didn't matter. "You stay in touch, Nacho. If you need anything at all, call me. You're Ben's friend, and my friend, and we will never forget what you did for us."

He smiled knowingly. "I'm guessing you think Ben told me about the baby. He didn't. And even Ben doesn't know you've decided to name him Ygnacio if he's a boy. I'm honored. Good night, Jackie." He closed the car door and went into the house. She sat in the car a very long time before driving away.

Chapter Twenty Three

Two days later Ben was still in the hospital. He was able to speak much more clearly and for longer periods. Jackie was with him, as she had been for about sixteen hours of each day.

There was a short rap on the door and Sergeant Yang walked in. "Hello Jackie, Ben. You're looking pretty good for a guy who was at death's door three days ago. I wanted to update you on our investigation. Internal affairs took the lead for obvious reasons. I'm relying heavily on our homicide dicks, though. They started as the lead investigators when it didn't look like you would make it, Ben.

"Geez, I apologize, Jackie. I hope this doesn't disturb you. I know you're Rod's sister but sometimes I forget you're not a cop."

She smiled. "It's all right, Ming. I've lived with Rod for so long I'm used to this kind of talk. Please go ahead."

"We originally broke into Tara's house under the "exigent circumstances" rule. We had reason to believe she might be holding Jackie hostage there, so we had the legal right to go in without a warrant. We found the house empty, then we left and posted cops at the doors until we could get a search warrant. Her lawyer fought it all the way and delayed us two days. The judge finally approved the warrant last night and we conducted the search early this morning. It was pretty ugly.

"In one large closet there was a shrine to Jackie, with pictures, candles, incense, the whole nine yards. Really spooky. We found a kilo of cocaine. The wrapping matches the rest of the load you impounded, Ben. And we found duplicate evidence locker keys. I'll be conducting a separate investigation into how Tara acquired them.

"The crime scene unit went into the tunnels and found the nine millimeter slug that went through your neck. It was too deformed to match to Tara's gun but it still has evidentiary value. You're damn lucky she used a nine. A .45 in the neck would have taken your head clean off. Sorry again, Jackie. The shell casing the first search team found has extraction marks that match perfectly to Tara's gun. Hotshot lawyer or no, she's toast.

"We had the lab do a special rush job on retesting your urine sample, Ben. We'll get a full analysis eventually but we already know the sample was adulterated with a female's urine. You're in the clear for everything.

"Now for the best part. As a result of our investigation the chief vacated your dismissal retroactively. In other words, you were never fired." He took Ben's badge out of his pocket and laid it gently on his chest. "Since you were a police officer in good standing when you were shot, you'll be eligible for a disability pension if you decide to go that route. Or, you can come back to work when you're healed up. You'll have to pass a physical exam, of course."

Sergeant Yang was nearly out the door when he stopped and said, "Oh yeah, I almost forgot. Your rookie year ended yesterday. You're off probation. Congratulations, patrolman." Even from behind Jackie could see the huge smile on the sergeant's face as he left.

Ben took her hand. "I know this has been a horrible experience for you. Barron is a wonderful place to raise a family. I'll take the disability retirement and we can go home to the farm."

Jackie smiled. "Not so fast, Officer Olsen. We'll talk about all that another time. Right now we've got a wedding to plan."

The end, but the adventures of Ben, Jackie and Nacho continue in *Ghetto Cop: Sophomore Jinx*, available at Amazon.com.

My newest thriller, *Small Ball*, a novel of Islamic terrorism, will scare the hell out of you. Every day, more and more of that novel comes true in real world headlines.

ABOUT THE AUTHOR

Don Geidel is a retired United States Navy officer, originally from Manchester, Connecticut. After the navy he joined the National City Police Department, retiring again in June 2008. He has a bachelor's degree in political science from the University of Washington and a master's degree in education from the University of San Diego. His wife Doreen is a retired United States Navy nurse corps officer, originally from Barron, Wisconsin. They live deep in the forests of the Pacific Northwest. You can email Don at Geidelfarms@gmail.com.

Made in the USA
San Bernardino, CA
18 June 2016